Extraordinary Praise
for
Kill Me First

"One knockout story. . . . Morgenroth succeeds not only in creating something different, but in doing it well."

St. Petersburg Times

"A relentless, read-it-at-a-gulp thriller . . . *Kill Me First* will have you up late, long after you've turned the last page, pondering whether anything you've learned about good and evil can possibly hold. Had Flannery O'Connor wandered the desert forty days and forty nights with Jim Thompson, this is the story they might have told."

Les Standiford,
author of *Presidential Deal*

"[A] shocking page-turner."
Baltimore Sun

"This is a terrific novel—fast-paced, totally absorbing and cleverly constructed. I was constantly surprised. I loved it."

Judy Collins

"Wholly fresh and absorbing."
The Economist

"This chilling and suspenseful tale of good and evil leaves the scent of sulfur in the air."
Hilma Wolitzer,
author of *Tunnel of Love*

"Mesmerizing."

Indianapolis Star

"Nicely turned phrases . . . invoke a fittingly noirish mood."
Washington Post Book World

"*Kill Me First* explores the gray area between good and evil and looks at how the media can indulge the perverse fascination that people often have with the gruesome accident by the side of the road."
Los Angeles Times

KILL ME FIRST

KATE MORGENROTH

AVON BOOKS
An Imprint of HarperCollins*Publishers*

For Gra

AVON BOOKS
An Imprint of HarperCollins*Publishers*
10 East 53rd Street
New York, New York 10022-5299

Copyright © 1999 by Kate Morgenroth
ISBN: 0-06-109774-8
www.avonbooks.com

First Avon Books paperback printing: August 2000
First HarperCollins hardcover printing: May 1999

Avon Trademark Reg. U.S. Pat. Off. and in Other Countries, Marca Registrada, Hecho en U.S.A.
HarperCollins ® is a trademark of HarperCollins Publishers Inc.

Printed in the U.S.A.

WC ❖/10 9 8 7 6 5 4 3 2 1

Nobody likes to see weaknesses in themselves, to realize what can happen to persons when they're put under stress . . . to think of themselves as doing anything to stay alive. They think they'd say, "Kill me first" . . .

—**Patty Hearst**

Prologue
An Easy Target

A row of figures stood in an empty field in the brittle dawn air. As the sky lightened on the horizon, their outstretched arms began to shake with the weight of the pistols they held.

One man stood apart from the others. In a low, lightly accented voice, he issued the command: "Fire."

The shots were staccato.

The man spoke again. "Just targets this time," he said. "You know your bullet only strikes wood. How would you feel if that were flesh?"

There were nine lined up. They faced their plywood adversaries bravely, and at the order, they raised their arms again and cocked their weapons.

Torrenson stood with his pistol trained on the target and tried to get a glimpse of his com-

panions without turning his head. He had
thought they would all look like thugs, but the
one next to him was a scrawny boy with terrible
acne, and the next one down was a woman. He
shifted from one foot to the other and felt his
black leather pants chafe against his thighs.

The speaker continued. "When you kill, you
are extinguishing a life. A life exactly equal to
yours. No better, no worse."

The edge of the sun burst over the horizon
behind the targets and sent a ray straight into
Torrenson's eyes. He raised his other hand to
shield his face and tried to focus on the man's
words. He knew that tense situations sometimes made the mind wander to trivial details;
he had heard that in one of his training classes
and had since discovered it to be true.

The man's voice changed with the rising
sun; he spoke in a normal tone, almost casual.
"It's easier to die for a cause than to kill for it.
One makes you a martyr, the other, a monster."

Torrenson had little doubt about this man in
front of him. He was a monster—Torrenson had
seen the file.

"Think about it carefully," the man said.
"Can you kill? If you think you can't, please
speak up now." The man waited for a response,
and when all remained silent, he gave the command for a second time. "Fire," he said.

Torrenson noted that few shots hit the plywood targets. He coolly steadied his pistol and

squeezed the trigger. The shape opposite vibrated with the impact.

The speaker paced along the line, squinting at the targets. "Nice shot," he said to Torrenson. Addressing the group he said, "It seems like others might be having trouble with the distance. That's all right, not all of you are marksmen. It's not a requirement of the job." The sun was full up over the horizon, brilliant and painful to look at. The speaker squinted into it for a moment, then turned back toward them abruptly.

"Well, maybe we can satisfy you with an easier target." In a couple of quick strides he reached the first two in the line—a man with ears that stood out from his head like jug handles and a big man standing next to him.

"Face each other."

Hesitantly, they obeyed the order.

"Take aim."

Neither moved. The man gently took the big one's pistol by the barrel and raised it to the other's forehead. Jug ears did the same immediately without prompting.

He moved down the line, arranging them with guns resting against each other's chests or nestled in the hollows of their throats. Each of the eight before Torrenson was paired. He was the only one without a partner.

The man came to stop in front of him. "Well, we seem to have an odd number. What do you think we should do about this?"

Torrenson shrugged, but his heart was plummeting into his stomach.

"Don't worry, we'll take care of it. I shall be your partner." He took a pistol from his pocket, raised it to Torrenson's forehead, and rested it lightly there.

Torrenson stood, frozen by that small circle of pressure about the size of a nickel. He knows, Torrenson thought. But there was nothing he could do about it now. He was vaguely aware of movement from the others in the line, a shifting, a tightening. Mechanically, he raised his arm.

The man smiled at him with white teeth, a little uneven on the bottom but otherwise perfect. From a distance his features had looked sharply chiseled, hard as flint. But now, close up, Torrenson could see the skin pouched thin and dry under his blue eyes.

"You give the word."

Torrenson realized the man was speaking to him. "Me?" His lips formed the word but no sound came out.

The man nodded, rocking the gun against his forehead. "On a count of three."

Torrenson wanted to know what the others were doing, but his vision had narrowed to the view of the eyes in front of him.

"Anytime," the man said quietly.

The sun felt warm on one side of his face. The other side was unbearably cold.

"One." Torrenson's voice was hoarse. He cleared his throat.

"Two." His voice was clearer, stronger.

"Three."

Shots rang out. Torrenson pulled the trigger and . . . nothing happened. He looked into the blue eyes so close to his own.

The man tightened his forefinger ever so slightly, and the gun exploded a moment after the rest. He had waited just long enough for Torrenson to realize that the outcome of the contest had been fixed. Torrenson's gun, as well as those of the other men who lay bleeding into the ground, had only two bullets. The rest—the ones who remained standing—had a full chamber.

The man spoke to the survivors. "You will bury your dead. The killing isn't done when the man lies on the ground in front of you. Go get bags from Karl." He gestured toward the truck that had been parked fifty yards away but now rolled to a halt beside him.

The man knelt by Torrenson's body, blood still pooling in the dust. He felt in the pockets of the black leather jacket. He found a set of keys and a pack of Trident gum. He tried the leather pants and came up with a bulky wallet. Glancing inside, he closed it and tapped it against his palm thoughtfully. Then he wiped it carefully against his sleeve, tucked it back in the pocket, and went to get a sack.

As a Praying Man Looks to God

It was years later that Tresler finally got the opportunity to meet and question the man he had been pursuing. Sitting out by a quiet pond, sheltered under the cascading branches of a weeping willow, Tresler was able to study Merec for the first time. He had a steep, cragged face with deeply etched lines. His eyes were a smooth, inscrutable blue. But it was his hands that drew Tresler's attention. They lay in his lap, his long slender fingers curled and quiet. And Tresler wondered—then asked, "How many people have you killed?"

"How do you mean?" He must have seen Tresler looking at his hands because he said, "Do you mean with these?" and he opened them, palms up, in a gesture of supplication. "Or do you mean by my order? Or maybe you don't even mean physically, but mentally, emotionally. We have perfected so many different ways of killing."

Tresler said he'd like to stick to the dictionary definition.

"Yes, that's simplest," Merec agreed. "I consider myself responsible for killing with my own hands," and he said this precisely, "eighty-two people." He tilted his head. "What is your reaction? A lot? A little? What you expected?"

"Less than expected," Tresler admitted, "for a lifetime's work."

"Ah, but those eighty-two are not the only ones. They are the ones I am responsible for killing with my hands, but not the only deaths that lie on my conscience, and certainly not the ones that lie most heavily." He rebuked Tresler gently, saying, "The simplest questions are indeed that—the simplest. But they are not usually the ones that give us the answers we most want to know."

They sat, listening to the buzz of the crickets.

"So tell me about the initiation tests," Tresler said.

Merec laughed suddenly, and he was handsome when he did. "I haven't thought about those in years. . . . But you must know something of the procedure."

"I know that half the men had two bullets, the other half had a full chamber. I know that the men left alive had to rake the grass with their fingers to get up the bits of meat and splintered bone."

Only Merec's eyes showed emotion, the lids dropping slightly, a contraction of the skin somewhere back near his ears. But he said simply, "It's not a glamorous job." He paused, then added, "You seem to be acquainted with the facts."

"From the Torrenson incident," Tresler said.

Merec nodded.

"So you know what I'm referring to."

He nodded again.

"Did you know who Torrenson was when he applied?"

"Yes," Merec admitted.

"But you contacted him anyway."

"I did."

"But . . . why?"

"Why?" Merec echoed. He laughed, rich and light, but it was not a laugh that invited company. "I think I have lost many of my whys and wherefores a long time ago. But let me see if I can answer your question. When I set up those initiations I researched all the participants very carefully. They came for various reasons, and I accepted them—also for various reasons. Many people do not see it, but there is a direct connection between what you desire and what you receive. Most came for violence, and that is what they received.

"I have a story that might clarify things. At

one session I had a man who came for the
money. It wasn't so much, but to him it must
have seemed a compelling sum. And he had an
unusually compelling reason. His little girl was
dying of leukemia. They didn't have any insurance. His wife and his mother both had given
all their money. This man had spent all his on
. . . other things. He was in debt, and the bank
refused him a loan. I could have—" he spread
his palms, "maybe should have—turned him
away. But I thought I could do something for
him.

"I pair myself with all the special cases. Of
course they don't have any bullets left in their
chamber, but they don't know that. Sometimes
in these special cases they will die no matter
what they do, as was the case with your man
Torrenson. In this situation I had decided that
if the man attempted to fire his weapon, I
would let him live. But he didn't even pull the
trigger. I made sure his child got the money—
far more than we had originally offered, and
he died honorably, which is more than most
can say."

"Honorably?" Tresler asked.

"He could not kill another man even to save
himself. Even to save his daughter. I call that
honorable."

"But if he had pulled the trigger, he would
have passed the test and been accepted into the
group?"

"He would have passed that stage," Merec conceded.

"So you don't accept honorable men."

"There's no room for honor in my profession."

"If you wanted to help him and suspected that he wouldn't pass the test, then why didn't you simply send him the money?" Tresler pressed.

Merec shrugged. "Nothing comes free—especially in this country of yours. I think," he paused, "no, I know if I had given him the money, he would not have given it to his little girl. A loan from a bank, yes, he would have given that because it wasn't really his, but if I had handed him the money, or placed it in his bank account, he would have used it for himself. Immoral, yes? Selfish, yes? But in the field he couldn't shoot me—a stranger—for money, or even to save his life. The beauty of humanity, wouldn't you say?"

Tresler leaned forward ever so slightly as he asked his next question. "Do you admire that quality?"

Merec rested one of his smooth, murderous hands over his heart. "I used to despise it."

"And now?"

"Now, I just don't know."

Tresler couldn't help but be fascinated by Merec's low voice and sad smile. "What was it that changed your mind?"

Merec leaned back in his seat and gazed out over Tresler's head to something far distant, as a praying man looks to God, and he said, "Sarah Shepherd. Sarah Shepherd changed everything."

A Shepherd's Life

Jonathan Shepherd's death was not as gruesome as many that Sarah later witnessed, but it was her first, and it was the one that shifted her life, like a switch thrown on a railroad track.

The day began like countless others before it. Both Jonathan and Sarah were early risers, and they were up by six. Sarah put the kettle on the stove and the slices of bread in the oven while Jonathan brushed his teeth. Then they switched places, and he set the tea to steep and buttered the toast while she dressed.

After breakfast, they sat in the living room and read the paper. Jonathan settled on the couch, his legs propped on an ottoman, a patched quilt over his knees. He spread the newspaper across his lap and traced the lines with a forefinger as he read. Sarah took the armchair, the paper creased and folded into a manageable square.

Dust motes floated gently, disappearing as they wandered in and out of bars of sunlight. The silence was broken only by an occasional hiss from the radiator and the rustle of newspaper as they turned pages or retrieved a new section.

Jonathan folded the paper on his lap and shuffled through the remaining sections on the coffee table. He flipped through again. Finally he said, "Sarah?"

"Yes, dear?"

"I'm looking for the 'Week in Review' section. Happen to notice it around here anywhere?"

She unfolded the paper on her lap, turned the page, and recreased it. "Maybe." Her eyes crinkled at the corners.

"Hmmm." He sat, frowning as though deep in thought. "Any chance you might have it?"

She took a sip of cold tea to hide her smile. "Maybe."

"Would you consider a trade?"

She put down the paper and crossed her hands over it protectively. "What do you have to trade?"

"The front page?"

"Already read it," she said.

"'Arts and Leisure'?"

"Read it."

"*I* know," he announced. "The sports section."

She laughed. "Deal." She gave him the "Week in Review" but declined the sports section.

When Jonathan finished with the paper—he always took longer to read than she—he said, "Ready for our walk?"

"I've been ready for about fifteen minutes," but she said it with a smile. She went to the closet and emerged with their hats and coats.

On their walk, Jonathan greeted the people they passed. Sarah kept her head down, watching the sidewalk. Often she took his arm to steady him where the tree roots buckled the concrete squares into crazy little hills and miniature cliffs.

After lunch they sat in the living room with the windows cracked open to a light wind and the faint roar of passing cars. Jonathan chose a straight-backed chair next to the couch and read aloud from a book he held in one hand, thumb and pinkie splaying the pages open.

Sarah perched on the couch, rubbing his bad knee. While listening to Jonathan's voice, she rubbed more and more slowly until she stopped.

Jonathan jiggled his leg.

She didn't seem to notice.

He jiggled again. Finally he lowered the book, looked pointedly at her, and cleared his

unloaded the stretchers they took Sarah down the hall one way and wheeled Jonathan in the opposite direction.

Sarah and Jonathan had been married thirty-one years. Their life together had been quiet, regulated, and ordinary. It was a life suitable to a seventy-one-year-old person—Jonathan's age when he died. Sarah was almost two decades younger, but she had adjusted to Jonathan's way of life without a thought.

That night, lying in the hospital bed, she felt as though her life had ended with his. She couldn't imagine a future for herself. That was just as well. In her wildest dreams she never could have imagined what lay in store for her.

Early the next morning the first of the bodies were found out in South Dakota.

A Lesson in Detective Work

The sheriff slid down the gravel bank into the ditch beside the road. "Where did you say it was, John?" he called over his shoulder.

"Over there. Down in those weeds." The old farmer remained by the road and gestured with his cane.

The sheriff waded into the waist-high weeds. "I don't see anything in here. I'm sure it's nothing."

"Don't tell me it's nothing. I know what I saw, and I saw a man climb down there in that ditch this morning real early, and he was carrying something slung over his shoulder. But when he came back up he didn't have nothin'. And I know it was something sneaky 'cause he looked around real sly like. I was behind my tractor over there in the field."

"What were you doing out that early anyway, John?"

"I got work to do, don't I? Besides, you shouldn't be bothering about what I was doing out here but what that other fellow was doing down there in that ditch."

The sheriff swept the weeds with his baton. "Well, I don't think there's anything . . ." but he broke off as his foot hit something. "Wait a minute," he said. He bent down, and the weeds bowed and whispered with the sound of something heavy being dragged. The sheriff backed out, pulling an enormous duffel bag. It was a drab army green but stained heavily all over with darker patches that had dried, stiffening the fabric.

"Nothing there, eh?" the old farmer crowed.

"Well, it might just be junk. But I'll give you this—it sure is heavy. Let's take a look here." He crouched and pulled open the zipper. "What the hell?" he scrambled back as a small river of liquid poured out. He laughed uneasily. "I bet you it's just some hunter dumped a deer back here 'cause it's not hunting season yet."

"The hell it is," the old farmer said.

"Well, let's see then." The sheriff grasped the other side and upended the sack. A man's body slithered out.

"Well lookee there." The farmer pursed his lips and observed, "Doesn't look like anybody from around here."

The sheriff glanced at the head. The top half of the face—the forehead and the eyes—had been blown away. Then the smell reached him. He felt something rise in his stomach and turned away, bending double. But he stood again quickly, and feigning nonchalance, he said, "Don't see how you could tell from that whether he was from around here or not."

"I mean the clothes, you idiot," the farmer said.

The sheriff noticed that the body was dressed like a biker in a black leather jacket, black leather pants, and thick boots. "You should have been a detective, John."

"Not me. Filthy work." The farmer made a face. "So what are you going to do about that one, seeing as he has no face and all?"

"We've got technology these days, John," the sheriff said. "There are things like DNA testing, dental records, computer reconstruction based on the bone structure. . . ."

"That's a load of horse shit," the old farmer said. "Look in the man's pockets, why don't you?"

"John," the sheriff said patiently, "when a man gets killed, the criminals don't usually leave convenient clues for us in the pockets."

John spit off to one side and said, "Betcha."

"For Pete's sake. You can't be serious."

"Ten bucks." The old farmer stared, challenging.

"Oh, all right. This will be a little lesson for you in detective work." The sheriff squatted near the body and gingerly stuck his hand in a pocket of the man's pants. It was empty. He tried the other side. Empty. "See," he said, "Nothing there."

"You didn't try the back pockets."

He sighed heavily and slid his hand underneath. He felt something hard and square. Reaching into the back pocket, he came out with a wallet. Holding it up he said, "Well, I'll be damned."

The sheriff leaned back in his chair and put his feet up. He was talking to the woman who sat at the reception desk. She was typing steadily, but she nodded to show she was listening.

". . . and old John says that we're going to have some trouble finding out who this guy is, and I say, 'You'd be surprised the kind of things criminals overlook these days, and there could even be something on the body itself,' so I start to check his pockets. And guess what? Whoever dumped him there left his wallet in his back pocket. And listen to this, Tammy. The wallet has a driver's license, social security card, birth certificate, credit cards—he even has his fishing license. So I've put a call in to find out who this guy is and where he's from. Then I called over to Davis—you know Sheriff Davis, don't you Tammy?"

Tammy bobbed her head, still typing.

"Well, I called him to let him know to be on the alert. Remember a few months ago when all those bodies were found around Topeka? They were also found in sacks like this one. So I'm thinking there's a chance there could be another rash of bodies around here. And what do you think Davis tells me? He already turned up two in his territory. One was down by Thayer Lake, and the other was in someone's barn, stuffed in a space beneath some bales of hay.

"I'll tell you, I got a hunch that this is one of those serial killers. Probably homosexual 'cause all the victims seem to be men. One got it in the throat, and Davis told me he didn't have much neck left to attach his head to his body, and the other had a bullet to the chest. From the powder burns they could tell that both were shot from close up. And they've identified the bodies too. One was a local boy, and the other come all the way from California. But both of them were bad news. They had rap sheets as long as your arm, according to Davis. 'Good riddance,' Davis said, and I tell you I have to agree."

"Maybe it's a vigilante instead of one of those serial killers," Tammy said, speaking for the first time, though she did not break off from her typing.

"You know, you may have a point there,

Tammy. Good thinking."

The phone rang. Tammy stopped typing and reached for the receiver. She listened for a moment, then said, "It's for you, Sheriff. They say it's about the search on the man you found."

"Great." He picked up and Tammy resumed typing.

"So do you have some answers for me?" the sheriff asked cheerfully. He listened and the smile slipped from his face. "What's that? What do you mean? I don't understand."

Tammy stopped typing and turned in her chair to listen.

"But the man had a driver's license, social security card—he had a *fishing* license. All right. Fine. Thank you very much," he said and slammed the phone down on the hook.

Tammy was staring.

"I don't believe it," the sheriff muttered. "Listen to this, Tammy."

Tammy was listening.

"Those idiots claim our man doesn't exist. According to them, he has a couple months of purchases on his credit cards and a recent speeding ticket, but before three months ago there's nothing. No record of him at all."

The next day two men in suits arrived at the sheriff's office. They flashed identification at him and announced that they had come to collect the body of the man he had discovered and that he no longer had to worry about the investigation. They would be taking care of it from now on.

"I'll need some—" the sheriff began to say, but one of the men had already produced the necessary documentation.

The sheriff studied it and sighed. "Well, he's down at the morgue. I'll come along and tell them to release the body to you."

He returned a half hour later and collapsed in his chair. "Well, that's over with now, Tammy," he said.

"Who were they?" she asked.

"Those were agents."

"FBI?" she whispered.

"No, CIA."

"CIA?"

"That's right."

"Wow. That was just like the movies."

"All I know, Tammy, is that it's someone else's problem now."

Agent Greene walked into his boss's office without knocking. As usual the air was hazy with cigarette smoke. Zackman sat with a cigarette dangling from his mouth and his feet up on the desk, watching the flickering television.

Greene crossed the room and lowered himself onto the tattered brown sofa. A wrestling match was playing out silently on the television. One of the wrestlers was gigantically fat and dressed all in black with a mask and a cape. The other was huge but all muscle; he wore tight shorts with the American flag stitched in sequins.

Greene said, "I didn't know you were a fan."

"Never seen it before," Zackman answered, his eyes still fixed on the screen.

"What do you think?" Greene was stalling, but he couldn't help it.

"Smart packaging. They're giving people just what they want—violence and easy morality. Obviously the fat fuck is evil and the Superman clone is the hero. Do they ever let the bad guys win?"

"I don't follow it," Greene admitted, "but I think the bad guys are generally the most popular."

Zackman grunted, stubbed out the cigarette in the overflowing ashtray, and lit a new one.

They sat in silence for a while watching the wrestling match. Finally Greene cleared his throat. "I have a report on Team Persi," he said.

Zackman's eyes slid away from the television and fixed on Greene.

"They found Torrenson," Greene paused, "in a sack in South Dakota. We found out when his alias was queried."

Zackman rolled his cigarette between his fingers. "We'll have to collect the body," he said.

"I've already sent some men. They're on their way back now."

"Have you notified next of kin?"

"Yes."

"Can we give them the body?"

Greene shook his head. "Shot to the face, point-blank range."

Zackman took a long drag of the cigarette. He turned his eyes back to the television, but Greene could tell he wasn't seeing anything on the screen. "Any word about our other man?" Zackman said.

"No. But it's possible that even if he has access to a phone it's not safe for him to use it."

"I realize that, Greene," Zackman snapped. "Shit." He pounded the table with his fist and the ashtray rattled.

"I'll go in," Greene volunteered.

"I don't need heroics. Right now I need men to follow up on the other angles."

"What other angles?"

"Any other angles, for fuck's sake. In the meantime we can just hope we don't get pulled off the case. The chief has taken a personal interest in this situation."

"But the chief won't pull the team off the case when we've still got the other man in," Greene protested.

"We think we do, but we don't know for

sure," Zackman corrected. "They don't think logically up there. There's more of a chance they'll leave us on the case for the sake of the fucking name. Those stuffed shirts with their inspirational fucking directives. Have you ever heard of a name like Team Persistence?"

Greene made a face.

"I don't know the history behind the chief's fixation on this guy, but he wants answers and he wants them yesterday."

"Why don't we just shut him down? If we can find out where he's going to be next?"

"Stop and think for a fucking second. Without some phenomenal luck we'd only be able to convict him on weapons possession. All he'd get would be a slap on the wrist, *and* he'd be alerted to the fact that we're watching him. No, we'll continue on with the present plan and hope our man comes through before the next job."

Perfect Health

Sarah could hear the whispered conversation between the two doctors from her bed by the window as though they meant her to hear.

"... severe depression and completely unresponsive. Physically we could have released her a week ago. Aside from her injuries she's in perfect health."

The other doctor's voice was a low mutter, but she couldn't distinguish the words. One half of the conversation was more than enough.

"No," the first doctor answered, "no living relatives that we can track. No, not for the husband either. You're right, the insurance company has already contacted me. And I can't tell them there's any foreseeable change. Come in and you can give me your opinion."

They entered the room, and Sarah's doctor crossed briskly to the hospital bed. He said a cheery good morning and pulled out his stethoscope. Bending over her, he slipped the cold metal disk under the collar of her hospital gown and listened.

He straightened and said, "How are you feeling, Sarah?"

She didn't answer him.

He nodded as though her silence was expected, scribbled some lines on her chart, and hung it back on the end of the bed. As he and the other doctor left the room—just before the door shut completely—a few words drifted back: "Give her a few more days. Then we'll see."

It was evening and the lights were off in the room. The door opened, laying a gradually fattening bar of light across the floor.

Switching on the overhead fluorescent, the doctor entered. He drew a chair up next to her bed.

"Sarah? Sarah, can you hear me?"

Sarah idly tried to comb her hair out with her fingers. Hitting a big snarl, she let her hand drop listlessly back into her lap.

"How long has it been now, Sarah? Almost two weeks, isn't it? And it's not getting better. You're not getting better."

She silently agreed. Nothing was better.

"Sarah, do you have any living relatives? We checked your files and there are none listed. Isn't there anyone we can call? Anyone?" He waited in vain for a response.

"Sarah, there's not much more we can do for you. Your hip is healing nicely. Your ribs as well. But we can't send you home. And we can't help you here. I think you need somewhere to rest. How does that sound? We found a place that has an opening. That's very lucky, you know. It's usually months on a waiting list. We've gotten a place for you at Willowridge Rest Home. It's very small, quite exclusive. I think you'll be happy there, Sarah. Sarah? Sarah, can you hear me?"

Where she expected to find indifference, she found rage and had no idea what to do with it. She traced one sharp nail across the inside of her wrist.

The doctor heard the sharp intake of breath and leaned forward. "What is it, Sarah?"

She turned dark glittering eyes on him.

He said soothingly, "This isn't forever, you know, Sarah. It's just until you get back on your feet, so to speak."

She knew he was lying. He didn't believe, once she entered the nursing home, that she would ever get out. Neither did she. They were both wrong.

A Familiar Tune

Merec phoned Karl first. They had not spoken since Merec had sent him on to New York. "How's everything?" Merec asked.

"Fine," Karl said with his usual brevity.

There was a short silence. Then Karl spoke again. "Rendezvous?"

Merec sighed. "Not yet," he said. "I'll let you know. I need you where you are. I have another job to complete first."

Next Merec called Tina. "How is your position?" he asked her.

"It's fucking awful. I can't believe you sent me to a fucking old folks home."

"Has anything changed since your last report?"

"Nothing ever changes around this fucking place," she complained. "Is this thing happening soon or what? I could take care of it myself, you know."

"No, I wouldn't advise that. My plans are a bit more elaborate. I'll contact you."

Merec hung up the phone and dialed again, leaving his phone number on the machine that picked up. Then he sat with his back to the window, the phone at his elbow. The light outside faded slowly. He heard a snatch of song, something hauntingly familiar, and crossed to the window, dipping his head out to catch the tune on the breeze. A moment more and he would have had it, but the phone rang. He waited until the fifth ring to pick up, and spoke into the receiver. "Have you deposited half of the money in the account? All right. Now I will take care of your little task as soon as the money is confirmed. Don't worry. I'll fix it so no one will ever suspect. Yes, I will be in touch."

Dead as a Doornail

Those who could still walk came out just before sunset every afternoon, emerging from the doorway with lightweight aluminum chairs. They gathered outside from early spring, when the first buds appeared on the trees, right through the fall, when the branches stood cold and dead against a gray sky. They came to escape the echoing hallways, to talk to the others who could still put words together into sentences, and to be recognized so that they would eventually be missed.

There were four of them on this chilly spring afternoon, the trees still skeletal and the grass more brown than green. Last fall there had been eight. But just as the days turned cold enough to whip their noses red, Harold Nussbaum, the sole male attendee, had died of his fourth heart attack. Then, sometime over the winter months, Rachel Merrywether had slipped desperately over into senility, and though she sometimes looked at them as though trying to remember something long forgotten, she did not know them. And just last week, Beatrice Spanner had died in her sleep. Bea had been quiet, but the way she lifted her face to the breeze had reminded them of what remained. They set out Bea's empty chair so that she could—by her absence this time—prod them into occasional thankfulness.

The sun was hanging low over the distant hills, and Emma Ness was still missing. They shifted in their chairs and offered up comments on the weather: the outlook (not a cloud in the slate-gray sky), the chill (a brisk fifty degrees), and the lack of rain (there never seemed to be enough in these dry years). Everyone had an eye on their watch. Finally Rose Tillman spoke.

"Dead," she pronounced in a loud, strident voice. "I say she's dead as a doornail by now."

Meg Litton gave a barking laugh, and Mattie Franklin shot them a disapproving glance.

Rose said, "What are you looking at me like that for, Miss Mattie Franklin? A person's allowed to express their own opinion. I do believe that the Russians haven't taken over yet, and it's still a free country. If my memory serves."

"The Chinese," Doris Morton said from behind her newspaper.

Rose transferred her glare from Mattie to Doris. Doris folded the next page back, snapped it straight, and held it up in front of her eyes.

"What's that supposed to mean?" Rose demanded.

Doris sighed and lowered her paper. "Either your memory or your knowledge of current events has failed you. The Russians are no longer a threat. They can't even quell an insurrection in their own country. The more acknowledged danger at the moment happens to be the Chinese." And she raised her paper again.

"Didn't I tell you not to speak to me?" Rose said. "Now you just need to remember that I will sit out here and like a proper Christian I will consent to share the same air with you, but I would ask you to remember next time that I specifically request that you not speak to me again. I, for one, don't care for your superior intellectual bullshit."

Mattie Franklin interrupted their argument. "Where *is* that girl?" she said, pushing herself up and out of her chair. "I'll go see what's keeping Emma. She's room twenty-four, isn't she?"

All eyes watched Mattie as she stood and walked toward the side door, her hips wide and comfortable in polyester knit.

But just then, farther down the walk, Emma's window slid up in its sash and her gray head poked out.

"You can go and sit back down, Mattie," she called. "I haven't kicked the bucket yet."

"All right," Mattie drawled, though the relief was plain on her face. "I was coming over to check on you. Everything okay?"

"Just fine. I'll be right out."

Mattie nodded and headed back toward the group.

A few minutes later the side door opened, but instead of Emma, Simon emerged. Simon was an attendant at Willowridge—young, lanky, and a great favorite with the women, even with Rose.

They called out "Simon!" and a few clapped their hands.

"Ladies," Simon replied. He crossed the lawn. "May I join you?" he said, and sat down in the empty chair that stood a little apart from the disorderly semicircle. He stretched out his long thin legs.

"What's this extra chair for?" Simon asked.

"It's Bea's," Mattie told him. "She wanted to leave it for the next person who came to Willowridge. The next person who could use it," she amended. "And we thought we'd bring it out until it got filled."

"It's a kind thought," Simon said. "And someone may have need of it soon."

"What?" several of the women exclaimed at the same time. New admissions weren't unusual. But a new patient who was a candidate for the group that met on the lawn—that was a rarity.

They demanded details. "I don't know much about her," Simon said. "All I know is that her name is Sarah Shepherd."

Sarah's Contribution to the Conversation

When Sarah arrived at Willowridge, she moved into Bea's room and Bea's bed, but as it turned out, Bea's chair remained empty; Sarah was still using her wheelchair, though her doctor had encouraged her to begin to walk. As she was wheeled through the hallways, she felt as if she were floating past phantoms. The corridors were quiet, and everyone spoke in hushed tones. Several other wheelchairs glided past, handled by attendants in white smock coats, and a couple of ambulatory inmates shuffled by with bent white heads and identical loose-fitting light blue pajamas.

There wasn't much pretense to amusement at Willowridge. The TV was situated in a long, narrow room packed with chairs, but when a bland-faced attendant tried to wheel Sarah in, she protested with a violent shake of her head. Instead she was parked near a window in a tiny sitting room with two faded chintz chairs and a sewing kit thick with dust atop a narrow sideboard. She fell asleep while watching a sparrow in a birch outside the window. A gentle hand on her shoulder awakened her.

"Excuse me." A lanky young man in a white smock bent over her. "The ladies are asking for you." He motioned out the window to the cluster of chairs at the edge of the hill. "May I?" he asked politely as he drew the chair back. He wheeled her out the side door and across the manicured lawn to where the small group sat clustered under the stand of trees. The branches swayed in a light breeze, and the slanting sun lit the old faces.

There seemed, almost, to be a place awaiting her—a break in the cluster of chairs. There were a few smiles, but otherwise her appearance went unmarked. It surprised Sarah. Though she had been willing to join the group to sit in the chilly breeze, she had been steeling herself to meet all advances with a cold stare. Instead she had not heard a word of greeting. The attendant was already halfway across the lawn, so she didn't have the possibility of retreat. She turned her attention back to the group. An ancient, brittle woman was reading a section from a newspaper held close in front of her nose.

"Under the agreement, which postpones a

final decision on Chechen independence, the Russians remain in the position of ceremonial partners in supervising the rebellious region. Although independence has not yet been achieved, the rebels have exposed the fragility of their mother country."

She lowered the paper and looked pointedly at a plump woman with a ball of knitting in her lap. Without pausing in the rhythm of her work, Rose said calmly, "Stuff it, Doris."

"Where do you find those expressions?" Doris asked with distaste.

"Certainly not in that damn paper."

"Who are you rooting for in this Chechen thing, Doris?" Emma asked, attempting to interrupt the two.

"For God's sake, Emma, it's not a tennis match," Mattie rebuked her. "We're talking about people dying."

"There's nothing so awful about dying," Sarah said suddenly, without even knowing she was going to speak.

All the women treated her to cold stares.

"And who asked you?" Meg Litton said. She narrowed her eyes. "You don't look old enough to speak without being spoken to."

"What I want to know," Rose pronounced in her raucous crow's voice, "is why we should give a shit about these foreigners killing each other in their own damn country. I bet they don't give a thought to us."

"They're in the middle of a war," Doris said.

"So?" Sarah interjected. "Would you rather be here?"

There was a startled silence.

"She's got a point," Rose leaned forward. "Are you going to answer the question?" When Doris did not respond, she turned instead to Meg. "What do you say, Meg?"

"I'd rather be there," Meg said.

"Aha," Rose crowed. "Emma?"

Emma laughed apologetically but agreed. "There."

"Mattie?

Mattie nodded.

Doris broke in. "That just goes to show how ignorant you are. You don't know what war is like."

"Do you think the Chechen soldiers would switch with us?" Rose asked slyly, and everyone laughed at the thought.

Fireworks

Sarah had been at Willowridge four months, and the weather had shifted from chill March winds to thick July heat. The morning of the Fourth was brooded over by low clouds. The light was yellowish, and the air had a breathless quality as it sighed through the trees. In previous years, from their vantage point at the crest of the hill, the old women could look off toward the city to the southwest and see the glow of the fireworks. Best of all, even from that distance they could hear the muffled booming and feel it reverberate in their fragile bones.

Mrs. Moodie, the head of the nursing home, was away on a long weekend, and she had left Martha Bell in charge. Martha was an earnest young woman with a flustered manner and a worried frown. Martha had been warned that she would be short-staffed on the Fourth, but when the day arrived it was worse than she had imagined. So when one of the new girls, Tina, arrived with two friends to help out, she didn't question providence. They were unusual friends for a young girl to have—a moon-faced balding man she called Fritz and an older gentleman with shaggy gray hair and startlingly blue eyes—but Martha was desperate and not inclined to look a gift horse in the mouth.

Martha settled down for the day in the video room, her eyes glued to the monitors, watching the faces of the weaker residents. She made a silent prayer, "Don't let them die while I'm in charge." She dreaded having to make the call to the relatives. She knew she couldn't summon the deep-throated sorrow that Mrs. Moodie had perfected while intoning the scripted speech "Your father [mother, brother, sister, cousin, great aunt] passed away early this morning [late this afternoon, in the early evening]. He [she] passed quietly in his [her] sleep." That part never changed. They all passed "quietly in their sleep," even when someone had a violent seizure in the middle of a roast beef dinner.

Martha watched on the screens as the harried staff helped everyone dress and get to breakfast. Lunch also was a success. They even managed to get everyone a bowl of vanilla ice cream with a dribble of canned blueberries and one maraschino cherry on top.

Outside, the clouds broke up, scudding off to the north. By afternoon the clouds had disappeared and the blue sky stretched vast overhead. But the observation room had no windows; it was dark but for the flickering light from the monitors. Martha stretched and rubbed her eyes.

The door of the room opened with just a whisper of sound. Martha was so transfixed by the screen that she didn't notice; she was staring into old Mr. Macy's eyes, silently willing him not to die. The two steps taken to reach the back of her chair were catlike and professional. She watched for death, but when it came, for all her vigilance, she didn't see it at all. At least she was spared when Mr. Macy met his end not too much later. Someone else had to make the call to the daughter, son, brother, sister, cousin, though this time they could not with impunity say he died in his sleep.

Sarah dozed in the sitting room during most of the afternoon. She woke when the light that came through the window was dusky gray. She assumed that with the excitement of the day, they had forgotten about her.

Not wanting to miss the fireworks she had heard so much about, Sarah wheeled herself laboriously down the corridor. When she reached the side door, an attendant she had never seen before—an older man with bright blue eyes—was turning a key in the bolt. He appeared mildly surprised to see her. "What's your name?" he asked.

"Sarah Shepherd."

"Weren't you in the TV room, Sarah?"

"Sitting room."

"Ah," he said. "I'm afraid you won't be meeting out on the lawn today. The other ladies have all gone on to the dining room."

She sat, waiting for him to take the handles of her wheelchair and escort her there. He stood and regarded her.

"I'm afraid," he said, "that you'll have to make your own way there. I need to wait for one more. Doris, I think it is."

She opened her mouth to question him, but something indefinable about his eyes made her hesitate. Slowly she pivoted the wheelchair and, without a word, pushed herself back down the empty corridor.

As she turned the corner, Sarah realized that the hall was unusually dim and gloomy. It took a moment to recognize the cause: all the doors along the corridor were closed. She rolled to a halt in front of one. With a quick glance over her shoulder, she twisted the knob. Wheeling herself in, she stopped to shut the door behind her.

"Hello?" she called. "Hello?"

The blinds were drawn and the room was

shadowy. It took a second for her eyes to adjust to the dim light. Rolling farther into the room, she saw that both beds were occupied. The first thing she noticed was the bright red pillows—Fourth of July colors. Then she focused on the faces, mouths tipped open, staring at a point in midair. In the center of their foreheads, right between their unfocused eyes, there was a neat round hole, singed around the edges with black.

Her hand rose to her lips, and she said, "Oh," very quietly. She could feel her heart beating hard against her ribs. Taking a deep breath, she backed the wheelchair away and turned from the bodies.

The corridor was empty as she slipped out. She bumped clumsily into the wall, backed up, and continued down the hallway to the dining room.

When she appeared in the doorway, she saw that everyone was waiting. They were grouped around the end of one of the long white dining tables. The man with the blue eyes smiled at her.

"Oh, we've been worried about you," Emma blurted out. "We didn't know where you'd got to. This man here was about to send someone to fetch you."

Sarah glanced at the other faces around the table. Rose was knitting and grumbling into her lap. Meg drummed her fingers on the table. Emma was tilted slightly in her chair to listen to something Mattie was whispering. Doris was reading the paper, raised like a shield between herself and the world. Only Mattie looked worried, her forehead wrinkled into crazy ruts and furrows.

"Come join us," the blue-eyed man beckoned from his seat at the head of the table.

Mattie leaped up to help her, but the man motioned her back down. "She can do it," he said. And Sarah rolled herself the last few yards across the room to a space beside Rose.

"We're waiting for a few more people to join us. Then we can begin."

"Begin what?" Emma asked.

"The festivities, milady," Merec said, with a gracious half-bow from his chair. "We will begin the festivities." Sensing something, Merec turned. "Ah," he said. "Jeremy has arrived."

A man stood in the doorway. He was thin and graceful and had long, glossy black hair that he wore pulled back in a ponytail.

"Jeremy, these are the ladies. Ladies, Jeremy," Merec performed the introductions. "Jeremy, if you would be so good as to get out the camera. We want to have these precious moments preserved."

Jeremy entered the room and silently bent over a black nylon bag. Sarah tensed as he pulled back the zipper and reached in, but he only retrieved a camcorder. Slipping one hand under the strap, he lifted the recorder to his eye. He swung the camera in the direction of the doorway, and everyone turned. Simon, their favorite attendant, stumbled forward into the room. He was followed by another attendant, Tina. She had come to work at Willowridge about the time Sarah had arrived. Tina helped Simon to a chair at the next table, and Sarah saw her slip something under her jacket before backing away.

Immediately afterward another figure appeared. Kevin, also a long-time attendant, though not so well liked as Simon, paused in the doorway, bent double, and vomited on the floor between his feet. In his sudden crouch, Kevin exposed the moon-faced man behind him—and the pistol in his hand.

Sarah knew that the others had seen it from the sharp intake of breath and the sudden stillness around her.

They all looked automatically from the gun to Merec. He said, "I guess the secret is out." Drawing from his waistband an identical weapon, he laid it on the table in front of him and added, "Come in, Fritz. And bring your guest."

The moon-faced man stepped carefully around the puddle of vomit and guided Kevin to a seat.

Merec clapped his hands. "Good. Everyone's here. Now we can begin."

The light had dimmed over the faraway hills, and the people around the table melted into gray paper cutouts. Jeremy flicked the switch on the wall, and hollow eyes and white knuckles instantly filled in the outlines. Emma took a breath, as if to speak, but Doris squeezed her hand and Emma subsided. A gulping sob escaped from Kevin. They all heard the beginnings of hysteria and looked anywhere but at his pale, contorted face.

Merec cleared his throat. "Fritz," he barked.

Fritz glanced up and, catching Merec's meaning, stepped forward to slap Kevin across the face. A crimson mark transformed the pale cheek, but it faded quickly and took with it the rising hysteria. Kevin settled into softer moans.

"I must say, on the whole, you are a very well-behaved lot," Merec said, rising. He tucked the gun back into the waistband of his pants, sauntered across the room, and grabbed the backs of two empty chairs. These he arranged tilted on an angle to face each other. "You couldn't imagine some of the company we've kept," he continued as he walked back for more chairs. "Screaming, fainting, hiding under tables." He took hold of two more and set them next to the first pair. "Tables don't generally stop bullets, you know.

"Oh, but the worst are the people who try to be heroes. Such an unfortunate term. It allows people to act under the guise of heroism when the real motivating factors are self-interest and panic. Human nature under extreme stress is a topic that fascinates me." He stopped to count heads, arranged two more, and stood back to survey the effect. "I've devoted quite a bit of my time and gone to no end of trouble to study it. They say the true qualities are brought out by stress." He minutely adjusted the last pair of chairs and looked up at them.

"I'm going to give all of you a chance to participate in one of my most long-standing experiments." He crooked a finger at Kevin, who was crying quietly, one hand clapped over the lower half of his face to muffle the noise. "You, what's your name?" Kevin drew a shuddering breath, but Merec said, "Never mind, never mind. Just come over here and take a seat." He patted the first chair invitingly. Kevin tried to rise, but his legs betrayed him, and he sank back down. Tina took one arm and Fritz took the other and they dragged him over to the first chair.

Everyone else was quick to take the seats assigned to them. Meg sat in the seat next to Kevin, Emma sat with Mattie, and Doris with Simon. Sarah and Rose were wheeled up to the line of chairs to make the last pair. Though Kevin was at the other end of the line, Sarah could detect the acrid odor of vomit. She wondered if it was something like what horses smelled when they scented fear.

"Now I want you all to listen very closely," Merec said, swinging a chair around to face them, "as this really is a matter of life and death.

Or should I say a choice between the two."

Jeremy stationed himself behind Merec, and the dark eye of the camera panned across their faces, freezing their fear on a tiny cassette.

"I am going to ask one person in each pair a question. You must answer in a complete sentence. That means subject and verb. I am enamored of proper grammar, and you'll have to indulge me." He scanned the faces. "You will have exactly two minutes to answer the question," he continued, tapping his watch. "Does everyone understand so far?" He paused, but no one replied.

In the brief silence they heard a low, thundering boom. Sarah saw joy light up the faces around her—in a second transformed from despair to deliverance. The instantaneous transition showed that in their hearts, each and every one had believed they would escape through some act of providence—that, like in the movies, they too would be rescued in the nick of time.

Sarah felt the thunder in her breastbone, felt the sound reverberate in her rib cage, but she knew that when she looked out the window she would see, not a cluster of police, but a fading, melting blossom of color in the sky. When she turned her head she caught the end of it, the pink and green stars that fell into insubstantial lines of palest light, like angels falling from grace.

As the next one, a bright, garish purple, exploded into miniature violets, Simon groaned.

"The fireworks," Mattie whispered.

Merec's rich laugh rolled over the group. "Just as you say, my dear. And here we all thought it was the cavalry arriving, didn't we?"

"I love the fireworks," Mattie said simply.

"Then you shall not miss them this year because of us."

"They'll take at least twenty fucking minutes," Tina protested.

Merec turned to Jeremy. "Do we have enough time before the night staff are due to arrive?"

"Yes," Jeremy answered from behind the camera.

Merec stood and shut off the lights. "You're missing them," he said to Mattie, motioning toward the windows behind her where a blood-red flower hung and wilted in seconds.

They twisted in their chairs to watch the spectacle. The woman Tina paced and smoked in jerky movements, Fritz picked at a scab on his elbow, and Jeremy circled and filmed their faces as they watched.

Sarah could not ignore the pacing woman, the camera, and the gun she knew was resting on Fritz's knee, but none of these things interfered with her enjoyment of the fireworks blossoming and dying on the faraway hill. And when the last melted into the sky, she acknowledged them to be very good fireworks—not the best she'd ever seen but very good.

They reluctantly turned away from the window. Jeremy flicked on the lights, and Merec rubbed his eyes wearily with one long, slender hand.

"All right, let's get on with it," he said, but he seemed to have lost his former spirit. He signaled to Fritz, who immediately went to stand behind Kevin and Meg. Kevin was the only one who had not watched the fireworks. He sat with one hand pressed firmly over his eyes.

Merec fixed his gaze instead on Meg. "My dear, my question is for you, as your companion does not look fit to answer. Remember that you have two minutes. I am going to kill one of you. I am giving you the choice. Will you die, or will it be the man sitting across from you?" He glanced down at his watch, and back up at Meg's face.

Meg didn't seem surprised or even much troubled. She looked at Kevin, who did not seem to have registered the question. She turned back and said clearly and distinctly, "Kill him."

Immediately they heard a soft "phft," and Kevin sagged even farther forward, tilting as though in slow motion. He landed on the floor with a dull thud.

"My dear," Merec said, "you have broken a record. It only took you six seconds to decide another man's life should be sacrificed for your own. I applaud your moral struggle."

In profile, Sarah imagined that she saw a tear glittering in the corner of one eye, but when he turned back, she concluded it must have been the light, for its planes and crags were like chiseled stone and the expression as impassive.

He looked to Emma next and asked the question of her.

"You're an evil, evil man," Emma said.

Her partner, Mattie, sat rigid and waiting, not raising her eyes from her lap.

When the clock reached one minute fifty seconds, Merec started counting aloud, "Fifty, fifty-one, fifty-two, fifty-three . . . you're going to die, my dear," and at that, Emma whispered, "Kill her," and Mattie fell onto the hard tile beside Kevin, blood pooling beneath her cheek.

And Jeremy, circling, recorded it all.

Merec glanced at Doris, then raised his eyebrows at Simon. A choking sound came from Simon's throat. "Kill her," he said finally, his voice high and unnatural. Doris collapsed forward and landed with her arm outflung, a fingertip touching Mattie's shoulder.

He turned to Rose and Sarah and looked from one to the other. Rose was knitting, her eyes stubbornly fixed on the needles in her lap.

"Well, what do you say?" he called to Sarah.

Sarah looked up into his blue eyes. "Kill me," she said.

Fritz hesitated and glanced at Merec.

"I will, you know. Don't think I won't."

Sarah's gaze rested on the crumpled figures she had known too briefly to call friends, and she said, "How could I not believe you?"

He stared at her, a frown gathering, then made a sudden motion. Sarah felt movement behind her and tensed involuntarily. But it was Simon, beside her, who fell, then Emma. It was done quickly, but before Fritz reached Meg, she caught on to what was in store. She didn't attempt to get up or even to duck. She simply opened her mouth and emitted a high keening. It ended as abruptly as it had started, and she too fell.

The sudden quiet rang with the echo of the last shot. A lake of blood crept across the floor, engulfing each sprawled figure.

Fritz started back over to Sarah and Rose.

"Not Rose," Sarah said.

Merec held up his hand, and Fritz stopped.

Rose doggedly continued with her knitting, her needles trembling and clicking against each other irregularly. But Sarah was prodded into speech. "What was that for?" she demanded.

"That?" Merec gestured to the figures on the floor. "It's for the best, really. In the past, when I've let those people go, twenty-five percent committed suicide within a year anyway. And another fifty percent never got over it."

"And the last twenty-five?"

"The last twenty-five percent, yes, they lived, as they say, happily ever after." He shrugged.

Jeremy circled with the camera.

"So now what are you going to do with me?"

"What indeed," Merec said. He pulled out his gun and ran his hand over the barrel. "I must confess that I am terribly curious."

She shifted in her chair.

"Could you tell me why you chose the answer you did? Was it a moral compunction? The thought of the guilt? What?"

"I didn't know there was a questionnaire," Sarah said.

He chuckled in delight. "You are extraordinary. But you really must tell me."

"Or you'll kill me?" She twined her fingers together in her lap. "Your bargaining position isn't very good."

"You think death is the only threat I can use? You think that's as bad as it gets? Everyone is so sheltered these days. Death is the best I have to offer. That is usually the reward, not the punishment."

"I'm not afraid of you," she said, chin raised.

"Really?"

She shook her head.

He pondered this and said, "We'll see."

Tina broke in impatiently, "We've got to get going."

Merec gave a look that silenced her. Then he addressed Jeremy. "ETA of the night crew?"

Without lowering the camera Jeremy replied, "Ten minutes."

Merec turned to Sarah. "What are we going to do with you?"

"I can tell you one thing you're not going to do," she answered.

"What's that?" he asked, as if playing with an enchanting child.

"You're not going to hurt Rose."

"Who says it hurts?" But he said to Jeremy, "We're done here."

Jeremy filmed a few more seconds, flicked a button, and the red eye faded. Lowering the camera, he ejected the cassette and handed it to Merec.

"Are you certain you didn't get any of our faces on tape?" Merec asked.

Jeremy nodded as he packed away the camera.

"All right, let's get going."

Merec crossed the room to Rose, who was still hunched over her needles. He laid the tape gently in her lap. "Make sure," he said slowly and distinctly, "that this gets to the media. And don't tell the police anything. If you do, you'll put her," he motioned toward Sarah, "in serious danger."

"I don't fucking believe it. You're leaving her behind?" Tina blurted out.

"Tina," he said in warning.

"But she can identify us, give a description to the police," Tina's voice rose.

"Fritz, can you shut her up?" he said, over his shoulder. He crouched before Rose and lifted the lumpy knitting. "What are you making here?"

Rose didn't answer, but she started violently at the sound of the shot.

When Merec straightened, Fritz was lowering Tina's body to the ground. "Thank you, Fritz," he said. "All right, let's move out. The other one comes with us."

Jeremy stepped forward and took the handles of Sarah's wheelchair. Fritz followed, leaving Rose alone among the bodies.

When they reached the parking lot, Merec called over, "Jeremy, you take her." Then he and Fritz veered off toward another car.

Jeremy halted the chair with a jerk before the passenger side of a dark blue sedan. He opened the door, lifted Sarah effortlessly—one arm beneath her knees, the other behind her shoulders—and deposited her on the seat. He collapsed the chair and stowed it in the trunk.

The other car was already pulling out of the lot as Jeremy slid in beside her. He started the engine and stepped on the gas. They raced down the access road and cornered the turn onto the slightly larger country road. Sarah felt the speed in the vibration of the car and the blurring of the trees that whipped by. She had been stationary, motionless for so long. Twisting in her seat, she looked back at the rest home perched on the hill. An appropriate position, she thought, for Purgatory.

As they edged onto the highway, thick with Fourth of July traffic, Sarah saw the lights of a car turn in where they had just emerged and knew it must be the first of the night crew arriving.

The Handoff

After parking the car, Charlotte Wilson went straight to the attendants' lounge. There she changed her shoes, put her purse away in her locker, and buttoned up her white smock. Sitting down on the old green couch, she extracted a cigarette from the box in her pocket. Usually the staff, eager to switch shifts, popped their heads into the lounge in search of their replacements. Charlotte sucked heavily at the end of the cigarette, expecting to get just a few puffs before being discovered. She was still sitting there ten minutes later when Becky ran skidding into the room. Throwing open her locker, she retrieved her smock and buttoned it with hurried fingers.

"God, I'm late," Becky said over her shoulder to Charlotte on the couch. "Are they raving?"

"No one's come in yet," Charlotte answered,

lighting her third cigarette. "Want one?" she asked, holding out the pack.

Becky shook her head. "That's strange. Did you check the video room?"

There was always someone in the video room.

"Haven't checked anywhere. Didn't want to mess with a good thing."

Becky shot her a disgusted look and went out into the hall.

A moment later Charlotte heard Becky's scream and dropped her cigarette on the floor where it burned a round black hole through the carpet. She hurried around the corner and discovered Becky in the video room, shivering and crying over the body of Martha Bell.

"Jesus," Charlotte said, backing away. "I'll go get somebody."

Running down the corridor, Charlotte called out, "Simon? Simon?" and heard her voice die out in the stillness. She noticed that all the doors along the hallway were shut. Opening one, she flicked on the light and saw the bodies. "Holy shit," she said.

Just then Becky's hysterical screams echoed again through the building. Charlotte found her sobbing in great heaving gulps outside the TV room.

"They're dead," she hiccuped, "they're all dead."

Charlotte glanced in. The room was filled

with slumped figures in the flickering blue light. She took Becky's arm, steered her back to the office, and settled her on a couch. Then she called 911. After waiting on hold, she finally got someone on the line. She gave them all the pertinent information in a low if not quite steady voice. When the operator told her they would do the best they could, Charlotte exploded, "I don't think you understand. It's a fucking massacre. Get someone over here now."

She was relieved when she heard the bell not more than five minutes later. She ran to the front entrance and pulled open the door.

There weren't any police cars or ambulances in the driveway. There were only two gray vans that had IBC on the side in large black letters. A knot of people clustered on the stoop, two of whom had huge cameras perched on their shoulders.

At first she was shocked. How could the camera crews arrive before the police? But she was glad to have someone else in the building besides the dozens of silent corpses, and she opened the double doors to let them in.

One camera crew rushed by her, the other stayed to talk. They pointed the camera at her face, thrust a microphone to her mouth, and shot question after question: When did she arrive? How did she discover the bodies? What was her first reaction? Were there any survivors?

The other camera crew ranged through room

after room, finding neat, quiet bedrooms and old men and women with neat, quiet holes in their heads. Then they reached the dining room and found Rose. She was still knitting, but she had been expecting someone ever since she heard Becky's screams.

The reporter crossed the room, stepping carefully over the bodies. He reached her side and asked, "Ma'am, are you all right? Do you need an ambulance?" Then, recognizing the amazing opportunity, he questioned her urgently. "Can you tell me what happened here?"

Rose's eyes slid past him to the cameraman who appeared in the doorway. "Are you with the news?" she asked.

He hesitated and admitted that he was.

"Then I have something for you," she said. Reaching under her knitting, she pulled out the tape and placed it carefully in his hand.

Visitor's Day
at Willowridge

A tall thin man in a crumpled gray suit approached the doors of Willowridge Rest Home several hours after the camera crew had been ejected by the arrival of the police. He walked to the building with a slow, slouching gait and mounted the steps. There were two police officers posted at the doors.

"Hold on there," the officer said. "Where do you think you're going?"

The man smiled slightly, reached into his inside jacket pocket, and produced his wallet, which he flipped open and handed over.

"Huh." The officer looked closer. "This is a federal ID."

"You're very observant," the man said.

The officer ignored the remark. "So you guys are horning in on this already?"

The man shrugged and waited patiently.

The officer scrutinized the ID again. "Agent Tresler," he read out. Tresler held out his hand, and the officer grudgingly returned the wallet. Tucking it into his pocket, Tresler murmured, "Thank you," and passed through.

Once inside, he found the main hallway thronged with officers. He strolled through, stepping quietly out of the way when small clusters of people hurried by.

He watched as dozens of men with loose, practiced wrists painted all the surfaces with a thin gray dust. There were men on their knees in every room, searching for bullet casings, for stray cigarette butts, for strands of hair. There were doctors bent over the corpses, exhausted and overwhelmed by the sheer number of bodies. The people with clipboards were too numerous to count. Coffee and sandwiches rolled through the halls on emergency gurneys, and sharp voices bounced off the slick walls.

Tresler poked his head into one of the few doorways without a surrounding crowd and found only a single plainclothes detective bending over one of the twin beds. An old woman lay in the bed, a hole in the center of her forehead.

"What do you think?" Tresler asked.

"No sign of struggle," the detective said, not even looking up from his inspection.

"And the other rooms?"

"Identical."

Tresler circled the bed, stopping at the foot. He pulled aside the blanket where it had fallen over the edge, thereby uncovering a plastic nameplate. It read "Harvey Desmond."

Tresler pulled the nameplate off and inspected it. It was a simple magnet that adhered to the metal frame. Tapping it on his palm, he crossed to the bureau against the far wall. He opened the top drawer. It was filled with ladies' underclothes. Tresler glanced at the man still bent over the pillow inspecting the bloodstains and said, "The nameplates have been switched."

The detective straightened and came over. He took the nameplate from Tresler. "So they have," he said, turning it over. "I hadn't noticed. That will slow us down."

"I believe that's the point."

The detective switched his attention to Tresler for the first time and frowned slightly. "Who are you? I don't seem to recall . . . "

"Agent Tresler," he supplied, taking out his wallet again to show his credentials.

"Ah," the detective said. "We've been sort of expecting someone to show up. Simmons," the man introduced himself. "And as interesting as this crime scene is, I should show you to the dining room. There's a live one there. And you'll probably be wanting to talk to Stanley."

Simmons led the way out and shouldered a path through the crowded hallway. The doors to the dining room were propped open. Within, another plainclothes detective was squatting beside an old woman in a wheelchair. The woman continued to work the needles in her lap as the man tried to talk to her.

"That's Stanley. He's in charge of this investigation." Simmons pointed. "As you can see, he's talking to the only survivor we've found. I don't think they've gotten anything out of her. Stubborn old bird." He shrugged. "Anyway, he's the man you need."

Tresler thanked Simmons and threaded his way through the sprawled bodies, stopping just behind Stanley. He stood listening to the conversation.

Stanley was saying, "I'm only going to ask you one more time, Rose. Let me remind you that we're the good guys here." His voice climbed in frustration. "Rose, listen, you're all we've got to go on here." He waited in vain for an answer. Finally he said, "I'm this close to hauling you in for obstruction of justice. Now what the hell went on here tonight?"

Rose went on knitting.

Stanley straightened and wheeled around, almost knocking Tresler over.

"What the hell?" Stanley snapped. "Can't you see I'm busy here?" He was ready to push past until he took a better look. He had to tilt his head back slightly as Tresler had a good few inches on him, though Tresler was also at least fifty pounds lighter than the burly police detective. "And who the hell are you?" Stanley demanded.

Tresler fished out his wallet once again.

"What's this?" Stanley snatched the wallet impatiently from Tresler's hand. He examined it closely. "Oh." Stanley flipped the wallet closed and gave it back. "Are you here to take over the investigation? Because I've got everything under control."

Rose cackled behind him, and Stanley's already ruddy skin turned a deeper, more vibrant red.

"I'm sure you do," Tresler said. "I'm here merely in an advisory capacity."

"Oh." Stanley paused. "Of course you are. Well, as you can see, we've got quite a little party. And no one's talking. Of course, everyone but this little lady has got a pretty good reason. Let me introduce you to Rose. Rose," he said, snapping his fingers, "Rose, look at me."

Rose ignored him.

"Rose, this is Agent Tresler. Rose . . . "

Tresler stepped around Stanley and past Rose and returned pulling a chair. He placed it next to the wheelchair and sat.

Stanley leaned against the end of the table and crossed his arms.

Tresler studied the old woman's face. The lines about her mouth were deep with determination, and her eyes were resolutely fixed on the knitting in her lap. Her hands trembled as she worked the needles. In the short time he watched, she dropped three stitches.

Tresler glanced over at Stanley. "Could Rose and I have some time alone?" he asked.

"Be my guest. But I don't think you'll have much luck with her."

The corners of Tresler's mouth twitched as Stanley walked away. He hunched over in the chair, his elbows on his knees. After a few minutes he heard Rose shift restlessly. A few more and the needles stopped. Finally she blurted, "Well, aren't you going to ask me anything?"

He looked up into her face. "Are you going to tell me anything?"

She stared. Then she snorted a short burst of laughter. "Ha. That was good. But you're right. Like I said to him," she jerked her head at Stanley, "I'm not going to tell you a damn thing."

He nodded.

"I won't," she repeated, more forcefully than before.

"All right," Tresler said.

They sat silent for a long time.

"They said they would hurt her if I told you anything," she said abruptly.

His attention sharpened at the information, but he kept his expression neutral and his voice calm. "They're very trustworthy, then? Did they say they wouldn't hurt her if you didn't?"

She didn't answer but looked stubborn. He waited her out.

"You'll know it all soon enough anyway," she said.

"Oh?"

"Everybody will know soon. Why don't you go bother those TV people?"

"You told the TV people?"

"Huh." She tossed her head. "I didn't have to *tell* them. And I certainly won't tell *you*."

"I understand," he said. "I won't trouble you any longer."

She glanced at him suspiciously.

Tresler smiled and stood. She had already told him all he needed to know: they had a hostage, and the media had some sort of inside information. He crossed the room to where Stanley was conferring with Simmons.

When Stanley asked if he had gotten anything out of the old lady, Tresler shook his head and said, "You were right. No luck."

Stanley nodded with satisfaction.

"Do you mind if I wander around?"

Stanley was generous in his triumph. "Of course not. Simmons, will you show Agent Tresler around?"

"No, that's all right," Tresler said. "I'll be fine on my own. By the way, who discovered the bodies?"

Within half an hour, Tresler had spoken to both women from the night crew and was back in his car on his way to the IBC building.

Prime
Time

They **sat** in an editing suite, their faces ghostly, the figures of the dead reflected in their eyes. The reporter glanced frequently at his companion, then back at the screen. He had watched the tape once already, and without even turning on the lights, he had picked up the phone and called the station manager at his home. When the manager answered, there were sounds of laughter and the buzz of conversation in the background. "Can't it wait?" the manager snapped. "No," he said. "This one can't wait." The phone on the other end of the line was placed in the cradle rather emphatically, and now the reporter sat with him, watching the footage again, anxious to be vindicated.

The tape approached the climax. The reporter tightened his grip on the arms of his chair, anticipating the dramatic sequence when the camera closed in and held on that one extraordinary woman. It moved about her, framing the shadows under the high cheekbones, the lock of hair lying soft against her jaw, the deep brown eyes, eerie in their calm. And then the camera tore away, swung to the right, and caught the bent head of Rose, concentrating furiously on her knitting. Finally it focused on those knobbed, cramped, trembling old hands, the knuckles whitening around the thin aluminum. The screen went dead.

The station manager let out a shaky breath. "My God, that woman." He laid his hand on the reporter's shoulder, as if for support. "Do you know what we have here? This is a gold mine. This," he said in awe, "is prime time."

Tresler showed IBC's receptionist his credentials and asked for the night crew.

"They've all gone home," she said.

"The morning crew?" he asked.

"Not here yet."

"You mean there's no one here?"

"What am I, wood?"

Tresler smiled but didn't answer. He clasped his hands behind his back and took a stroll around the room. He stopped by the glass doors and looked out into the parking lot. He inspected the plants (fake) and the framed photographs of disasters (real). Then he walked back to the desk and slouched against it. "So," he said. "There are five cars in the parking lot. Are you sure there's no one here for me to speak to?"

"All right, wise guy," and she lifted the receiver to dial.

Tresler left the building an hour later with two videotapes tucked under his arm. He returned to the rest home just in time for the early morning news.

When Tresler entered Willowridge for the second time, he had to pass through the guards at the doors, but now the halls were deserted. There were trolleys with sheeted bodies seemingly abandoned. He peeked into a few rooms, but these also were empty. The mystery was solved when he reached the lounge. All the people in the building were packed around the television watching the news for coverage of the event. Stanley was at the forefront of the crowd.

Tresler edged inside the door and stood with his hands in his pockets. He arrived just as the program cut to footage the cameramen had taken at the nursing home before the police arrived. Even from his position back against the wall, Tresler could hear Stanley groan.

On the screen, an earnest but sorrowful

anchor announced that IBC had in their possession exclusive, uncut footage, taken by the perpetrators of this awful crime. It would air this evening at eight o'clock.

"What?" Stanley jumped up. "Son of a bitch." He violently kicked a metal filing cabinet, which boomed hollowly back at him. He searched the crowd. "Why didn't anyone inform me of this?"

No one answered him.

He let off another kick, this time at the couch. "Shit," he said, already halfway out the door.

Tresler slipped out after him. He caught up with Stanley in the hall.

Stanley jerked around at the touch on his arm. "Oh," he said. "It's you . . . "

"Agent Tresler," he supplied.

"Yes, that's right," Stanley said absentmindedly. Returning to the topic on his mind, he said, "Did you see, did you *see*? How could they . . . ? The old woman, damn her. Now we've got to . . . The TV station . . . "

"I've got the tape," Tresler interjected.

"Of course we've got to go get the damn tape. I *know* that. You bureau guys all think local police are idiots."

"No," Tresler said.

"Oh yes you do, and don't try to deny it," Stanley turned fiercely on him.

"I meant—" Tresler stopped and tried again. "I mean that you misheard me. I didn't say that we need to get the tape. I said that I already have the tape."

"You've got it?" Stanley repeated.

"You've got it." Tresler held it out to Stanley. Tresler didn't mention that he had another copy in his car.

Stanley took it, still looking as if he wasn't sure what he held. Then he threw his head back and laughed. "Well, how about that? You slippery little weasel," and Stanley clapped him on the shoulder.

Tresler winced.

"How about *that*! So they made their big announcement, and come eight o'clock they'll have nothing to show. Hah."

"No," Tresler said, trying to get Stanley's attention. "Listen, that's just a copy."

Stanley stopped chuckling and frowned.

"They'll still be airing the footage tonight."

"But they can't. We have to stop them."

"How?"

That halted Stanley in his tracks. "Isn't there some law we can invoke?"

"Think," Tresler said softly. "Just think. Do we even want to stop them from airing it?"

Stanley frowned again. "But—"

"What do we have to go on right now? What sort of evidence have your men gathered?"

"Well, it will take a while for results to come back from the lab," Stanley said.

"What do we really have?"

Stanley ignored the repeated question. "But we've still got to stop them from airing that tape."

Tresler shook his head gently. "I've got a better idea."

On Pins and Needles

Sarah woke to find her head resting on Jeremy's shoulder. Startled, she pushed herself upright. Jeremy's face was just visible in the light reflected from the dashboard. He had the blue shadow of a beard, and there were dark circles beneath his eyes. The window was cracked open, and the cool morning air blew through the car, ruffling the wisps of hair at his temples and brushing across her own face. He looked relaxed, driving with one hand on the wheel. He was flexing and clenching his other hand, but not in a menacing way. She realized she must have been leaning on his arm for a long time.

Glancing out the window, she could just make out the dark shapes of trees and the contour of a dirt road, whose jolting had roused her. It felt—there was no other word—cozy in the car, winding through the trees in the half darkness.

She recalled the last time she had been in a car without knowing the destination. Years ago, Jonathan had taken her for a drive for a birth-day—she didn't remember which. He had taken her to an amusement park where they had a mar-velous time until he bought her cotton candy, then coaxed her onto the Ferris wheel. She had gotten sick all over his pants.

The memory of her ride on the Ferris wheel summoned the more recent memory of Kevin and the scent of his vomit. She lifted her head and sniffed the clean morning air. By all rights she should be lying next to Simon on the disin-fected tile, maybe even obscenely draped over him. She knew that the thought should evoke emotion, but she felt nothing.

Sarah watched the trees gather complexity, their twisting branches emerging dark gray against a lightening sky.

Jeremy's voice made her turn away from the window.

"What's your name?" he asked.

She glanced over at him, and his face, which had seemed so impassive in the midst of the killing, now looked softer, almost melancholy.

"Sarah Shepherd."

"Sarah Shepherd," he repeated.

Suddenly, from his lips, it sounded like the name of a stranger.

"Well, Sarah Shepherd, we're almost there."

She nodded but didn't ask him where "there" was. She found that if she didn't know where she was going, it was easier to bear.

The
Pitch

Tresler parked next to Stanley's jeep outside IBC's main office. Neither had slept or changed, and both looked the worse for wear.

They entered, and Stanley flashed his badge at the receptionist. "Police," he barked, "I need to see the director, pronto."

The girl looked about fifteen and had a bored, seen-it-all expression. "We already had one of you around last night," she said.

"Well, honey, you got some more of us right now. Get the goddamned director on the line."

She snapped her gum. "You could see Mr. Elis."

"Who is Mr. Elis?"

"He's the station's public relations liaison."

Stanley decided to play along. "Honey, if you had important business, would you go talk to Mr. Elis?"

She laughed at the suggestion, her frosted pink lips curling.

"Right," Stanley said, pleased. "Now who do I want to see?"

The girl giggled and picked up the phone. "Some policemen here to see the director."

Stanley leaned over the desk. "Tell him it's Detective Stanley Wall."

"It's Detective Stanley Wall." She listened for a moment, then put the receiver down. "Wait over there," she said, with a dismissive flick of her wrist.

"You should learn some manners, young lady." Stanley stood over her. "Maybe I'll write you up for truancy."

She rolled her eyes. "It's summer, dummy."

They waited twenty minutes, Stanley pacing restlessly, Tresler slouched in a chair.

When the phone at the reception desk rang, the girl answered it, listened, and hung up without a word. She went back to her magazine and said, "Eighth floor, to your right at the end of the hall."

Stanley gave her a menacing look, which she didn't notice.

They went up and were met by a secretary with hair sprayed into a helmet, who opened the door into a huge corner office. Director

Morgan was sitting behind his desk. A man in an expensive suit—the lawyer, Tresler surmised—already occupied one of the chairs in front.

The director stood and with a slight motion of his head told the other man to do the same. "Ah, Detective . . . Detective . . . "

"Wall," Stanley supplied, automatically reaching into his pocket for his identification, but the director held up a hand.

"That's not necessary. Not necessary at all."

Stanley awkwardly withdrew his hand from the inside pocket. He cleared his throat and announced, "Agent Tresler."

"My, my, an agent also? Gentlemen." The director motioned toward other chairs. He made no attempt to introduce the other man present. "Now, I think I may know what you have come about. It's the nursing home incident, isn't it?"

Stanley cleared his throat again. "Yes, as a matter of fact—"

"Of course," the director interrupted. "Of course we'll get you a copy of the tape." He leaned forward and pressed an intercom on his desk.

"We already have a copy," Tresler said.

The director took his finger off the intercom. "Oh really? Well, then I can only assume that you have come to try to stop me from airing the footage." He stared hard at Tresler as he said this.

"On the contrary," Tresler said. He stopped and looked at Stanley.

Stanley nodded. "Quite the opposite," he said.

"Really?" the director drawled, glancing from one to the other and lacing his hands together on his desk. He glanced over at the man in the suit. "You can leave us now, Frank."

"I would suggest that I—" the man began, but the director cut him short. "Out," he said, very quietly. Frank rose immediately and left the room.

"So," the director leaned forward, "let's hear what you have to say."

Charlie's
Package

Jeremy pulled up in front of a sprawling
one-story wooden building at the end of a
deeply rutted dirt road. Just as he cut the engine,
the screen door banged and a boy, hardly eigh-
teen, leaped down the steps two at a time.

"Merec said you brought a package I was to
take care of," he said, coming up beside the car.

Jeremy opened the door and got out, stiff from
the long drive. "You?"

"What's wrong with that?" The boy glanced
at Sarah, and his eyes flicked away through the
rest of the car and back to Sarah. "That it?"

Jeremy leaned against the side of the car and
loosened his hair. It fell around his face like a
curtain.

"All right, then." The boy opened Sarah's
door. "Guess you're it. Come on." He grabbed
her by the arm.

Jeremy was around the car and beside him in a moment. "You get the wheelchair. It's in the trunk. I'll get her." He leaned over and slid one arm below her knees.

"That won't be necessary."

Jeremy froze. Sarah looked over his shoulder to where Merec stood at the top of the steps.

"Let Charlie take her."

Jeremy slid his arm out and stood.

"I'd rather Jeremy," she said. Merec ignored her. So did everyone else.

Charlie abandoned the wheelchair, dropping it carelessly back in the trunk. "I told you Merec said for me to take care of her." Walking back toward Sarah, he said to Jeremy, "Get that wheelchair for me."

"I need Jeremy." Merec's voice was sharp with command. "You can get the wheelchair." He turned on his heel and reentered the house. Jeremy climbed the steps slowly and followed Merec inside.

"You," Charlie said, pointing a finger straight at Sarah's nose. "Don't you move." He circled to the trunk and heaved the wheelchair out. It clattered against the bumper, and he lugged it up the steps.

The sun on the windshield was strong. A bead of sweat trickled down Sarah's temple. Another broke over the bridge of her nose and slid down into the corner of her mouth. A fly buzzed around the door and got stuck, bumping against the inside of the window. She watched the fly until the screen door banged again and she knew her escort had returned. Charlie was muttering as he stomped down the stairs.

"How am I supposed to know how to work a damn wheelchair." He yanked the car door wide, took her legs and swung them out facing him, and knelt before her on one knee, as before a queen. Fitting his shoulder into her stomach, he hefted her over his back, her head hanging upside down, feet waving in the air. He secured them with an arm, grunted, and kicked the door of the car shut. His shoulder was all jutting bone, and it jolted into her stomach with each step. He climbed the steps and propped open the door. The floor was hardwood stained a dark mahogany.

"Hey, Charlie's gone and brought himself back a woman."

She saw two pairs of feet step out of the way as Charlie pushed by.

They progressed farther down the hall, into a room with more pairs of feet.

"Whoa, look out for old Charlie, comin' through."

Charlie continued on to another room and across a carpeted floor. Over in the corner, Jeremy and Merec sat at a table. They both glanced up as Charlie passed through with Sarah slung over his shoulder.

Charlie passed through one more doorway. Again he slammed the door with his foot, and she was hoisted roughly into the wheelchair.

Sarah found herself in a small, bare room, about eight by ten feet. There were no windows. Track lighting was bolted into the wall near the ceiling, illuminating large, disturbing cracks in the plaster.

Charlie stood over her. As her ride had indicated, he was thin—his shirt hung on his shoulders almost as it would on a wire hanger. He had a heart-shaped face and a dusting of acne on his forehead, but his eyes were beautiful: a chocolate brown with thick black lashes and dark arching brows. They were even more striking because he had shaved his hair to a military fourth of an inch. Now he backed away and took a packet of cigarettes out of his pocket. He extracted one and lit it. She noticed that his hand trembled a bit. He took a long drag and exhaled. "You're my package," he said and took another drag.

"So you've said." She kept her voice deliberately colorless, but he crossed the room and slapped her anyway. The sting brought angry tears to her eyes.

"Look at me," he commanded.

Charlie stood over her, obviously trying his hardest to be menacing. It was partly nervousness, partly her sense of the ridiculous—she laughed.

In the next room, Merec and Jeremy looked up at the sound.

"They are perfect for each other. Listen," and

Merec raised his pen.

A moment later they heard a cry, then another, and cursing.

"Splendid. They're getting along just fine."

Sarah turned her head to one side and spit blood onto the floor. She was surprised at the pain.

Charlie leaned against the opposite wall, glaring at her. She watched him take greedy drags and wondered what it was like to smoke. She spit again and asked, "May I have a cigarette?"

"You bum," he said.

"What?"

"You bum a cigarette. That's what you say. 'Can I bum a cigarette,' not 'May I have a cigarette.'" In this last, he tried to imitate her refined speech.

"May I—" she stopped when he shook his head. "I don't believe this," she muttered. "*Can I* bum a cigarette?"

He nodded approvingly and pulled one out of the crumpled pack. Crossing the few steps to her wheelchair, he held it out, and she took it from his fingers. He bent from the waist, struck a match, and out of habit curved a hand around it to protect it from the wind. He held the flame steady and waited for her to draw.

"You've got to inhale for it to light," he said.

She did, tentatively.

"Haven't you ever smoked before?"

She awkwardly took the cigarette from her mouth with her thumb and forefinger and shook her head.

"Jeez," he said, half laughing, half scornful. "You really don't know anything. That's not how you hold it. That's how you hold a joint." He saw her incomprehension. "Never mind." He squatted next to the chair. "When you want to take it out of your mouth, you do it like this," he demonstrated, holding his palm flat toward his face and seizing the cigarette between his middle finger and forefinger. "Try it."

She did.

He made a face. "You need a little practice. But now, when you want to drop ash, flick the end with your thumb." He demonstrated. She watched and repeated.

He smiled for the first time, and she saw his teeth were ugly, crowded, buckled mouth, and stained a dark, unhealthy y

"All right now, take a puff." He to drag on his.

She did the same, and immediat explosively.

He grinned. "That's it."

In the next room, the tw heads again. The laugh this time by Sarah's low

Merec said, "What th

"Just like a pro," Charlie proclaimed.

Sarah sucked dramatically on her cigarette and blew out over Charlie's head. Then she stared in the same direction.

"What?" Charlie scrambled up from the floor.

Merec stood in the doorway. He smiled, but his smile was not yellowed and vulnerable. It was sleek.

"What's this, a tea party? How touching." He strolled into the room. "Charlie, I said I wanted you to take care of her, not be her nanny."

Sarah broke in, "I just asked for a—"

Charlie turned on her in a rage and hit her a ___nded blow with his fist. "The boss is ___ said through his teeth and pivoted ___ spine straighter.

___ moving closer, "yes, thank ___ I can see you've done ___ stopped in front of ___ her swollen

___ the ___ the ___ ber- ___ led

___ us." He ___ held them ___ ou. Charlie,

"Well, you'll have to do without for now." He glanced over at Charlie. "Out," he said, jerking his head at the doorway.

Charlie shot a surly look at Sarah and left the room.

Sarah noticed that her cigarette had burned down to the filter. She extracted a new one from the pack Merec had given her and placed it in her mouth. Merec stooped and lit the end with a heavy gold lighter. He straightened, leaned comfortably against the wall, and regarded her with cold blue eyes.

Her head throbbed, but she smoked intently, concentrating on the unpleasant sensation.

"How do you like smoking?" he asked. "It is your first time, is it not?"

"I think it's very unpleasant," she answered truthfully.

He nodded. "Will you keep it up?"

"I think I shall."

He gazed at her a moment, then turned and left without another word.

Sarah sat, the smoke twining intimately up through her fingers, rising to hang before the light. She felt herself suspended like the smoke. No sound reached her from the other room. No one came. The door remained closed, and finally, the cigarette fell, the ash scattering, and she dropped her face into her open hands.

• • •

Sarah was not, however, as alone as she might have hoped. A camera was hidden high in the wall, and Jeremy watched from a monitor next door. What is worse, he recorded it.

Half an hour later, the door opened and Charlie lugged an iron cot into the room. He was scowling and kept his face averted as he assembled the cot against the wall opposite the door, where the video camera could best catch her. Then he stomped out of the room and returned with an armful of bedding, which he deposited on the cot. "I ain't makin' your bed," he said. "You got to make your own damn bed."

"I agree. As I have to lie in it."

Watching, Jeremy caught Sarah's allusion and smiled.

"Well, I sure ain't," Charlie repeated. He moved to the door and paused. "You're supposed to knock twice when you have to go."

"To go?"

"To the toilet," he said, and left.

She wheeled herself over to the door and knocked twice, very hard.

The Season Premiere

The tape aired at eight o'clock Wednesday evening, the night after the massacre at Willowridge. It would be untrue to say that the entire country or even a large portion saw the tape that evening. But Rose watched—the nurses at the hospital could not keep her from it. "I lived it," she said. "I think I can stand to watch it." If she had stormed at them, they would have been able to prevent her, but her quiet words left them with nothing to say.

They showed the tape in full, and she witnessed the fireworks on the distant hill one more time. As she gazed at the faces of her friends bright with terror, she saw them as she had never seen them before. They shone, they melted, they were fragile and beautiful, and she wished with a fierce contraction that *she* had been able to finish her life so spectacularly prodded back into emotion—as a shooting star is brightest just at the instant before it fades.

Stanley watched the tape sitting on the couch next to his wife. He hadn't told her anything of it beforehand, especially about his part in the program. He had just pulled her down on the couch next to him, saying, "Honey, you've got to see this."

"Is this the new case you're working on? I think I heard something about that today," she said. "Let me go get some wine." She started to rise, but he pulled her back down.

"Just watch, Mary," he said. "Just watch."

Mary shifted and yawned during the short introduction. But she sat up a bit straighter when the camera cut to Stanley, sitting in a chair next to the host of the show. She looked over at Stanley on the couch beside her, then back at the screen.

"We taped it this afternoon," Stanley explained.

"Shhh," Mary said. "I'm trying to listen."

The Stanley on the screen, in a dark suit and tie, was talking in a solemn tone about the grave and horrific nature of the crime that they were about to witness. He said that if anyone had any information—any information at all—in connection with the case, they should call the hotline number that appeared at the bottom of their screen. The number, he added, would appear again at the end of the program.

Mary turned to study Stanley as though to make sure he was the same person. "You were good," she said, sounding almost surprised.

Stanley looked pleased but said only, "Tresler thinks that the perpetrator of the crime will call in."

"That doesn't sound very likely. Who is this Tresler?"

"My partner on this case." Turning back to the television, he saw that they were starting the footage. "You've got to watch this, Mary. It's the most incredible thing I've ever seen."

After eating, Tresler checked his watch and pulled a straight-backed chair up to the television. A small table and a narrow twin bed were the only other furniture in the room.

Retrieving a notebook, Tresler watched Stanley's performance closely. On the screen, Stanley came off as a concerned officer in deadly earnest. Tresler was sure that the man who had made the tape would hate Stanley's moralizing and would certainly resent the intrusion. And Tresler was betting that he wasn't the type to let someone like Stanley have the last word.

When the tape started rolling, Tresler focused not on the drama but on the detail. He watched hands. He studied faces. He took notes and compared them with his case file. By the end of the tape he had his lead: the girl attendant who lay among the sprawled bodies in the cafeteria, whose face had not appeared even once on the screen.

Zackman watched the program from his cramped, smoke-filled office at CIA headquarters. He continued working through a thick folder of papers on his desk throughout Stanley's speech, but when the footage started to roll, his attention was drawn to the screen. He watched fixedly for the remainder of the program. And afterward he scribbled down the hotline number on a scrap of paper.

All the men milled around the makeshift bar, pouring drinks. Merec perched on the arm of a couch, swirling the ice cubes around and around in his scotch, just as the men swirled respectfully around him. He spoke a word to one here or there, and they listened gravely, staring down into their drinks and nodding.

Jeremy sat next to Merec on the couch, silent and watchful.

Tonight Charlie, scowling furiously with pleasure, was the center of attention. The men pressed drinks on him and nudged him roughly with their elbows, saying things like "Tonight we'll see how Merec caught your bird" or "Your little package is on TV."

The program came on, and they found seats, cradling their glasses against their stomachs and making jokes.

The host ran through the story of the brutal attack on the tranquil rest home outside Arlington, Virginia. The hoots and calls of the men drowned out most of the introduction. But when Stanley appeared on the screen, Merec hushed them violently. They quieted, and Stanley's voice came through loud and clear.

"Who is that goon?" one of the men asked. But no one answered him. Merec's body had tensed, and his eyes were fixed on the screen.

"Merec?"

Merec turned to look at Jeremy, his eyes still burning.

"That guy's nobody," Jeremy said.

"Quite right, Jeremy," Merec agreed. "But whoever planned that little episode is not."

"But—" Jeremy began.

Merec cut him off. "Let's not let this little interruption spoil our enjoyment of the real show."

The tape had started rolling, and everyone's eyes were on the television. When the camera focused on Sarah, Jeremy leaned forward a bit. When she stared, eyes glittering, into the camera, someone whistled. Later, when she said coolly, "How could I not believe you?" another man muttered, "That's one tough bird."

"Not bad-looking either," someone else chimed in.

"She doesn't look so hot anymore," Charlie said.

But instead of the approval and admiration he expected, the men turned on him. "What the hell did you do to the lady?" The speaker grabbed Charlie by the shirt.

"Let me go, Jody. I just roughed her up a little."

Jody gave him two sharp slaps. "That lady, she's ten times the man you'll ever be."

"Merec?" Charlie appealed.

Merec was watching the little scene play out. "Perfect," he said, "perfect. Let Charlie go, Jody."

Jody shoved, and Charlie stumbled backward into another man standing behind him, who gave him a shove into someone else, who stuck out a fist, and Charlie went down.

"Let him alone, boys." Merec took a sip from his glass. "He roughed her up on my orders."

They stood back reluctantly, and one gave Charlie a parting kick in the ribs. He grunted and stayed down.

"She was magnificent, wasn't she?" Merec smiled. "That little lady is going to bring us a heap of money."

"She's rich?" someone asked.

"No, as far as I know, she hasn't got a cent. But this program aired nationally tonight, and I would bet that it's going to air again—several more times, I would think. And I imagine that the rest of the viewers may have the same reaction as you. I have plans for her. When we're done, there won't be a person in this country who hasn't heard of Sarah Shepherd."

The national media did not miss the event. Sarah's story made for great headlines, and some reporters, even in the depth of their cynicism, found themselves moved.

IBC aired the video again and again, and it is safe to say that the entire country (or at least a large portion of it) at one time lowered the lights and sat down in front of their televisions. They were mesmerized, their horror excited, their bloodlust gratified, and their need for a hero fulfilled.

The press had a field day. They spoke to psychiatrists, criminologists, and other siege survivors. They printed articles, commissioned Op-Ed pieces, and took dozens of polls. They went out on the street with cameras and questioned the people that walked by. It was amazing how many people said, "I would have done exactly the same thing in Sarah Shepherd's situation." Or, when asked about their own aging parents, swore, "No, under no circumstances would I put my mother or father in a nursing home."

But as soon as the police were done with Willowridge, it was scrubbed, disinfected, and reopened. It was full in weeks.

Waiting by the Phone

Tresler and Stanley met early Thursday morning. Tresler had commandeered a small, windowless room at FBI headquarters, equipped with four desks and as many phones.

He introduced Stanley to Helen, the stiff-faced lady sitting behind the nearest desk. She was the head of the night shift and had handled the flood of calls immediately after the program aired. Stanley had wanted to remain at the phones during and after the broadcast, but Tresler had pointed out that neither had slept for almost forty-eight hours and that nothing would come in that night anyway. "Besides," Tresler soothed him, "they will be recording, tracing, and logging all the calls. And if anything important comes up, they know where to reach us." What he didn't say was that Helen had been at the agency for over thirty years and could probably handle anything that came up as well as or better than they could.

Helen acknowledged Stanley with a nod and handed Tresler the stack of phone logs. "Nothing," she said. "We logged three hundred and twelve. Two hundred and ninety-seven were 'What has the world come to?' calls." She saw Stanley looking puzzled and explained for his benefit that these were mostly old ladies wanting to talk about how shocked and outraged they were. Suddenly Helen's rigid face was transformed into a wicked grin. "Amazing how they want to go over all the gruesome parts in great detail," she said, winking at Stanley.

Before Stanley had a chance to reply, the next shift arrived, and the women on the night watch gathered their things together while the new group settled themselves. The supervisor of the day group was a small, stooped woman named Irene, even older than Helen.

"Irene will take care of you," Tresler said to Stanley. "I've got some other things to do, but I'll be right next door in the computer room, extension six-three-five if you need me. All right?"

"No problem," Stanley said. "I've got it under control."

"You know, the girls can handle it. You don't really have to stay."

"You said they'd be rerunning this number on the regular news?"

Tresler nodded.

"Then I should be here," Stanley said.

"Suit yourself," Tresler said, and disappeared through the door.

Stanley sat down at his desk to wait. The room was quiet but for the rustling as the women turned the pages of their magazines. Stanley drummed his fingers but stopped when one of the women looked up. She smiled sympathetically. "Want a magazine?" she asked.

Stanley was deep into an article in *Elle* about how to *really* please a man, when the phone rang for the first time. He started in his chair and looked up. Irene answered it on the second ring, "Willowridge hotline."

Stanley listened intently.

"Yes," Irene said after a pause. "Yes, it was a terrible thing that happened. Yes, thank you for calling to express your concern. No, I'm afraid I can't tell you how much blood they found on the floor."

Stanley sighed and went back to the magazine.

At one o'clock, Stanley poked his head into the room where Tresler was working. "Lunch?" he suggested.

Tresler glanced at the computer. "I had planned to work through."

"Oh no," Stanley protested. "God knows I

need a break. Besides, you need to show me where you can get some food in this building. It's like a maze."

Tresler sighed and stood to lead the way to the cafeteria. They sat at a table tucked in a dark corner of the room.

Stanley looked at Tresler's tray. "Is that all you're having?" he asked.

Tresler had only a cup of coffee. Stanley's own tray was loaded, and he attacked his food with relish.

"Amazing how hungry you get doing nothing," he said with his mouth full. "What have you been doing all morning?"

"Just following up on a few ideas I had."

"You bureau types. So closemouthed about everything," Stanley said, shaking his head. "How long have you been working here?"

"Oh, a while." Tresler took a small sip of his coffee.

"What's your story?"

"My story?"

"Yeah. Every law enforcement official seems to have one. You know—how they first got interested in the business. Like a guy I know on the force, his father was killed by a bank robber in a heist. They never caught the guy. That kind of thing gets under your skin.

"For me, it happened when I was ten. I was walking down the street, and I hear this lady start screaming that she's been mugged. I see this kid running toward me, and I stick out my foot and down he goes on the pavement. I jump on top of him and manage to keep him down until a couple of adults reach us. That was it. I was hooked. Never felt better than when I nabbed that kid and gave the lady back her purse. Nothing beats that feeling."

"Did you ever find out the kid's story?" Tresler asked.

"What?"

"Did you find out why the kid was stealing? Maybe he was hungry, his mother was sick, his father just got laid off."

"No, he was just a punk kid."

"What happened to him afterward?"

"I don't know. That wasn't any of my business. Still isn't. I just catch them. It's up to the courts what to do with them."

Tresler only nodded.

"But what about you, Tresler? What got you into this?"

Tresler tilted his head to one side and said, "I always wanted to be a criminal. But I didn't have what it takes, so this was the next best thing."

Stanley stared at him for a moment, then he laughed. "You almost had me going there. A criminal. That's a good one."

Taking another big bite of his sandwich, he chewed while Tresler watched the activity in the cafeteria. Stanley swallowed and said, "How can you stand it?"

"What?"

"This part of the job. The nitpicky details, the waiting."

Tresler blew on his coffee. "What else is there?"

"Anything else—a stakeout, a raid, an arrest."

Tresler shook his head. "This, right now, this is the meat of the case. This is the part where you pit your mind against your opponent. This is the real test."

"But it's all a matter of luck really," Stanley protested.

Tresler looked at him but said nothing.

"Like this case," Stanley continued. "We don't seem to be left with much to go on. And it doesn't look like anything will come of this hotline idea. But we've got to solve it. For Sarah Shepherd's sake we've got to crack this thing."

"I find," Tresler said, "that it helps not to get emotionally involved in the cases I'm working on, at least not with the victims. You need to think like a criminal, not like a victim."

Stanley looked at him as if he'd just sprouted horns. "How could you not think of a woman like that? She's what keeps me going on a case like this. I mean," he explained quickly, "the thought of saving her keeps me going."

"But what then?" Tresler asked.

"What do you mean, 'What then?'"

"Once you save her, what then?"

"Then? Well, then I'll be a hero," Stanley said simply.

Tresler smiled into his coffee.

A Proper
Beating

Sarah woke Thursday morning from a surprisingly sound sleep. Her face was tender from Charlie's blows, but otherwise she felt fine. She slid herself from the bed back into her wheelchair and waited.

Jeremy and Merec watched from the other room. Merec rubbed his chin. "It's not good enough," he said. "The swelling has gone down, and she didn't bruise very much. I'll need more for the video."

Jeremy fiddled with the controls on the monitor, heightening the red tint.

"No," Merec shook his head. "Have Charlie try it again. And make sure he does it right. I don't want to waste any more time." He straightened. "I'm going into town. I'll be back in an hour to check on things."

● ● ●

In the room, Sarah tried to occupy herself tracing the cracks along the wall. Did her eyes jump automatically from the end of one to the beginning of another, or was it all connected? The chasm never seemed to end.

A little while later the doorknob turned and Charlie entered. She scowled at him, but he wouldn't even meet her eyes.

The first blow was like the burst of sun over the horizon.

Merec drove the twenty minutes to the nearest town and stopped first at the stationery store to buy a copy of every newspaper. He took them back to his car and spread them out on the front seat. The story about the tape of events at Willowridge made the front page in all but one.

A plan had started to form in his mind. He started the car and drove to the gas station to use the pay phone in the far corner of the empty lot. Retrieving a handful of change from the ashtray, he dialed Karl in New York. Luckily Karl was in and picked up on the second ring.

"It's Merec."

"Mmm," Karl acknowledged.

"How far have you gotten on your assignment?" Merec asked.

"Got the supplies."

Merec smiled. Karl made succinctness into an

art form. It was part of what made him so valuable—that and his particular skill with explosives.

"Listen," Merec said, "I'm calling because I want you to suspend work on the job. I have a new project for you." Over the next few minutes he explained to Karl what he wanted.

When Merec returned to the compound, he went straight to where Jeremy sat outside Sarah's cell. Dropping the newspapers on the desk, he leaned over to peer into the monitor.

"Perfect," Merec said. "That's perfect. We'll do it tomorrow. By then those bruises will look impressive."

Lost and Found

Early Thursday morning, when Tresler had left Stanley to oversee the hotline, he settled down in front of the computer in the next room and logged onto the bureau's system. Then, laying the case folder on the desk, he sorted through the contents. He shuffled through dozens of photos of the bodies with small round holes in their foreheads until he came to the attendant with the short blond hair and the pink lipstick. Her eyes had rolled back in her head, and her mouth was slack-jawed and loose. He extracted it and propped it on the keyboard.

It took him just minutes to find that the young woman was a recent hire at the rest home and that she had given a name that did not match her social security number. The social security number belonged to an eighty-five-

year-old woman living in Naples, Florida. The
name itself was certainly false.

Extracting scissors from his briefcase, he picked
up the photo and carefully cut around the curve of
the face, across the forehead, and around the one
visible ear. He lifted away the hair, the body—and
only the face remained. He taped it on the side of
the monitor, pulled up the missing persons data-
base, and started to scroll through pictures.

When Stanley interrupted him to go to lunch,
he was still sorting through the enormous data-
base but with no luck.

Tresler had been searching for almost twenty
hours when he finally found her. He sighed,
took a sip of cold coffee, and pulled up the
information. Name: Mary Louise Morton. Age:
twenty-two. Disappeared five months ago. Last
seen in Albuquerque, New Mexico. It gave an
address and a phone number. Tresler checked
his watch; it was almost two in the morning. He
calculated the time difference—still too late to
decently call. But he picked up the phone and
dialed anyway.

"Hellooo?" The voice that answered the
phone was loud, but it needed to be to compete
with the music blaring in the background.

"I'm trying to reach Mrs. Collins," Tresler
said.

"What, darlin'? Can't hear you. Just a sec." It
was obvious now that the voice was slurring a
little bit. "Honey pie, turn that down a bit. No,

down," she screeched as the music pulsed louder. "Hold on there, babycakes," she said into the phone.

Tresler waited.

The woman picked up again and yelled for the other receiver to be hung up. At last there was a semblance of quiet. "Now, what can I do you for, darlin'?"

"I'm trying to reach Mrs. Collins," Tresler repeated.

"Ain't no Mrs. Collins here," she laughed hysterically, "God forbid."

"I'm sorry," Tresler paused, then tried, "Ms. Collins?"

"Now, that's me."

His eyes burned from staring at the computer screen, and he rubbed them with the back of one hand. "Ms. Collins, I wanted to ask you a few questions about Mary Louise Morton."

"Oh no, not that again. I swear that girl has been more trouble than I bargained for, I'll tell you that. Shouldn't never have agreed to take her on, but I did feel sorry for the poor thing, having my sister as a mother. But it's been no end of trouble, reporting her missing and dealing with the police. And you'd think that would be the end of that, but then people just keep bothering me about it. Who are you anyway?"

"Ms. Collins, I'm with the FBI, and I—"

The woman broke in, "Now that's just what that other fellow said to me. He claimed to be with the FBI too, when he came around bother-in' me not too long ago. Now here's another one of you back for more."

Of course, he thought to himself, the nursing home wouldn't have been their first crime; someone was already on his trail. But all he said was, "Someone else from the FBI has been asking you questions?"

"Jeez, you're nosy."

"They pay me to be," he said.

She laughed at that. "All right, Mr. FBI Man. What do you want this time?"

"Well, let's start with the other investigator. When did you speak to him?"

"Maybe a month ago. He came around here asking the same old questions the police asked. And I told him the same old things I said before. Probably the same things you'll ask me. So unoriginal—they pay you for that too?"

"Well, how about this. If you can remember his name, I won't trouble you any longer. I'll just call and ask him."

"That'd be a nice change," she agreed. "Let me see, he left me his card. You know, somehow I didn't imagine FBI guys having business cards. But hold on, I think I have it around here somewhere." Tresler heard the sound of rum-maging. "Here it is," she announced. "Let's see, the name is Dick Martins. Oops. It says here CIA. Well, CIA, FBI, how can anyone expect a person to remember letters?"

"Is there a phone number?" Tresler asked.

She read it out. "Is that it?"

"That's it," Tresler said. "Thank you." But she had already hung up. Without, Tresler noticed, asking if he had any information about Mary Louise.

No Appeal

When Sarah woke Friday morning, she found that her right eye had swollen half shut. She raised her hands to her face and gingerly explored the bruises. Her bottom lip was split, and her right cheekbone had disappeared beneath swelling. To add to her catalog of discomforts, her tongue was stiff with lack of moisture, and she definitely needed the use of the bathroom. In his assault Charlie had targeted her face, leaving her body untouched, so she was able to shuffle from the cot to the wheelchair without difficulty and roll across the room to tap on the door.

When Charlie first entered, his eyes flicked over her face, and embarrassed, he quickly looked away. Silently he helped her to the bathroom, then wheeled her back to her cell. He exited but returned a moment later with a tray of food and a pitcher of water.

As he bent to set it down on the floor beside her wheelchair, she extracted a cigarette and put it in her mouth. He noticed and fished in his pocket for matches. When the end of the cigarette glowed orange, he lifted his beautiful eyes to hers. "When this one gets low," he said, "you can light another one from it. You put it to the tip of the new one and inhale. That'll do the trick." He hurried out.

She smoked three in a row before she let the third one extinguish itself against the filter. Her face throbbed. She fingered another cigarette, rolling it across her knuckles. She dozed, and woke with a start to nothing. She knocked once more for the bathroom.

Sarah must have drifted off again, for she found herself waking, and she was not alone in the room. A camera was balanced on a tripod in front of her, the red eye glowing, and Merec stood behind it.

A quarter of an hour later, she repeated, "I can't do this." She raised her chin and looked beyond the camera at Merec. "I won't do this. I'm not going to ask people I don't know to give you money."

"It's to ransom you," he pointed out. "It just so happens that I'll be receiving it."

"I can't," she said again.

"You're too modest."

Sarah didn't reply.

"You'll do it sooner or later."

"Later then," she shot back.

"That wasn't a choice," he informed her. "But we'll have to find something for you to do in the meantime. Chances are it will be unpleasant."

There were no windows here to gaze out of, and she had decided that she didn't like to look at the walls, crawling as they were with unsteady fissures wide enough to lose your faith in. So she answered him.

"What could be worse?" she said.

At that, he laughed.

"Did you catch that?" Merec asked Jeremy a few minutes later.

"Got it all," Jeremy replied.

"I couldn't have planned it better. Imagine what will happen when they air that? I'm going to have to raise the amount to ten million. God, she's worth twice that."

"So, do you want me to edit the tape to send in?"

"No, not yet." Merec rubbed his chin. "Not quite yet."

• • •

Sarah was restless after the confrontation. She
shifted in her wheelchair, settled, and shifted
again. For the first time since her husband's
death, she craved activity. She had shuffled
around her room at Willowridge, but for any
distance she had reverted to the wheelchair.
Frowning, she tried to lift one leg, straighten it,
and let it down. She repeated the movement as
many times as she was able, and when she
couldn't lift it again, she switched to the other
leg. Straighten, down, straighten, down.

She tried a few steps, starting from the bed,
using the handles of the wheelchair to help bal-
ance. Then, letting go, she took three uncertain
steps on her own.

Stanley's Discovery

When Stanley returned to the office on Friday at nine-thirty, the calls had slowed to a trickle.

"Anything?" he asked.

"Nothing that has checked out," Irene said.

"And last night?"

She shrugged.

"Is Tresler around?"

"He said he'd be in this afternoon."

"Oh." Stanley cleared his throat. "Very good." He settled himself at his desk. Today he had come better equipped. He extracted the case folder from his briefcase. Opening it, he bent over to study the information. Two hours later, head in his hand, he was still flipping through the pages of data. Types of weapons, markings on bullets,

times of deaths, numbers of bodies, psychological profiles, voice analysis—all led to nothing. He
smacked his palm against his forehead softly and
groaned. Then abruptly he stood.

"If Tresler comes back, tell him I've gone to
the lab."

Five minutes after Stanley left, Irene took a
call for him from a man who gave his name and
number but declined to say anything more.

Tresler had been trying to reach Dick Martins,
the CIA agent, all morning, and he felt like he
was getting the runaround. He tried once again,
and the woman who answered the phone told
him that Mr. Martins had just gone out to lunch.

"Maybe it would be best if I just sent him the
information."

"Oh yes," the woman agreed, a shade too
heartily.

"Could you give me your address?" Tresler
jotted it down in his notebook. "Thank you," he
said. And he gathered up a few things and
headed out to speak to Mr. Martins in person.

Stanley didn't return until early evening. He
shrugged out of his coat and sat back down at
the desk with a sigh.

"You got a call," Irene said. "Early this morning just after you left."

Stanley looked up. "Man? Woman?"

"A Mr. Zackman. Here's the number."

He took the log from her. "Thank you, Irene." He dialed.

"Zackman here," a hoarse voice answered.

"This is Detective Stanley Wall returning your call."

"Wall? I don't think I . . . oh yeah. You're working on that nursing home incident."

"That's right," Stanley said.

"Well, I wanted to talk to you about that case. I saw the tape on television last night. Now I couldn't swear to it, but from the MO, the general behavior patterns, specifically the sadistic games, I think we're following the same man."

"The same man?" Stanley repeated. "Who do you work with?"

"Central Intelligence," Zackman said. "We've been following this case for over six months now. Lost a man already in the operation."

"What happened?"

"Can't reveal that. Sorry. Agency policy." Zackman made a face that Stanley couldn't see.

"Oh."

"In fact, strictly speaking, I shouldn't even be calling you now."

"But that's ridiculous," Stanley said.

"True," Zackman agreed. "But in this case I need to put my men's lives ahead of company policy. I wanted to alert you to the fact that we have a man in deep cover with the organization."

"So do you know where they're located? Do you have information on the operation?" Stanley asked eagerly.

"We haven't heard from our man in some time."

"Well, it's good to know that there's someone on the inside looking after Sarah Shepherd's interests."

"Whose interests?"

"Sarah Shepherd. The woman who was kidnapped."

"Oh, yes, her." Zackman doubted that his man would be able to do anything for her, but he refrained from mentioning it.

"Wasn't she fabulous?"

"I hadn't thought about it," Zackman admitted. "But I suppose she wouldn't make a bad agent."

"That's all you have to say about her?"

"In my opinion," Zackman said seriously, "that says a lot."

Bruce Lee, a Miracle, and the Seeds of Disaster

Less than an hour after Merec's interview with Sarah, the recruits arrived. Merec emerged from the house just as the three men piled out of the windowless van, blinking in the light. One was bowlegged, his skin like dark canvas, his eyes recessed so you seemed to see them only when they caught the light. The second was broad-shouldered with a handlebar mustache. He cleared his throat often and had a habit of licking his lips. The third was a stocky young man in his early twenties.

Merec approached the driver. "Maude," he said and leaned over to kiss her on both cheeks. "You are invaluable. What have you brought us?"

Maude accepted the salute gravely. "Alan."

She nodded at the small, wiry figure. "Pat," she said, flicking her finger at the second, who licked his lips nervously. "Lee," she said of the last.

"Fritz, Jody, Parker—see these men to their rooms," Merec ordered.

Fritz took Lee by the arm, and Lee knocked him flat on the ground.

"We're getting soft," Merec muttered, turning away from the sudden crowd of men around Lee, who was punching and kicking in a fair approximation of a martial arts film.

Merec started back into the house. Maude followed.

"So you finally got tired of that poor little thing, what was her name?" Maude said.

"Tina? You brought her in."

"True," she agreed. "I thought she might be useful." She clarified, "Or at least expendable."

"Indeed. But have you heard? I brought someone else back in her place."

"Yes, I heard. It was hard to miss. The networks can't get enough of it. But . . ." Maude reached out and laid a hand on his shoulder, "was that wise?"

"That's not something I generally consider." Merec loosed her hand with a shake of his shoulder.

She caught up to him outside Sarah's cell. Merec was leaning over Jeremy's shoulder, staring at the monitor. On the screen Sarah was taking baby steps around the room behind the wheelchair.

"What's this?" He straightened. "I thought she was crippled."

"It's a miracle," Maude said. "Now, are you going to tell me what's going on here?"

Merec ignored her question. He spoke instead to Jeremy. "Why don't you go with Maude to make sure our new arrivals are settled in properly."

They walked down the narrow hall, Maude leading, Jeremy behind. Maude had been with Merec longer than anyone, and she took pride in this. When Merec needed something special, he called Maude. But recently Jeremy had begun spending long hours with Merec alone. Then on the last job, in the midst of the action, he had extracted a video camera and started recording. After that, he was always there, recording everything—either with his camera or with his beady brown eyes.

She had been momentarily reassured when Merec had told her he wanted her to take over this next recruiting session. But outside the power of his influence, she had lost focus, lost impetus, and deep down she knew that the recruiting session had been a half-done, lackluster affair at best.

Stepping to one side, she opened a door leading to a room off the corridor. It was sparsely furnished with two chairs and a table. She crossed over to the window, staring out at the trees that pressed up close against the sides of the house. The forest was young and dense with green underbrush. She heard Jeremy close the door and the creaking of one of the chairs as he settled himself.

"So?" Maude demanded. She turned to face him. "What the hell is going on here?"

They had never spoken alone before, and she could have been referring to any number of things. Jeremy surprised her by saying, "I had nothing to do with your situation, Maude. That was in the works way before I came on the scene."

"What the fuck do you know about my situation?" she spat.

He was silent.

"Tell me what happened at the rest home," she demanded. "It was supposed to be an easy mark: one old man, five hundred thousand in the bank. That's about as easy as it gets. Send in a point person to determine the lay of the land, then in and out, and it's over. Instead you go in and kill nearly everyone in the damn place, you leave the point person dead on the floor of the cafeteria, and you bring out this crippled woman. What's wrong with this picture?" She paced across the wooden floor, her soles squeaking.

Jeremy shrugged. "You know him better, but it doesn't sound so out of character to me."

She stared at him hard. "Let's go see the new recruits," she said and led the way out.

Sarah had been installed in one of the cells usually used for the new arrivals. They had four other identical rooms in the interior of the house, barely larger than walk-in closets, all equipped with an iron cot and a video loop. When Maude and Jeremy made the rounds, they found Lee jogging in place, punching the air, Alan sleeping, and Pat hunched over the edge of his bed, chewing on a thumbnail.

Back in her room, Sarah lay on her cot, her eyes closed against the bright track lighting. She longed for darkness, for the hum of crickets, for a night breeze, or for an uncompromising sun, for curved blades of grass, for a warm salt bath. Instead she rose painfully and took another turn around the room, tracing the cracks on the wall with her fingertips.

Tresler's Discovery

Tresler got into CIA headquarters on the strength of his federal ID. He brought with him a newspaper and a cup of coffee as camouflage and went in search of Martins' office. When he found it, he walked by, and from the corner of his eye he saw it was occupied. Veering toward the open door, he smiled at the woman sitting outside.

"I'm just going to pop in and say hello," he said as he sailed by. Once in, he turned and shut the door behind him. Then he faced the man behind the desk. "Hi," he said brightly, setting the coffee and the newspaper down on the man's desk.

"Hello." Martins was obviously puzzled.

Tresler sat in one of the visitors' chairs and crossed his legs. "How are you?"

"Fine, I'm fine. And yourself?"

"Just fine."

"Excuse me, but I'm afraid I've forgotten your name," Martins admitted.

"That's because I haven't had the pleasure. I'm Tresler." He leaned forward and extended his hand.

"Tresler, Tresler, the name sounds familiar," Martins mused.

"I've been trying to reach you most of the day," Tresler admitted. "But I had trouble getting through to you, so I thought I'd use it as an excuse to come meet the man himself."

"I must admit I don't know what you're talking about."

"Well, I work over at the FBI," Tresler flashed his credentials, "and I've heard your name mentioned several times in connection with cases we've had an interest in."

"Oh really?"

"Oh yes. You come highly recommended."

"Oh?" Martins said, obviously pleased.

"Yes. And I was just assigned to a case, in a purely advisory capacity, mind you, and I was a little worried about the efforts of the local law enforcement."

"No surprise there," Martins remarked.

"Exactly. So you can imagine my relief when I heard that you were already on the job. I just thought I'd stop by and speak to you about it. I wanted to make sure that the local efforts didn't interfere with your operation."

"Of course."

Tresler waited expectantly.

"Um ... which investigation?" Martins asked.

"The one relating to the recent nursing home incident."

"I don't have anything to do with that case."

"It's connected with the disappearance of the girl Mary Louise Morton down in New Mexico. And correct me if I'm wrong, but I believe that you are working with that one." Tresler saw that Martins had not connected the two cases, but he tried to bluff it.

"I can't exactly say you're wrong there, but you must know company policy. I can't talk about my cases. I will tell you this—you can rest easy. We've got that one under control."

"Wonderful," Tresler said. He pretended to hesitate. "May I ask how ... ?"

Martins glanced at the door and leaned forward over his desk. "Easy as taking candy from a baby. We cracked their organization. We've got a man in." He sat back, smiling broadly.

"One of yours?" Tresler asked.

"Oh no. Just a dupe. We offered him a suitcase full of money and he took the bait. How's that for a neat little piece of work? On the case just over a month, and it's almost a wrap."

"Do you know how many men? How they're armed? Where they're located?"

"I'm afraid that's information that I can't share."

"Do you know that he's got a hostage now?"

"Don't you worry, we'll be taking all the factors into consideration," Martins said with a superior smile. "And I hope you'll excuse me, but I've really got to get back to work."

"Certainly. It's been a pleasure." Tresler left the office and, closing the door behind him, muttered through his teeth, "Idiot."

The woman sitting just outside the office heard him and said under her breath, "Hear, hear."

Work as Usual

"**Y**ou want me to what?" Lee asked Merec. The new recruit stood bouncing lightly on his toes in the doorway of Sarah's room.

"It's one of the perks of the profession. We want to make sure you're able to enjoy it," Merec said.

"Okay, okay, but how do you want me to do it?"

"Don't you have any favorite techniques?"

"Splinters? Under the fingernails?"

"Not very original, but that should do fine." Merec paused and seemed to be waiting for something. "Well, go on. Go get some splinters then."

"Oh." Lee bounced once more and bounded away.

Sarah was left alone with Merec. He stepped

forward and offered her a light. She reached
into her breast pocket and retrieved a new pack.
With her hands anchored firmly in her lap, she
grasped the gold cord. She had to rub her fingers together to free them of the cellophane.
Then she pried out a cigarette. All her movements were calm, but as she raised the cigarette
to her mouth, her hand trembled. It was only
the smallest flutter, but Merec found he had to
turn away. He almost left her then, but her voice
called him back.

"My light?" she said.

He lit her cigarette. His own hand, he
noticed, remained steady.

"So, do you want to reconsider that little
request to the American public?" he asked.

She took a drag. A couple of days, he thought,
and she looks like she's been smoking for thirty
years. She offered him a cigarette from her pack.
He took one but didn't light it.

"It wouldn't make a difference anyway," she
said. "You'd still go ahead with this."

It wasn't a question, but he answered nevertheless. "No, it wouldn't make a difference."

"This is what you do, after all. This is all you
do."

All you do. She made it sound so small. He
wondered what her life had been, to make his
sound so insignificant. He had touched thou-
sands of lives all over the world, sinking them
suddenly and violently into tragedy.

He opened his mouth to say something—he didn't know exactly what—but Lee returned, his palm cupped around some long chunks of wood.

Merec shook his head. "Those are much too large, and you'll never get them out. Let's forget the splinters. Needles will work much better. They'll come out cleanly and you can sterilize them. That should reduce later complications."

"Can I borrow your lighter to sterilize the needles? I don't have anything else," Lee said, scattering the useless wood chips on the floor.

Merec handed it not to Lee but to Sarah. Then he went to fetch the needles himself.

The lighter was heavy, and Sarah hefted it as one might a good throwing stone. She rubbed her thumb over its surface and felt a roughness on the underside. Holding it up to the light, she could see that there had once been an inscription on the bottom, but it was so worn that it was illegible. Flicking back the lid, she spun the wheel and the flame leapt up, a bright pale yellow. The center, the shape of a slim pinkie finger, was darker, duller, but edged by a vibrant violet blue, the color you might imagine for a halo.

Merec spent a while poring over the needles in the sewing kit, trying to select the thinnest. He needn't have bothered, as they were all factory made and all identical.

Instead of returning to the room, he stopped outside, where Jeremy sat at the monitor. He opened his palm and said, "Take these in to the new man. And keep an eye on things, of course. This will be important for the tape."

Jeremy nodded and avoided his eyes.

"Are you all right on this job?"

Jeremy stared stonily at the monitor.

Merec threw the needles down on the desk. Some rolled off the edge and onto the floor. "Work as usual, Jeremy. Just as usual."

Merec strode off, one hand bunched into a fist. Within that fist, tucked into the deep crease in his palm, he held one of the thin needles.

Continuing out of the cabin, he walked into the surrounding woods. It hadn't rained in weeks, and the branches snapped under his feet.

He stopped when he couldn't see the walls of the house and leaned against a tree. Holding out his left hand, he studied the innocent pink of his nails. Then he held out the needle, turning it in the light. Wiping it on his shirt, he inserted it under the nail of his pinkie. Just a little bit. He drew in a breath and pushed it deeper. Was this what she felt, or was pain subjective also? The blood welled up around the needle, ran over his finger, and dripped on the brittle leaves. He licked it, tasting the iron.

Would Lee go this deep? He pushed it farther. Or this?

Abruptly he pulled the needle out, tossed it away, and started back to the house. Braced for screams, he frowned when all he could hear was the dry rattling sound of leaves thrown together by the wind. A chill raised the hair on his arms, even in the sluggish heat. Blood was dripping steadily from his finger, and he went to the closet where the first aid kit was kept. It was missing. Of course—she would have need of it. Instead he wadded a piece of tissue around his nail.

Merec felt a strange reluctance to return to Sarah's room, so he went to check on the new arrivals. Jody sat outside one cell with his feet up, snoring lightly. Merec looked at the monitor; the man within was stretched out on his cot, one arm thrown across his eyes, his chest rising in a slow, steady rhythm. Without waking either, Merec continued down the hall to the next cell. Fritz was at his monitor reading a magazine. When he saw Merec approach, he rose almost ceremoniously.

"What have you got there?" Merec asked.

"Just a magazine," and Fritz tossed it away onto the table.

"I can see that." He moved around Fritz to pick it up. "Sailing. Fritz, I didn't know you sailed."

"I don't."

He turned the magazine over in his hands. He had researched every potential candidate, but now he realized that for all the information he had gathered, he knew Fritz as a soldier and that was all. He had no business with anything else.

"Sir?" Fritz shifted uncertainly.

He focused on Fritz's broad, bland face, now twisted with unease. Merec found he was still holding the magazine on sailing in his right hand. His left, despite his precautions, was dripping blood steadily on the floor.

He set the magazine down on the desk and leaned over to peer into the monitor. In the cell, Pat paced back and forth across the tiny room, his head bent, blowing noisily into his mustache.

"Well?" he said. "Your report?"

"Right. Sorry." Fritz was businesslike now. "He's been pacing for two hours now, ever since we put him in there. Seems a bit anxious for the job to me."

Merec stared at the pacing figure on the screen. "He may surprise you."

"If you say so," Fritz agreed quickly.

Merec hesitated, then asked, "Do you think you could do my job?"

"Ah, no," Fritz responded immediately and emphatically. "No, I haven't got your genius."

"Genius?" Merec said, surprised and a little pleased.

"Yeah, genius for bringing out that side in people."

"What side is that?" He didn't know what he expected, but whatever it was, it wasn't Fritz's answer.

"The worst side," Fritz said.

"The what?"

"I mean," he stuttered, "I mean, what is it you always say?"

"The true side," Merec said softly.

"That's it. That's what I mean. I never see that so much as when you're there to point it out to me."

"What is it you see?"

"I just see people, you know. Just ordinary people."

"Of course you do." Whatever genius Fritz had, it was not in his way with words, Merec consoled himself.

"Genius, that's what it is," he repeated, sensing somehow that Merec was not pleased. "I'm sure you're right about that bugger in there. Bet you're right about him. Sure as anything."

Double Booked

"**W**hat did you say?" Tresler wheeled around and stared at Stanley. He had just returned to his office from his talk with Martins.

Stanley explained again, "I said that I got a call this afternoon from a man from the CIA. He said that he's on the case, and he wanted to alert us that they have an agent in deep cover. But I couldn't get anything else out of him."

"What was the man's name?"

"They would never tell me who they had sent undercover," Stanley said, horrified.

"No," Tresler corrected, "I mean who called?"

"Oh. A man named Zackman."

"And this agent in deep cover—it wasn't one of theirs?" Tresler questioned him sharply.

"Yes, I'm sure it was. He said he was breaking with agency policy to call me because he had to put his own men's lives first."

"The name wasn't Martins?"

"No, I told you his name was Zackman. You could ask Irene if you don't believe me. Well, you'd have to call her at home since she was off at six."

Tresler asked impatiently, "What else did this Zackman say?"

"Not much. I told you, getting anything from this guy was like pulling teeth. He just said that they'd been following this case forever and that they had a man in deep cover."

Tresler frowned. He started to turn back to his desk again, then froze.

"Tresler? Are you okay?"

"How long did he say he was on the case?" Tresler asked.

"A while. I forgot to record it when I called him back, but I still have his number."

"Approximately," Tresler prodded.

"I don't know. At least six months. Maybe more."

Tresler looked at Stanley but as though he didn't even see him. "They double booked," he said under his breath.

"What?"

Tresler actually focused on Stanley this time. "Double booked," he repeated, louder. "When one team isn't getting results, they put a second team on the scent."

"You mean there are two CIA teams?"

"That's what I mean. The man heading up the second team is an idiot, and if I'm not mistaken, I'll bet that Zackman's man is in a pretty precarious situation right now."

"We should call Zackman. Let him know."

"That is exactly what I intend to do," Tresler said.

Too Many Westerns

When Merec approached the door to Sarah's room, he saw that Jeremy's chair was empty. Lowering himself into it, he looked at the monitor.

Sarah was sitting in her wheelchair, and Charlie and Jeremy were both kneeling before her, each bent over a hand, the first aid kit open between them.

"Both hands," Merec whispered.

Sarah's head was bowed. Jeremy finished his bandages and moved over to check Charlie's work.

"Thank you, Jeremy," she said. Her voice was low and graveled.

"There you go." Charlie got up off his knees. "Just don't go getting into any fights with anyone for a few weeks and let those sluggers heal."

Each finger was swathed with bandages, some of which were already darkening. She waved them in the air as though playing the piano. "Good as new. Thank you, Charlie."

Jeremy and Charlie both turned to leave.

"You forgot this." Sarah scrabbled in her lap with her thick, clumsy fingers. She held up the gold lighter.

Jeremy lifted it delicately from her hand.

When he found Merec sitting in the wooden chair by the monitor, he put the lighter on the table in front of him.

"How did it go?" Merec asked.

"It went great," he said, unsmiling.

"And Sarah?"

Jeremy leaned over, popped a tape out of the player, and laid it on the table next to the lighter. "See for yourself."

Merec picked it up and tapped it against his palm. "I've done much worse," he said. "Many times."

Merec kept a television in his room with a hookup to play the recordings. He retreated there, inserted the tape, and rewound—much further than he knew he needed to. He watched Sarah as she ate, as she practiced walking, and as she tried to brush her teeth with her finger and water from a jug. Merec watched as he and

Lee entered the room. He had known to stay back, out of camera range, but Lee stalked in, his face captured in profile, three-quarter, and full-on views.

After Jeremy delivered the needles, Lee held one between his thumb and forefinger and showed it to Sarah. "Very thin, see here? Shouldn't be too bad. I'm sorry about this and all."

"I'm sure," she said.

"Listen, why don't you just tell them what they want to know? Then we could skip this whole . . ." Lee waved the needle, searching for an appropriate word, ". . . business."

"I'm afraid," she said, "that there isn't anything to tell."

He approached, stopping just in front of her chair. "Are you agency?" he whispered.

"What?"

"Of course you wouldn't tell me. But you must be." He moved closer and glanced furtively at the door. "I'm supposed to tell you that help is on the way."

Merec stopped the tape and rewound. He watched the scene again, and just as he passed the part where Lee whispered, "Are you agency?" there was a knock. He hit pause and opened the door to Maude.

"Jeremy said you were watching the tape and that maybe I should see it."

"Yes, indeed you should." He opened the

door wider, motioned for her to draw up a
chair, and rewound again.

Maude watched, leaning forward. When
Merec paused the tape again after Lee said,
"Help is on the way," Maude cursed.

Merec turned on her. "Is there any way he
could have brought anything with him?"

"I followed all the procedures," she said
aggressively, all the while thinking about how
lax she had been throughout the operation. "We
had them strip, as always, and gave them new
clothes."

Merec continued to press for details: How far
could they have been tailed? Did any heli-
copters fly overhead during their drive? When
could Lee have been contacted between recruitment and departure? Her answers were less
than satisfactory.

"So what happened here, Maude?" he
demanded, leaning forward over his knees.

She was silent. Merec stared at her, then
turned back to the television and pressed the
play button.

On the screen, Lee unfroze and finished,
". . . is on the way."

Sarah just looked at him.

At her less than enthusiastic response, he
repeated, "I said, help is—"

"I'm not hard of hearing. But I assume it's
not here yet. So—" Sarah held out her left hand.

"Okay. Okay." Lee emptied the pins into the

breast pocket of his shirt, keeping one. He fumbled with the lighter and held the needle above the flame. It blackened. He cursed.

"Try another, and this time hold it higher," Sarah suggested.

"Right." He repeated the procedure, this time with better results. He grasped her wrist, and she covered her face with her other hand.

Watching, Merec and Maude held their breath.

Lee fitted the needle under her thumbnail, but again he hesitated. "Lord forgive me," he muttered and shoved.

And there was . . . silence. Sarah lowered her hand from her face, and stared at the needle stuck deep under the nail. Tears stood in her eyes but didn't fall. Her lips were white, and moved as if she were speaking, but no sound came out.

"Doesn't it hurt?" Lee sounded almost disappointed. "I thought you'd scream."

Sarah took a gulping breath and settled her face back down in her hand.

Lee left the needle in her thumb and took out another from his pocket. Setting her wrist on the arm of the wheelchair, he carefully roasted the next point and inserted it into her forefinger. The blood dripped steadily on the floor. Seemingly unconcerned now, Lee worked methodically. When he finished with the left hand, he laid it in her lap and took up the right.

At the thumbnail, Sarah moaned, low and deep in her throat. He had completed nine fingers when he ran out of needles. He rummaged in his pocket but came up empty.

"Now, that can't have been so bad," he said. Sarah had a needle bristling from every finger except the pinkie on her right hand. He stepped back to survey his work.

Watching, Merec gritted his teeth.

Though the position of the camera couldn't record it, they heard the door open, and Charlie's voice said, "All right, you, that's enough."

The camera focused and closed in on Sarah's face, now unshielded. Her mouth was a tight line, a slight frown gathered between her brows, as though she was trying to remember something that had slipped her mind.

Maude looked over at Merec and found him focused intently on the screen with a peculiar expression on his face—an expression she had never seen there before. She felt a pang of something she didn't care to identify. "I suspect," she said, "that woman has watched one too many westerns. She can't be for real." She glanced at Merec. "I've never seen someone go to such lengths for the camera."

He tore his eyes away from the television. "You forget, Maude. She doesn't know the camera is there."

• • •

After bandaging Sarah's fingers, Jeremy brought her a glass of water and left two pills alongside. She took them without question and fell gently to sleep. Jeremy was sitting, watching her, when Merec returned and said, "Do you have a minute?" Leaving Charlie in charge of the monitor, Jeremy followed Merec out into the woods, where they could talk without being overheard.

Merec stopped and sat on a fallen log. Jeremy put his hands in his pockets and leaned against a maple tree.

Merec said, "You watched the whole thing, didn't you?"

Jeremy nodded.

"How long do you think we have here?"

Jeremy grimaced. "Not long."

"Well, we can't worry about that. I'm going to talk to Lee, find out exactly what he knows. I want you to gather up everything you need to put together the second tape. When you're done packing, just stay out of the way, and I'll take care of the rest."

Mustering
the Forces

Tresler and Stanley met Zackman at CIA
headquarters. He led them through the
corridors to a conference room where five of his
men were already waiting. "Just in case,"
Zackman said.

Martins arrived fifteen minutes later, looking
defensive. He had barely taken a seat when
Zackman started in on him.

"Let me get this straight," Zackman said,
"because I don't believe my fucking ears. One
of your men made contact with a recruit that
was headed in? Just some random guy you fingered, and you wired him with a transmitter
and promised him a suitcase of money? And
my man is in there?"

"No one told me you had a man in there,"
Martins said. "No one told me that anyone else

was on the case. The chief wanted information quick, so for fast information, you have to take risks. You know that, Zackman."

"All right, calm down gentlemen," Tresler broke in. "Let's concentrate on the facts. Martins, when do you expect to hear from your contact?"

"We won't hear from him. Too risky. We just sent him in with a tracking device."

"When do you expect to get a lock on his location?"

"We have one," Martins mumbled.

"Jesus Christ," Zackman stood.

"I was waiting for approval."

Zackman leaned over Martins. "Give me the coordinates for that fucking signal."

"I don't have the authorization to do that." He was flushed but firm.

Zackman exploded. "If you don't give me those fucking coordinates, I'm going to rip your fucking head off."

"This is my case, Zackman. It's been my work that got the information, not yours. Your man hasn't come through with a thing."

"And you're doing your best to screw up the chance you have."

Martins shrugged.

"Fine." Zackman spat out the word. "You can have the fucking credit. Just give me the coordinates."

Martins' eyes narrowed as he stared at

Zackman. "All right," he said. "It's close. I have the exact position in my office."

"Vans, gear, out in front. Now," Zackman snapped at his men, and they disappeared from the room. Zackman, Stanley, and Tresler accompanied Martins to his office. He unlocked a drawer in his desk and dug out a plain manila folder. "Have fun doing my work for me," he said, handing it over.

Tresler and Stanley were in the van with Zackman when it pulled out of CIA headquarters less than thirty minutes later.

Pincushions
and Pistols

It took five men to tie Lee down to a chair when he understood what was in store for him.

"You should be ashamed," Merec's mocking tone was back. "All this fuss when, in your own words, 'It can't have been so bad.'"

It took Lee a few seconds to understand the significance of having his words repeated back to him. "But you weren't . . ." He trailed off as he remembered the other words he had whispered.

Merec confirmed his worst fears. He said, "There is no help on the way for you, my friend," and drew from his pocket a needle and his gold lighter, caked with spots of Sarah's blood.

Binding Lee at the wrist to the arm of a chair

wasn't enough. Merec needed to tape down his hand to the very fingertips.

"I would suggest that you at least attempt to keep still. I'm not sure I'm as skilled as yourself, and I might make a complete mess of it." He raised the lighter and flicked open the top with his thumb.

Lee tried to lean forward but was restrained by the tape. "What if I tell you everything, right now?" he said.

Merec lowered the needle and lighter. "Go ahead."

"Um . . . "

Merec calmly raised the needle to eye level and flicked on the lighter, roasting the tip.

"They came to me, man. They came to me."

"When was this?"

"Well, after I got rid of, you know, the body."

What the hell had Maude been doing? Merec wondered, but all he said was, "Go on."

"It was a weasely little guy. I went to see my girlfriend, and he like ambushed me on my way out of the building. I was headed back to my place, so I let him walk along with me. Let me tell you, you should raise your prices. Even the government has got you beat by a mile. You'd have to be crazy to turn down the kind of money they were offering. And all they wanted was for me to smuggle in this transmitter."

"Where did they put the transmitter? In your clothes?"

"No." Lee grinned triumphantly. "My hair."

They undoubtedly already had a lock on the location. So why hadn't they made their move? There really wasn't any time to lose, but Merec decided that he would make time for this one little task.

"What do you imagine is going to happen now?" he asked Lee.

"Now?"

Merec took the pin and held it just above the flame, enjoying the look on the man's face. He had brought many more than nine this time, and Lee screamed until he fainted. But Merec continued until every finger bristled with needles.

He waited patiently until Lee woke again. When he did, the first thing he saw was Merec's smiling face. Then he looked in horror at his fingers and opened his mouth to scream again. But faster than the sound could escape, Merec lifted his pistol and calmly shot him through the heart.

Fritz met him at the door. As Merec closed it behind him, Fritz said, "The dirty son of a bitch deserved it, sir."

Laying a hand on his shoulder, Merec replied, "Don't we all, Fritz, don't we all?" then raised his pistol and shot Fritz under the chin. Merec phrased it as a question, and if the bullet hadn't traveled up through his brain and killed him instantly, Fritz would certainly have reassured him—would certainly have agreed, "You're right, sir, I'm sure you're right."

An hour later Merec had taken care of almost everyone. One fighter—they called him Peanut because when he shaved his head it was the sprawling, untidy shape of a peanut—almost got Merec. He came into the room where Merec stood over the bloody bodies of Jody and Henry. Peanut already had his pistol out, but he hesitated. Merec didn't hesitate. He never had.

Then only Maude, Jeremy, Sarah, and Charlie were left. Merec found Maude in her room. She was standing at the window when he knocked and entered. Without turning, she said, "Merec, I'm sorry."

"So am I."

She looked over her shoulder, surprised by the apology. She saw the pistol in his hand, and her mouth twisted in a bitter smile. "No you're not," she said.

Jaws

As Merec was leaving Maude's room, pistol still in hand, he met Charlie in the hall.

"They're all dead," Charlie said, his voice high. Then he noticed the gun and took a step back. "Oh. I guess you know." He backed up to the wall. "I can take care of Sarah. I mean, when you and Jeremy need to go out, I can watch her."

"What if I don't plan to take Sarah?"

Charlie was silent.

"Can you cook?"

He shook his head.

"Don't you know when to lie, boy? Come

on," Merec motioned for Charlie to precede him toward Sarah's room. The seat before the monitor was empty, but just then Jeremy appeared in the doorway. "Car's packed," he announced.

"Good." Roughly Merec pushed the boy forward. "What do you think about Charlie here?"

Jeremy turned cold eyes on the boy. "He could be useful."

"Well, if Jeremy wants you . . ." Merec clapped the boy on the shoulder and, raising the pistol, shot him in the nape of the neck. Charlie's body collapsed, and his forehead hit the floor with a thick, heavy sound. Merec sighed. "He's the last," he said to Jeremy. "Let's get the hammers and the kerosene."

Half an hour later, Merec entered Sarah's cell. "We're going now." He held out his hand to her. "Coming?"

The question was, of course, a courtesy. But she refrained from a sarcastic comment; she was too busy thinking about the implications of the outstretched hand. He knew she could walk. He must have watched her stumbling steps. What else had they seen?

She let him help her to her feet and lead her through the door of her cell. Immediately outside they came across the first body. She saw Charlie's beautiful eyes, half closed as though sleepy. Then she looked at his mouth, once crowded with yellow teeth—the one part of his face that had seemed vulnerable. It was open at an unnatural angle; the jawbone must have been broken at the hinge. Inside it was a bloody mess. The teeth that remained were sharp, jagged pieces jutting out of the gums, bloody and ragged like the jaw of a shark.

It shook her, the destruction of his sad, humble teeth. Her knees weakened, and she needed to clutch at Merec's arm to steady herself.

"Does that upset you?" he inquired.

She avoided the question by turning it back on him. "Doesn't it disturb you?"

He stopped to contemplate the body. "I don't know," he said, and strangely, she heard honesty in his response. "I have lost . . . perspective, I suppose you could say."

"Why did you do that to his teeth?" she asked.

"So they can't identify the body."

"Oh."

Jeremy appeared around the corner. "We'd better move," he said.

Merec led her through corridors, past other bodies, all with their bloody jaws agape. One of the bodies twitched; the jaw worked and emitted a groan. They stopped beside him. Merec glanced at Sarah and said, "Would you like to take care of that?" Reaching for the shoulder holster tucked under his arm, he offered her a pistol, a strangely familiar expression on his face.

She paused, trying to place the expression. It struck a long dormant chord, and the recognition floated to the surface of her mind; he was flirting with her. She flushed and took the gun gingerly with her bandaged fingers, carefully fit her forefinger through the trigger, and aimed. Merec reached over and undid the safety.

Sarah leveled the gun again and pointed it straight at the man's heart. When she pulled the trigger, she wasn't ready for the recoil. The pistol jerked, and the bullet went through the man's nose. Right before her eyes, his nose disappeared into fragments of cartilage and blood.

"That was messy." Merec reached out and retrieved the gun. "Your eyes are very bright right now," he observed. "What are you thinking?"

"I was wondering," she said deliberately, "how many bullets there were in that gun." She did not tell him about the strange thrill she felt. She wasn't sure if it was disgust . . . or something else.

He laughed, delighted. "I am so glad I decided to keep you for a while." He offered his arm again. "You are charming when you lie."

As they emerged into the soft, humid night, Jeremy was coming up the steps with two more jugs of kerosene.

"Leave one for me by the door," Merec said.

He guided Sarah down the steps and to the car, where she sat with the door open, perched on the edge of the seat. Merec headed back to the house and picked up the jug on the way in.

Sarah tilted her head for a view of the stars and took a deep breath. The air smelled of kerosene and hummed with the sound of crickets.

Jeremy returned first. He leaned against the car, the door propped open between them. Sarah had the feeling that Jeremy was on the brink of speech, but at that moment Merec emerged, tossed the empty can over the railing into the bushes, and took the steps nimbly, two at a time.

"Jeremy, do you have our cocktails?"

Jeremy pushed himself upright and went to fetch two glass jars with rags stuffed in the tops.

"How is your pitching arm?" Merec said, turning to Sarah. "Would you like to do the honors?"

She solemnly took a jar from Jeremy and cupped it between her bandaged hands as Merec took out his lighter and held it to the rag. It blossomed with flame, and Sarah needed to hold it at arm's length. She walked toward the house like that, the jar held ceremoniously before her like an offering. The flame lit her face with flickering intensity. She walked to the base of the steps and, grasping the jar firmly in one hand, cocked her arm and threw.

It didn't go far. It landed just inside the door

and exploded in flames that ran like a snake, sliding along the path of the kerosene.

Hearing her name, Sarah turned to look at the two men, their skin golden in the light from the fire. Merec approached with the other cocktail held casually in one hand. He drew her away and circled the house, tossing the jar in one of the windows.

The flames in the front had climbed the walls and fed greedily on the roof. Some low-hanging branches of one of the trees caught and were outlined in a glow of deep orange. From the corner of her eye, Sarah saw Jeremy step forward, and she felt cool fingers on her arm. "Let's go," he said, but she could barely hear him as the noise of the fire had grown from a murmur to a roar.

Jeremy did not offer her his arm. Instead he took her hand like a small child or a young lover. He held her palm, avoiding her bandaged fingers, and led her to the car. His clasp was light and gentle as a whisper. The backdoor of the car stood open, and she slid in.

Merec jogged over. "Let's get going. This place will be hotter than Hades in a few minutes."

Jeremy stood one second longer, staring at the blaze. Then, making sure Sarah was all the way in, he swung the door closed.

She looked out the back window as they bumped away over the dirt road. She imagined that the flames must be crawling over the bodies by now, a voracious lover licking them clean.

The Northern Lights

They were about fifteen miles away when Stanley said, "Look, it's the sunrise."

Zackman glanced up through the windshield, down at his watch, and back up to the glow on the horizon. "But it's only three o'clock," he said, his lips thin.

"And that light is in the north," Tresler added.

They drove on, all watching the light flickering above the trees, fading the stars. They were stopped five miles from their destination by a police car parked slantwise across the road.

Zackman got out, approached the car, and bent over to talk to the sleepy young officer in the driver's seat. He returned to the van. "We missed them by an hour," he said. "A fucking hour."

Tresler suggested quietly that they head back.

"But the evidence," one of Zackman's men protested.

"Won't be accessible probably for days. With the heat and size of that fire."

Zackman climbed back in the passenger seat. He said, "Turn it around, Bill," in a tired voice and didn't speak again.

When the van arrived back at headquarters, Tresler asked Stanley if he wanted to be dropped back at his jeep. To save time, they had driven to CIA headquarters in Tresler's car.

"No." Stanley rubbed his eyes. "No, that's out of the way. My house is much closer. I'll get the car later." He gave directions in a subdued voice, and on the drive back both were silent.

Tresler pulled up in front of the house and shifted into park but didn't shut off the engine. They sat, the car vibrating gently beneath them.

Stanley didn't immediately make any move to get out. Through the windshield they both saw Stanley's wife appear at a window.

"My wife," he said.

"Ah." Tresler nodded. There was another long pause. "What does your wife do?" he asked politely.

"She's a criminal defense attorney."

Tresler chuckled.

"What?" Stanley said. "What's so funny?"

Tresler couldn't answer—he was still chuckling.

Stanley snorted, then also began to laugh. "Oh boy," Stanley said a minute later, wiping his eyes. "Okay. So what do we do now?"

"Now we get some sleep."

"I mean on the case. How are we going to find them?"

"Well, how do you catch a fox?"

"Is this a riddle?" Stanley asked suspiciously.

Tresler shook his head. "You study the habits of the animal."

Camera crews paced the perimeter of the smoldering fire. Eventually they were able to reach the house, and the information trickled out to the public. Ten men and one woman were found, but there was some difficulty in identifying the bodies. There was no question that the fire was arson, and the police were assuming, from bullet holes through the skulls of many of the victims, that they were all dead before the fire occurred. There was even a rumor—unsubstantiated—that an undercover agent had died in the blaze. Of course, the most heated question revolved around the identity of the woman.

IBC aired their video footage from the Willowridge Rest Home twice more, and clips from it ran almost every night. As Merec had predicted, everyone in the country had heard of Sarah Shepherd.

Secret Files and Frank Sinatra

In Merec's FBI file there were five pictures. One was of a man whose sharp features seemed to lean together like the blade of a hatchet. Another showed a man whose thin, aquiline nose flared at the nostrils as though he scented something unpleasant. A third photo was of a heavy-jowled man with hard pebble eyes. The pictures were so varied that someone, as a joke, had included a picture of Frank Sinatra. There was also, at the bottom corner of the dusty accordion folder, a tiny snapshot—just the blurred jaw and ear of a man turning away in a crowd. It was a picture of Merec taken more than a decade before in a small town in the Netherlands, but it was impossible to make out anything but the approximate shape and size of the ear.

There were also details in the CIA file, in

faded ink, typewritten documents, and yellowed slips of newspaper articles in a dozen
languages. These held Merec responsible for
two dozen terrorist attacks, ranging from presidential assassinations to guerrilla wars in
Africa.

The one thing all the reports agreed on was
that he had a reputation for being unpre-
dictable. Merec wasn't affiliated with any particular organization or ideology, nor could he be
chalked up as a gun for hire. He rarely went to
the highest bidder and might even do a job for
free if it appealed to him.

Tresler glimpsed the folder when he met with
his contact within the CIA, Bob O'Berski. Bob
chose the back corner of a dark, cavelike bar
where smoke hung in low clouds just above
their heads. Tresler placed an envelope on the
pitted wooden table, and in exchange, Bob slid
the accordion folder across to him.

"Don't know what you want with it," he said.
"I told you this folder is old. They've got a new
one somewhere I can't get to."

"That's fine," Tresler reassured him.
Extracting the contents, he found the pictures,
the articles, and the scribbled notes. He took a
few minutes to skim through the material. Bob
waited, dipping lower and lower into his beer.
By the time Tresler was finished, Bob's glass
was empty. Tresler went to the bar and ordered
two more.

"You know the agency, they don't pay shit," Bob said, accepting the beer. "Can't live on the pension, and there's never enough to save. I don't know how the guys with families do it." He took a long drink. Wiping his mouth with the napkin that served as a coaster, he put the glass down on the bare wood to add his own milky-white ring to the circles upon circles upon circles. "So what do you want to know?"

"Just tell me everything," Tresler said.

"But you probably know most of it already," Bob cautioned. "You still want to hear the whole story?"

"As if I didn't know a thing about it."

"Okay." Bob took a sip of his new beer. "Well, the whole operation was a fiasco from the beginning. I'm not sure why the agency got involved in what seems like a bureau case, but I heard the command came from the top. The rumors hinted that the chief had some sort of personal vendetta against this guy.

"Anyway, as you know, Zackman is assigned to the case. He creates Team Persi, and they track their man through a recruitment buzz going through the soldier of fortune scene. Zackman sends two men in. But one turns up a couple weeks later in a sack. The other man they don't hear from, but they had him in deep cover—that means no backup, no radio contact, no nothing. They're counting on him being able to get out and get them the info. So they're not worried when two months, even three go by.

"But someone high up is impatient. It's been months with nothing to show but one dead Persi, so what do they do? They put another team on it. That's fine, but they don't tell Zackman. And the other team decides not to sink a man into the organization. Probably 'cause it eats up too much time. So they do heavy surveillance, and I don't know the details of how they come up with this info, but they have a lock on some Joe who's headed in. They make contact, offer him an absurd amount of money that they never would have paid even if the sucker made it out alive, and they thread a tracking device into his hair."

He took another deep drink.

"So this schmuck goes in, and they get a read on his location. Do they follow up? No, they fuck around. I never did get the real story on why. Anyway, when Zackman finds out, he goes ballistic and tears out of headquarters like a bat out of hell."

Bob stopped to drain the rest of his beer, then continued. "They saw the light from the fire at least ten miles away. The forest around it lit like a fucking tinderbox. Hadn't rained in a month. It burned a quarter-mile radius around the encampment, and they couldn't get anywhere close for a day because of the heat of the thing."

He solemnly rotated his empty glass on the table.

"This guy you're tracking is one crazy son of a bitch." He looked up at Tresler as though expecting an answer.

Tresler shrugged.

"Listen," Bob said, leaning forward, "I've known you a while now, and I've seen the way you work. You catch these guys by figuring out what makes them tick. That's why you wanted that old file, right?"

Tresler agreed.

"But that's exactly why you don't have a chance with your man. You saw what it said in the file. He's not affiliated with any known organization. He's not working for some liberation group, or to get buddies out of prison, or to alert the world to some crisis. Usually with that kind of profile, the guy is a hired gun. But this one's not out for the money. My theory," he said, "and mind you, this is only my theory, is that he's a killer. Plain and simple."

"But what about those games he plays with his victims?"

Bob waved his hand as if he was shooing a fly. "What do I know about that shit? I'm not a psychiatrist."

"Okay, so what's the standard opinion?" Tresler inquired.

"That he's really working for someone or something, and they've just buried it so deep that we can't see it. I've heard that even in the real file we don't have much on him. But word is he came over here because he couldn't get people to work with him anywhere he was known. No one in their right mind would sign up with him—his men have close to a one-hundred-percent fatality rate. That's part of the reason why almost no one has any idea what he looks like. If they're not killed in the operation, he does the job himself."

"What about this woman Rose, who was left behind at the rest home?"

Bob laughed. "That's the biggest joke. The one person who knows what he looks like, who could positively identify him, and she's not talking for anything. She claims the leader said that if she helped us, it would put Sarah Shepherd in danger. Can you believe that shit? I mean it's not as if she's exactly safe now. But I'll tell you, that Rose is one stubborn old lady."

"What about Sarah Shepherd?" Tresler asked.

Bob clapped his hands to his ears. "Aw, God, I knew it. I knew it was coming."

"Where did she come from?"

"I wish we knew," Bob said. "I wish we knew."

Musical Chairs

On the drive Merec had Sarah lie down in the backseat of the car. At first she lay on her side, knees drawn up, eyes staring at the silhouette of the seatbacks. She soon tired of the view and shifted onto her back. From there she could gaze up through the rear window into the night sky. She amused herself by remembering that the light from the stars was millions—hundreds of millions—of years old. She knew that relative to the stars, her life would flash by faster than the time it took for a shadow to strike the ground. But the trip in the car that night seemed interminable.

The next morning, Merec called Karl from a pay phone just half a block from Karl's apartment.

Without identifying himself, Merec said, "Leave the apartment immediately and go to your local post office to pick up a package." He hung up and waited.

Obligingly, Karl appeared at the door of his building and stepped out into the street. Merec scanned the faces on the block. Some glanced up briefly as Karl passed, but most ignored him, and none seemed to follow. Fifteen minutes later, Merec intercepted Karl on his way back, falling into step with him.

Karl glanced over but showed no outward sign of surprise.

"How is the work going?" Merec asked.

"Almost done."

"Can I come up?" But the real question was "Is it safe?"

Karl nodded.

They climbed three flights. Karl had secured an apartment with two rooms connected by a long, narrow hall. The room at the front of the building had a clear view down to the street. The back room was dark, with only a tiny window onto an airshaft.

Merec took the measure of each in three long strides. He flipped the mattress, inspected the undersides of the table and chairs, and rapped his knuckles along the walls. A second later someone rapped back. Merec jumped and peered suspiciously at the spot. He knocked again, and again it was echoed back to him.

"Thin walls," Karl said.

"Then we will need to talk softly."

"You're staying?"

"We're staying," Merec corrected.

In the backseat of the car, Sarah had managed to squirm into a pair of black slacks and a cotton T-shirt. Merec also had her tuck her hair up into a large straw hat, put on tortoiseshell sunglasses to cover her black eye, and apply some lipstick—a dark, dramatic burgundy—to distract from the fading bruises.

When Merec returned from Karl's rooms, Sarah was sitting up and craning her neck to get a glimpse of the street sign. She had been lying down in the backseat for the entire ride and consequently had seen very little of the landscape. But the street sign confirmed what she had already suspected—they were in New York City.

Merec opened the door, and for the second time he offered his arm and tucked her fingers into the crook of his elbow. She needed help up the three flights, and on the second landing he passed his arm around her waist. By the time they reached the door, he was supporting almost all her weight. Only her toes touched the last few steps.

He opened the door, took Sarah straight into the back room, and lowered her onto the mattress. His breath smelled of peppermint and smoke, and she drifted off to sleep on the scent.

• • •

With Karl's help, Jeremy transferred his equipment from the trunk of the car to the front room of the apartment. Merec stood by the window watching the process.

Testing the table, Jeremy found that the legs were unsteady, so he set up on the floor. He had brought only the simplest things: a TV, a VCR, remote controls, headphones, and the video camera. With everything plugged in, tested, and working, Jeremy joined Merec by the window.

"How long before you can finish the edit?"

Jeremy shrugged. "It's a very crude setup, but the footage is good."

"It had better be. Today is Saturday. I want the tape finished by Monday."

"It won't be my best. What's the hurry?"

"I have plans for that tape."

"It will be more effective if it's well done," Jeremy said.

"No, that doesn't matter. Just make sure it's not boring."

It was Jeremy's turn to laugh.

"And," Merec continued, "I want a few tears from our viewers for our little hero. We need to get it to Sarah's public before she's passé."

"And that means by Monday?" Jeremy said.

Since the equipment was on the floor, Jeremy lay on his stomach, propped up on his elbows, eyes shining in the light of the screen. Absorbed in his work, he paid no attention to the honking of horns outside the window or the shouts and cries of people from the sidewalk. Jeremy was dazzled by the image of Sarah Shepherd—not Sarah the woman but Sarah the hero. He saw the gem shining in the rough, unpolished stone. And he polished.

When Sarah woke, she stretched and raised herself on her elbows. Merec was sitting on a chair in the corner with a newspaper spread on his lap and a single earphone in his left ear, the cord leading to a small radio. She could see his eyes follow the lines, his legs elegantly crossed, his foot flexing gently.

She watched him. A moment later she asked abruptly, "Are you going to sit there all day?"

He looked up at her. "Yes," he answered. "Why?"

She hadn't had anything particular in mind. She searched for a retort. "You happen to be sitting on the only chair in the room."

He glanced down as if surprised. "Sorry. Do you want it?"

"Yes," she said, though she didn't.

Instead of leaving the room, he merely transferred himself to the floor next to the chair. "There you are," he said, going back to his paper.

She had no choice but to struggle up from the mattress, cross the room, and sit in the chair. Now they were sitting side by side.

"I don't actually need the chair," she said.

"That's all right. I'm perfectly comfortable on the floor."

"I mean, I would prefer that you leave."

"Don't beat around the bush now. Tell me how you really feel," he said, grinning up at her. He reminded her for a flashing second of Jonathan—her gentle, peaceful Jonathan who closed his eyes when killing spiders with his slipper. It wasn't until later that she realized what had caused that lightning connection. But now she didn't smile back, and Merec's own teasing grin leaked away.

"I can't," he said simply, almost, she thought, apologetically.

"Why not?"

He opened his mouth to answer. Shut it. Frowned.

She watched the transition from man to captor. She knew what was coming.

Quick as a rattlesnake, his hand whipped out and hit her across the face. Even though she had sensed it coming, still it was so fast, so firm, that her head snapped around, smacking against the wall, and the pain came flooding back. At the same time the pain in her fingers, which had lulled to a dull throbbing, flared up hot and fiery. She raised a bandaged hand to her cheek, cupping it tenderly. "I didn't know you cared."

"Oh, deeply, my dear," he said in his old smooth tone. "Deeply."

She kept her palm pressed against her tingling skin. Far off, a motorcycle roared at a whisper.

"Do you have any cigarettes?" she asked.

He patted his pockets and came up with a pack. He handed it to her along with the heavy gold lighter.

She fumbled with it but managed to produce a flame with her bound fingers. She lit a cigarette, exhaled, and watched the lazy smoke twist to the ceiling.

The Hound

Tresler found Michael O'Connell's name in Merec's file. There was only one thing that made O'Connell stand out from the long list of people suspected of having had contact with Merec: O'Connell had an address attached to his name. He was entombed in a high-security prison in England serving two consecutive life sentences for the assassination of a political figure. Once known only by his nickname, the Hound, O'Connell was suspected in dozens, maybe hundreds of murders across five continents and spanning a quarter of a century.

Tresler left Stanley in charge of the case and flew out of JFK to Heathrow. When he arrived, he was taken straight to the prison.

As he checked in, Tresler was waved over by a wand that beeped at his keys and his zippers. He had already handed over his pistol.

"Well, this is an event," the guard remarked. "O'Connell hasn't had a visitor since I've been here."

"How long is that?" Tresler asked.

The guard considered. "Seven years now, almost eight."

The prisoner was brought to the other side of the window, shackled at the wrists and ankles. They bound his hands in front of him so that he could cradle the telephone receiver between his two palms to bring it up to his ear.

O'Connell was a little man, bowlegged, with a fringe of gray hair lying neatly around his ears and a trim, dapper beard. His eyes were bright, and he regarded Tresler expectantly.

"How are you?" Tresler asked politely.

"Grand," O'Connell said with a cheerful smile. "Just grand. Do you think you could tell us a little bit of what's going on in the world? We had our TV and radios all confiscated about seven months ago, and we're dead lost."

Tresler realized that O'Connell was talking about all the inmates and not, as he had first thought, about himself, using the royal "we."

"Of course. Do you want to know anything in particular?"

He did. He wanted to know everything about the recent elections in the States, which Tresler could tell him, and in Italy, which he couldn't. He wanted to know about any natural disasters, any manmade disasters, any prison breaks, and any assassinations. After Tresler mentioned the blinding of a dignitary in a recent bombing, O'Connell launched into a heated discussion of the importance of the different senses. He contended that he would rather lose anything rather than his sense of smell—eyesight, hearing, anything. "Imagine Helen Keller," he said. "Imagine the things she must smell. What sense would you be least willing to part with?"

"Sight," Tresler replied.

O'Connell shook his head as though disappointed. "That's what so many people think."

"You disapprove?"

"I think it lacks imagination. It's as if you can only know, only trust, what you see. In fact, that is the one thing you can't trust. Imagine what you could know if you weren't allowed to rely on what you see." He closed his eyes briefly and said, "It's time for me to go."

Sure enough, a second later a guard came to fetch him. "Time for lockdown," the guard explained to Tresler.

O'Connell said, "I imagine you didn't come to chat. You can come again tomorrow," and he gave Tresler a slight nod before he was led out.

But the next day Tresler had to wait for three hours before the guard brought O'Connell to the visitor's room, and when he appeared, one side of his face was battered a deep purple and one bright eye was swollen shut. A cut snaked along his forehead and down around his brow, stitched up with neat black sutures.

"Sorry," he said, awkwardly cradling the phone against his other ear. That was the only reference he made to his horrific appearance. "You were a good sport my last visit. What is it you want to know?"

"Merec," Tresler said. O'Connell showed no visible reaction to the name. "I want to know about Merec."

"Even if I did know anything, why do you think I'd tell you?"

"I'm told you have video facilities here." Tresler reached into his bag and pulled out Merec's videotape. "I have gotten permission for you to watch this. I will wait here until you're done."

While he was waiting, Tresler went out to chat with the guard. During their conversation he asked casually what had happened to O'Connell. The guard frowned. The cut, the bruises, Tresler said.

"Oh that? That's nothing. No one can touch him."

"Looks like he got touched to me," Tresler remarked.

The guard laughed. "The other guy got shipped out in a bag."

Forty minutes later O'Connell returned to the room. He placed the videotape on the table, cradled the phone against one cheek, and without preamble started to speak.

"I worked with Merec when I was first starting out in the business. He was just a few years older than I was, but he had already made a name for himself. My father was in armed robbery, and that's where I got my chops, but I didn't want that as a career, and my father agreed. He said you had to rely on too many other people, and there were too many circumstances that you couldn't control. Success in that business was at least as much luck as it was skill. He wanted to see me in something a little more stable. He was the one that set me up with Merec to try out this new gig.

"On the first job we were after a Belgian businessman. Beforehand Merec tells me who he is, what he does, where he lives, all about his family. He tells me little details like how often he travels, how much money he makes, what he likes to do in his spare time. I sit and listen; I'm supposed to be learning from him. But when he was done there were two things I thought I had to know: I wanted to know who wanted this guy dead, and I wanted to know why. So I asked Merec . . . and he laughed at me. He told me things didn't work that way. I didn't understand him at the time." O'Connell paused here, keeping the phone cradled close to his cheek.

"Merec was meticulous with his jobs. He'd do surveillance as long as he needed to. I heard a rumor later that on one job—mind you, it was one that everyone said was impossible—he did surveillance for five years. I never doubted it. He had infinite patience.

"On our job with the Belgian businessman we only needed to watch for about two months. That's about average, though at the time it seemed like forever. When we decided to go ahead with the job, we entered at midday when the kids were out and the wife was shopping. She was always out shopping for at least three or four hours in the afternoon. As soon as she went, the housekeeper made a beeline for the bar on the corner. She kept an eye out for the car, but she didn't have too much to worry about, as the wife's shopping wasn't always shopping, if you know what I mean.

"That's what's so amazing about the job. You get to know so much about these people, about their lives, their deceptions, the deceptions practiced on them, their failings, their successes—all the little details. You put a tap on their phone and listen to their conversations. You bug their house and listen to them make love to their wives and put their children to bed. Then you kill them. I don't know if you ever get over the wonder of it.

"We stowed away in the attic, and we stayed there until about four in the morning, trying to keep our muscles from cramping, and pissing into plastic cups. At four we crept down into the living room, and Merec told me that if I didn't do exactly what he said he would kill me. He disappeared down the hall and returned a minute later with the children. They were six and nine, both girls. He had one nestled in the crook of his arm, the other he led by the hand. He sat them on the couch and disappeared again. He reappeared with the housekeeper. She had something stuffed in her mouth. It was red, with lace. I think it was a pair of her own underwear. Then he came back with the husband and wife. He managed to squeeze everyone on the couch. 'Remember,' Merec said to them, 'not one word or I'll—'

"The wife had this awful habit of interrupting. We'd been listening to it for the past two months, and before he could even finish his sentence the wife opened her mouth. She said, 'But—.' She didn't ever get out another word. Bam, just like that, he shot her right between the eyes from ten paces away. That's not as easy as you might think. But the scariest thing about it was that he didn't hesitate—not for one second. Just 'But—,' and she was gone. That's more than just skill: that takes an iron will.

"As long as I knew him, Merec always had the advantage because he'd kill in an instant, without hesitation. Everyone—and I mean everyone—hesitates at least a second before killing. Now I couldn't say why. I know it of myself. I've tried to fight it, but I still do it. Maybe it's simply the lag time between the will, the decision to kill, and the execution. And the only way I can think that Merec got around this was that his finger would decide to kill before his brain. Don't ask me how that's possible.

"Killing—sometimes it's simple, sometimes it's complicated, but I guarantee it's never the same every time for anyone. I've known men who have killed for a decade, then one day they freeze and can't pull the trigger. You never know when it's going to happen. Sometimes it's trying to kill someone you know—sometimes it's a complete stranger. But killing, it's a religion, not a science.

"Anyway, so Merec shot the wife. One of the kids started to scream, and Merec killed her too. Though she didn't make a sound, the housekeeper got it next. She slumped over with those panties still in her mouth. Finally he takes out the businessman. Now there's this one little girl left—the nine-year-old. I wanted him to finish it off, but I'll tell you the truth, I was afraid to open my mouth.

"The little girl just sat there, her eyes squeezed shut. Merec went right up to her and said, 'Make sure you do something interesting with your life, little girl.' And he left her sitting there, wedged between her mother and younger sister.

"I worked with him for a couple of years, and we did ten or fifteen more jobs together. He was always the same. Meticulous to a fault before the job went off, but once we were in full swing, he was a loose cannon.

"Why did I stay with him so long? You should have known him back then. He was like Helen Keller. He could scent things. He could smell fear, smell betrayal, smell intention. He was always calm on the surface, but inside he was on fire. I remember he liked me by the end, at least as much as he could like anyone. I kept my mouth shut, didn't fuss, backed him up, followed his lead, and made a lot of money. Then I got offered a job on my own, a one-man thing. I guess I got a reputation as the steady half of Merec's operation.

"The next job Merec took on after I left, he turned on his own men, shot down every single one, and left the mark alive. After that he tracked down his employer and shot him instead. Then he took off to Africa or something. Some crazy fucking place. It was just as well. You couldn't trust him for anything but havoc. Out of his head, the grapevine said.

"A few weeks after he left, I got a letter. It had a certified check for one million signed with some name I didn't recognize, but I knew it was from him. There was a little scrap of paper in there also. It said, 'You too could be an artist.'

"I banked the money and retired. I thought, What do I need this shit for? I'm young and rich, and I can do anything I want. But I only lasted eight months. A man needs a profession. He needs his work.

"I got back in the business gradually. I didn't

go for the big-money jobs, at least not necessarily. I built up my reputation. I did what Merec said never to do: I asked why. Then I found out that asking didn't get you the answers. And it never would. I didn't need the money, so I made up my own hits, my own questions, and supplied my own answers. I realized that was what Merec had been doing all along. His own questions, his own answers. I realized what Merec had meant by that note."

Now Tresler broke in. "So he's not crazy?"

O'Connell raised his eyebrows. "You came here to ask me that?"

"Can you tell me what motivates him?"

"God only knows. I certainly don't." He grinned. "Makes him devilish hard to catch, doesn't it?"

"Does he have anything that he's sensitive about? Anything that gets to him?"

O'Connell thought for a moment. "It's been a while," he said, "but I remember once a member of our team confessed to Merec that he had talked to a shrink about our latest job. Merec shot him. Later I asked him if it was because the man had snitched. But Merec said no, it wasn't that. Even if the man hadn't told the shrink about the job, he still would have shot him. He killed him just for admitting he went to one. Merec hated the whole idea of psychiatry. Said it was ridiculous to have someone try to explain you to yourself. Ridiculous to expect it but even more ridiculous for someone else to think they could."

"Is that right?" Tresler said. He sat lost in thought. Then he looked up. "It's tempting, isn't it? To try to figure him out. Did you ever attempt it?"

"Sure I did," O'Connell admitted.

"Conclusions?"

O'Connell scratched the new scar on his forehead. Then he brought the phone back down to his mouth. "I've had a long time to think about this, as you can probably imagine. And I believe," he said slowly, "that Merec is blind in a sightless world, but while everyone sits still, afraid to stir, he is walking around. And what happens when you walk around without being able to see where you're going?" He answered his own question. "You bump into things."

"You don't think he's . . ." Tresler paused, as if ashamed of his question. He tried again. "You don't think he's evil?"

O'Connell laughed, and his small white teeth bared themselves in a snarl. "You're asking a man who is allegedly responsible for personally slaughtering one hundred and forty-seven people for his opinion on evil?"

"Yes." And Tresler wondered if he had misjudged him. "Who else would know so well as you?"

O'Connell sobered immediately. "Who else indeed," he said thoughtfully. "All of us, who do what we do, we're taking a big gamble. We must believe that there is no order in the world, no real reward or punishment for our actions. But if there is such a thing as evil, and that's a big if, Merec is certainly the most evil man I know."

A Damn
Good Reason

Saturday passed, and Merec didn't stir
from the room—at least not when Sarah
was awake. When she went to the bathroom, he
accompanied her and stood outside in the hall
reading yet another newspaper. She could feel
his presence there as she lingered in front of the
mirror, inspecting the fading bruises on her
face.

On Sunday Merec sat on the floor in front of
Sarah and removed the dressings from her fingers. The nails had all fallen off, and the tips
were scabbed and sensitive. She kept them folded into fists because whenever they brushed
against the wall or the mattress they felt strange
with too much feeling.

To pass the time she paced the small room
and napped in between. Occasionally she

would smoke, filling the air with a hazy, cloudy quality that made it seem like one of her dreams. Often she would look up to find Merec watching her. It unnerved her, though she would have done anything to keep him from knowing it.

On Monday the weather took a turn for the worse. A heat wave hit the city, and the air in the back room was thick. She had difficulty breathing and could hear the sound of the air in her throat. She couldn't stand the noise. She tried to quiet it by lying down. It didn't work. She could still hear it—the passage of air through emptiness. The feeling in her chest built until she had to jump up from the mattress and begin to pace again. Finally she spoke to mask the noise.

"Do you still want to make that tape?" she said.

Merec froze, alarmed. How did she know what Jeremy was doing? Then he realized that she was referring to the ransom plea.

"Why? Will you do it now?"

She stood a little straighter. "No."

"Why did you bring it up then?"

She didn't answer.

"I see. You wanted to know if there was more of this," he wiggled his fingers at her, "in store."

"Yes."

"Well, that all depends on you."

"Hah." It was a forced, violent sound. She leaned toward him, her face close to his own.

"You didn't even do it yourself. Was it the idea you liked? Were you standing outside waiting to hear the screams?"

"Is that what you thought?" She saw the revulsion on his face. "I would never do something like that if it wasn't necessary."

"I saw you kill six of my friends before my very eyes, for no reason I could fathom. Or you ordered them killed. It's a matter of semantics."

"But that was clean, fast," he said. "They didn't feel any pain."

"So let me make sure I understand you. You only kill people for no reason. But you're assuring me that you need a damn good reason before torturing them?"

"Yes. Now what's going on here? Why the inquisition?"

She didn't answer.

"You're angry," he said in sudden wonder.

"I'm not angry."

"Then what are you?"

"I'm . . ." She hesitated. "All right, fine. You're right. I'm angry. I'm not just angry, I'm so mad I could spit."

"Spit, if it will make you feel better."

"I couldn't."

"And why not?"

She considered that. "Because I'm a lady."

He let out a peal of laughter. For once it was not mocking. "So that's what you are," he said, still chuckling. "I was wondering."

She didn't respond but gazed straight ahead.

"Don't be so afraid," he whispered.

Her head whipped around. "I am not," she said, her voice icy, "afraid of you."

"I believe you told me that once before. I haven't forgotten. That was not what I was referring to. You shouldn't be afraid of what you may discover about yourself."

A knock interrupted them, and Jeremy stuck his head around the door. He looked at Merec and said simply, "It's ready."

Media
Savvy

U pon returning from England, Tresler called Stanley. He was about to propose meeting in the morning at the office, when Stanley eagerly suggested a late dinner.

"I know a great little diner not far from my house. Do you want the address?"

Repressing a sigh, Tresler took out a pen.

Stanley was waiting just inside the door when Tresler arrived.

"I don't know about you, but I'm starving," Stanley said, leading the way to a table. He beckoned the waitress over. "I already know what I want. I'll get the meatloaf dinner. What will you have, Tresler?"

"Just a coffee," Tresler said to the waitress.

"Don't you ever eat? I don't want my partner dropping dead of starvation. Better make that two meatloaf dinners." He turned back to Tresler. "So, how did your long-shot lead in England pan out? Things here have been crazy. You know, I've spent the last few days up at the arson site. We've lifted ten sets of tire tracks from the dirt road leading in, and I think that's going to be a great lead. We've also got descriptions from witnesses of some suspicious cars out that night."

"Suspicious cars?"

"It could lead to something," Stanley protested. "And we recovered some things from the fire—weapons, electronic equipment, something that looks like an internal security system."

"Bodies?"

"Yes, we've recovered the bodies. We're still working on identification, but we have positively confirmed that the one woman found could not possibly be Sarah Shepherd. Too tall by at least four or five inches."

"The undercover agent?"

"They don't know for sure, but they think he's there. You see, there's not much to go on. No hairs, no clothing," he paused a beat, "no teeth."

"So you would say that we have . . . "

Stanley tapped his fingers on the table. "Nothing," he admitted. "We've got nothing."

The waitress approached with the two meatloaf dinners. She set one in front of Stanley and the other before Tresler. She poured Tresler's coffee. He moved his plate slightly to one side and curled his fingers around the warm mug. Stanley stared morosely down at his food. Then he shook himself and started eating. In the next few minutes Tresler watched as Stanley managed to devour all of the food on his plate with astounding speed.

"So," Stanley said, talking around a large piece of meatloaf. "Did you come up with anything?"

"Yes. I found out that our man doesn't like psychiatrists."

"Oh." Stanley stopped chewing to think about it. "So?"

Tresler told Stanley his plan.

"But," Stanley interrupted, almost before Tresler had finished speaking, "that didn't work last time. You said he was going to call after the hotline segment aired, and he never did."

"And he might not again. But I would say we can be sure he's monitoring the media coverage of the case, and it would not be out of character for him to call in a response."

"But it wouldn't make any sense."

"True," Tresler agreed. "It's a long shot. But we don't have anything else to go on."

Stanley had no answer to that. Instead he pointed at Tresler's untouched meal and said, "Are you going to eat that?"

Tresler shook his head.

"Then if you don't mind," Stanley said and reached for the plate.

Merec decided to send Karl to deliver the tape personally. "IBC," he directed him. "Front desk. I want you to drop it off in person. Do you understand?"

"Yes."

"Before you go, are the plans of the cathedral done?"

Karl passed over a cardboard poster tube, sealed at both ends with wide pieces of duct tape.

Merec took it and bounced it thoughtfully against his palm. "What about the other little task?"

Karl handed Merec a small rectangular plastic object.

Merec flipped it open, saw the white button inside, and closed the box. "Range?"

"Fifty meters," Karl said. Digging in his pocket, he produced a key and held it out to Merec. "If you want to watch," he said. "It's marked on the plans."

Merec laughed. "You are a treasure, Karl. Thank you. You know where we're scheduled to meet next week?"

Karl nodded, and Merec tossed him the keys to the car.

• • •

Tresler lined up the radio station for Tuesday evening. Then he arranged for the tracking equipment and the personnel to run the equipment and found a psychiatrist. Stanley took care of print advertising in every major city. The radio station was nationally affiliated and promised to advertise the event. Everything went smoothly until Stanley found out that Tresler planned to conduct the interview himself.

"But I did the other program," Stanley protested.

"And you did very well," Tresler agreed. He did not add that Stanley had been exactly what he wanted at the time.

"I have media experience," Stanley said, his voice rising.

"As do I," Tresler replied.

"Fine. But you are supposed to be an *adviser*."

"And I am advising you to let me conduct this interview."

"And if I don't?"

"Then I'm afraid I will have to withdraw my services from the case."

"What? You can't do that."

Tresler didn't answer, because, of course, he could.

"All right," Stanley said, with bad grace. "You can do the interview. But I think you should watch out for this media obsession of

yours. I think you're a little too fond of the spot-
light there, Tresler."

Tresler nodded gravely and said, "I will
take that under consideration."

Tuesday evening an alarm on Merec's watch
began to beep. Sarah looked up from the mattress and watched Merec open the paper and
riffle through its pages. He seemed to find what
he wanted and, closing the paper, adjusted the
dial on his radio.

Sarah sighed and shifted onto her side to gaze
out the small, dirty window into the airshaft.
When she glanced back at Merec a few minutes
later, she was instantly aware that something
unusual was happening. Merec's relaxed slouch
had straightened, and he was concentrating
intensely. She looked around the room, but she
couldn't see what held his attention. In fact his
eyes seemed unfocused, as though he were staring into the air. Then she realized that, of course,
it must be something he was listening to through
the small earphone.

He stood suddenly, pocketed the radio, and
tucked the newspaper under his arm. He met
her eyes for a brief second before leaving the
room. She heard him walk down the hall, but
he returned a moment later.

"Where is Jeremy?"

"You sent him out for food," she said, puzzled at his lapse of memory.

"Right." Merec checked his watch. "Well, I can't wait." He turned and disappeared again down the hall. She heard the door of the apartment open, and Merec's voice floated back to her. "I'm going out."

Sarah started up from the mattress. "Where?" she called out but only heard the door click shut behind him.

She stood in the middle of the room uncertainly. "But what about me?" she said, to nobody in particular.

On
the Air

The interview aired at five. The program's host introduced the participants and then turned it over to Tresler. They had only a five-minute segment, so Tresler quickly ran through the doctor's credentials and launched into the interview.

"Dr. Meadows," Tresler said, "tell us a little of how you go about interpreting the information from a crime scene."

Dr. Meadows was a thin, nervous man with a toupee and a habit of talking too quickly. He launched into the answer eagerly. "Well, I have to admit that it's true many people think that what I do in an investigation is only a step away from voodoo. But you see, what they don't understand, and what I always have to explain, is that the methods I use closely resemble a judicial court. And no one claims that our courts here in

America measure out justice with voodoo, now do they?" He didn't stop for an assent.

"You *see*, in the courts they look at the evidence and rely heavily on precedent. That means looking at rulings and conclusions from earlier cases that bear a similarity to the one in question. Perfectly logical, don't you think? And that is *exactly* what I do. I examine the details of the case and compare it to other criminal cases I have overseen in the past. I give my opinion, and the authorities either take it into consideration or they discount it. And let me tell you, they find that more often than not my advice is materially helpful in solving a case."

Tresler smoothly inserted himself into the rapid speech. "As I'm sure will be true here also." He directed the momentum away from the doctor's eager self-justification and asked, "Would you talk a little bit about what you saw in this particular case?"

"This case, oh yes," he said, rubbing his hands as if to warm them. "This case is quite a gold mine of information. Let me explain. Now, criminals always leave behind some sort of trail. The more bizarre the crime, the more distinctive the trail. *But*," he held up a finger for emphasis, "they're not generally so obliging as to document the event."

"You mean the videotape," Tresler guided the doctor gently.

"What? Oh yes, of course. This videotape very

carefully does not provide much in the way of traditional 'clues' for the police to pursue, but what the perpetrator does not realize, at least not on the conscious level, is that he has left behind a psychological road map to his mind. And this is where *I* come in," the doctor placed a hand on his chest.

"When I am called in on a case, first and foremost I consider motivation in all striking factors, and in this case the most striking factor happens to be, in my opinion, the videotape. So I ask myself, *Why* does the perpetrator leave behind something that can only implicate him and help his pursuers? And the answer that comes to me is that the criminal most likely thinks that he is flaunting his bravado before the world.

"*But,*" his finger went up again, "there is a deeper psychology operating here. This man wants to distinguish himself from the rest of the psychotic element by taking on the guise of scientist and professes in what he calls his 'experiment' to test the true qualities of human nature. However, if you will observe, unlike true science, he has already formed his conclusions and arranges his test so that his opinions will most likely not be challenged. He forces his victims to participate in his moral degradation." The doctor's voice rose a decibel.

"But of course this does not make him feel better, it only exacerbates the issue. He *claims* to despise society, but he doesn't really hate society.

He is projecting his own vile proclivities onto society, and his anger and aggression are really a result of intense self-hatred." The doctor finished up grandly and slightly out of breath.

"Insightful," Tresler said. "And what is your opinion of Sarah Shepherd's role in this?"

"Who?"

"The hostage," Tresler clarified.

"Of course. Thank you for refreshing my memory. You have pointed out an even more intriguing twist to the drama. Unexpectedly our criminal is presented with someone who does not conform to his carefully scripted version of events. And when presented with this anomaly, he is unable to act. She represents a refutation of all his ideas, and I guarantee that his next move will be to try to destroy everything she stands for."

The station manager gave Tresler a signal.

"Thank you very much for your interpretation of events, Dr. Meadows," Tresler said. "I firmly believe that your analysis will be invaluable to this investigation. And listeners, stay tuned because we will be taking calls from anyone who wants to speak to the doctor."

The program host took over, and Tresler slipped out. He joined the staff in the back room into which he had squeezed his people with their tracking equipment. He sat down in a chair and put on the earphones that allowed him to listen to a portion of each call that came in.

The first was from a woman who was outraged at the doctor for talking about this sicko as though he were an actual person with thoughts and feelings instead of the animal he had proved himself to be. They patched her through to speak to Dr. Meadows on the air. The next caller said that he thought a valuable service had been provided because the people killed were old and therefore useless to society. He was also patched through. For the next five minutes Tresler listened without result until he heard a smooth voice with the hint of an accent saying, "No, I'm not calling to speak to the doctor. Yes, I know that this is what the line is for. I was hoping to speak to the other man. Yes, the investigator."

Tresler caught the operator's attention and indicated that he would take the call. Then he motioned at his team to start tracing immediately and picked up the line.

"Hello?"

"May I ask to whom I am speaking?"

This time there was no doubt—Tresler recognized the voice from the videotape. He gave the thumbs up to his people and spoke into the phone. "This is Agent Tresler."

"Hello, Agent Tresler," Merec said. "I have a hunch you are an intelligent man. Do you know who this is?"

"Yes."

"Good. I was just listening to your little program, and I figured that since you seemed so interested in me, it would be good manners to call and find out a little bit about you. So, tell me something about yourself."

"What do you want to know?"

"Well, for instance, do you have a wife? A family?"

"No. No family."

"Ah, so you're like me. A man who lives for his work."

"Yes, you could say that."

"So how did you come to be a federal agent?"

"That's funny," Tresler said. "Someone else asked me that just a few days ago."

"And what did you tell them?"

Tresler remembered his words to Stanley. "I told them that I had always wanted to be a criminal. But I didn't have what it takes, so this was the next best thing."

Unlike Stanley, Merec did not laugh. There was a short silence following this statement. Then Merec asked, "What does it take?"

"A large ego."

Now Merec laughed heartily. "Yes, yes, you're right."

"Why did you choose your present occupation?" Tresler asked.

"Someday I will tell you but not today."

"All right." Tresler glanced over at his team, huddled around the equipment.

"So how is your trace going?" Merec asked. "Have you pinpointed the state yet?"

Tresler smiled. "I'm not sure. Shall I ask them?"

"Don't bother. It doesn't matter. But it is interesting to note that you were expecting my call."

"Hoping," Tresler said modestly.

"Did that psychiatrist tell you I would phone in?"

"No. That was my idea."

"Well, in any case, it has been a pleasure, Agent Tresler."

"You could always call again. I can give you my number."

"I'm sorry, but I think I will have to decline that generous offer. But I will tell you this. When the time comes, I'll make sure you can find me. How does that sound?"

"Fine," Tresler said.

"I have one more question for you before I go."

"Yes?"

There was a pause. "Did you really believe all that nonsense the doctor was spouting?"

Tresler smiled. "I don't generally think in those terms. Belief or disbelief is not useful to me in my job."

The band of people huddled around the equipment burst apart suddenly and scattered to the phones. One of the men gave Tresler the thumbs up.

"But surely you must have an opinion," Merec pressed.

"I try my best to avoid it."

"Then you have the wisdom of Solomon, my dear fellow, ... and you're definitely in the wrong profession." The phone clicked, and Tresler was left with a dead line. "Hello?" A second later he heard a dial tone. He swiveled in his chair. "What's happening, Stanley?"

Stanley held up a finger and continued speaking quickly into the phone. When he hung up, he relayed the news to Tresler. "We got a fix. Downtown New York City. We've got three different police stations in the vicinity on the lines now, and they're mobilizing."

"Chances are we won't get him," Tresler said. "But we know where he is."

"But he also knows that we know," Stanley protested.

"That was his intention."

"Why would he do something like that?"

"The doctor might say it is a cry for help."

"What would *you* say?" Stanley asked.

Tresler just smiled and shook his head.

A Dearth of
Christmas Cards
and a Decision

When Jeremy let himself back into the apartment with the bag of groceries balanced on one hip, he found Sarah pacing the hallway just inside the front door.

He started and almost dropped the bag.

"What took you so long?" she demanded.

He shut the door quickly and, ignoring her question, said, "What the hell are you doing out here?"

"Waiting for you."

"Where is Merec?" He looked down the hall as though expecting Merec to appear at the question.

Sarah threw her hands up. "He left."

"He left?"

"Gone."

"Where did he go?"

"Damned if I know. He didn't happen to mention it."

"But . . ." Jeremy trailed off, momentarily confused. "Okay. Just tell me exactly what happened."

"We were sitting in the back room. Then he got up and left."

"Did he say anything?"

"He said, 'I'm going out.'"

"That's it?"

"That's it."

"And you have no idea what made him leave?"

"It looked like he might have been listening to something on the radio," she said.

At that moment the front door swung open. Jeremy and Sarah jerked around and saw Merec.

"Where did you go?" Sarah demanded.

"What's going on?" Jeremy said at the same time.

Merec walked past them and down the hall toward the front room. "No time to talk," they heard him say before he disappeared through the doorway. He reappeared with the cardboard tube Karl had given him and a duffel bag. "We're going."

"What, *now*?" Sarah said.

"Yes, now." He turned to Jeremy. "Bring only the absolute essentials."

Jeremy, catching the note of urgency, nodded and slipped by Merec toward the front room. "We'll met you outside," Merec said. He opened the bag and pulled out the hat and sunglasses that Sarah had worn previously.

"Will you tell me what . . . "

He shushed her, shoved the sunglasses into her hand, and perched the hat on her head. She instinctively reached up to fix it. Then Merec produced a lipstick from his pocket and held it out to her.

When she reached for the lipstick her hand was trembling. So Merec uncapped it, twirled the base, and applied it for her. He retrieved another hat from the bag, pulled it low over his eyes, and motioning for her to put on the sunglasses, opened the door to the apartment.

"Ready?"

She nodded, and he led her down the stairs and out to the street.

When they hit the sunlight she paused, blinking furiously behind the tinted lenses. Merec's hand wrapped around her upper arm like a band of iron and propelled her relentlessly along.

Then she saw them—a line of police cars, their lights revolving silently, in a procession down the street. To her surprise, Merec stopped as they passed. The last car in the line slowed to a halt just half a block away.

Sarah watched, tense with anxiety.

"All you have to do is call out," Merec said to her.

She turned toward him. His hand had loosened its hold, and now it dropped from her arm.

"What?" she said.

"Call out to them. Just walk over to them. Take off the hat and sunglasses so they recognize you."

"Why would they recognize me?" Merec had forgotten that she knew nothing of the videos. But she didn't wait for an answer. "You want me to walk over to them so you can shoot me."

"I don't need you to walk away to be able to shoot you," he pointed out. "Besides, I don't have my gun with me. I left it in the apartment."

"You didn't," she said, but her voice was unsure. She looked at him, then over to the group of police clustered together on the sidewalk.

He followed the direction of her gaze. "Idiots. I could have picked them off like tin cans on a fence by now."

She reached up and took off the sunglasses. The skin around her left eye was still tinged yellow from the last lingering bruise. "What's going on?"

He shrugged. "I simply no longer wish for, or require, a hostage."

"What about the ransom?"

"I don't need money. I already have more money than I could ever possibly spend."

A woman approached and glanced at Sarah

as she passed. She continued a step or two, stopped dead, and turned back to gape. Sarah couldn't help but notice, and she returned the woman's stare. Merec dipped his head, but he needn't have worried, for the woman's eyes never left Sarah's face. When the woman didn't look away, Sarah snapped, "Where are your manners? Didn't your mother ever teach you that staring is rude?"

Merec choked slightly, trying to hold back his laughter. The woman must have thought it was adequately unhostagelike behavior because she frowned and walked quickly away, only glancing briefly over at the police clustered near their cars.

Sarah slipped her sunglasses back on without Merec having to ask and said, "Have you ever had a hostage stay with you by choice?"

"I've heard of it happening, but no, it has never happened to me personally."

"Well, I don't suppose you've ever had an old woman with no family for a hostage before."

"No, I can't say that I have."

"Well, that explains it."

He regarded her steadily. "You'll have to pull your own weight."

"Do you mean I'll have to kill people?" she asked matter-of-factly.

"Do you think you could?"

She pursed her lips, but she said nothing.

"It might not be necessary," Merec continued. "Jeremy does his video. There will be something suited for you."

Just then Jeremy sauntered out the door, his canvas bag slung over his shoulder. He walked past the policemen then, glancing back over his shoulder, he spotted Merec and Sarah. He nodded at them and continued in the opposite direction.

At that instant the officers huddled in the group scattered, and two headed toward Merec and Sarah. Without a word, Merec turned and began to walk away. This time he didn't offer Sarah his arm. He didn't even look back.

Sarah knew it flew in the face of all reason that she should follow this man. She knew that most likely, almost certainly, it would mean her death. But now she found that death was not the thing she dreaded above all others. She dreaded her life at Willowridge, the yawns that had opened her mouth wide enough to crack her jaws apart, the flickering light of the television, the old watering eyes, the emptiness. Back in that world she would be completely alone. She didn't have a single friend with whom she exchanged yearly Christmas cards. If death was truly a void, then at least it was an unconscious one.

The man before her, moving away down the sidewalk, was a refuge. He would provide an existence for her this side of the grave. While he watched her with those sharp blue eyes, she blossomed. And when he no longer wished to observe, he would not let her slip unnoticed back into that world alone. No. With swiftness he would deliver her to the next.

She hurried after him, and his footsteps slowed for her. That alone made the tears start up in her eyes.

Horseshoes and Hand Grenades

Just before boarding the plane to New York, Tresler received a call informing him that the police sweep had turned up nothing.

Tresler related the information to Stanley.

"I don't understand why we bothered in the first place," Stanley burst out. "Now he'll just run somewhere else, and we're no better off than we were before."

"I don't think so," Tresler said.

"Why the hell not? I would if I were him."

"That's assuming he simply wants to escape. But if that were the case, he never would have called in. No, he's got something else on his mind. He's planning . . . something."

"What?"

"I don't know. But I'm pretty sure he'll find some way of letting us know."

"And why on earth would he do that?"

"Can't you tell? Our man likes an audience."

"An audience," Stanley snorted. "Well, he's certainly made sure of that already. What do we give him that a million TV viewers don't?"

"Someone to appreciate his skill."

"His skill! The man murders people."

"But you have to admit," Tresler said, "he is very good at what he does."

Just as Tresler landed at JFK he got another call. This time it was Irene, still manning the hotline back at headquarters.

"I've been trying you for almost an hour," she said. "We got a call from a woman in New York who claimed to have seen Sarah Shepherd on the street. Sounds like a throwaway call, right? But wait until you hear where the woman allegedly saw her. She was a block away from the phone booth where Merec called you."

"Hmm," Tresler said.

"She said at the time she wasn't quite sure if it was Sarah—it seemed so unlikely. But when she got home, she took out an old paper with a story on the kidnapping and checked the picture. After that she didn't have a doubt about it. She mentioned that there was a group of policemen not ten yards away, which was the second thing that convinced her at the time that it couldn't be who she thought."

"And the first?" Tresler asked because he knew Irene was waiting for it.

"When she caught sight of Sarah, she stopped and was going to speak to her, but before she could say anything, Sarah turned to her and said, 'Where are your manners? Didn't your mother ever teach you that staring is rude?' So what do you make of that?" Irene asked. But before he could reply, she answered her own question. "You know, when I first heard it, I thought the same thing as the woman—it couldn't possibly be Sarah. But when I thought about it, I realized that that little piece of information was the most legitimate part of the whole story. It's something no one could ever make up, but it fits."

"Mmm," Tresler said in agreement. "Did she see anyone else with Sarah Shepherd?"

"She says she seems to remember someone standing off to one side, but she was too busy staring at Sarah, and she thinks he was probably wearing a hat."

"Most likely."

"Doesn't lead anywhere, but I thought you might like to know."

"Yes, thank you, Irene." Tresler turned off his phone and again related the details to Stanley.

Stanley groaned. "Ten yards. Jesus, they were so close."

"You know the saying."

"What?"

"Close only counts in horseshoes and hand grenades," Tresler said, deadpan.

Stanley laughed despite himself. "No," he admitted. "I hadn't heard that."

Dangerously Good

When **Merec** and Sarah rounded the corner, Jeremy was waiting for them in a cab. They climbed in beside him. "The Plaza," Merec said grandly.

Sarah leaned close to the window and watched the city flash by. The air seemed bright. They were on a one-way avenue, so it gave the impression that everyone was rushing in the same direction, to the same end. And she supposed they were.

While they were stopped at a light, Sarah spotted a street vendor with a table full of hairpins that looked like instruments of torture, "I love New York" T-shirts, Yankees baseball hats, and row upon row of bright, gleaming sunglasses. She leaned forward and touched the cabby on the shoulder.

"Stop here for a minute." She turned to Merec. "May I have some money?"

He considered, then took out his wallet and handed her a twenty. She stepped out of the cab, pulling her hat more firmly down over her face. Inspecting the rows of sunglasses, she chose a pair. She spoke briefly to the man stretched out next to the table in a deck chair and held out the twenty. He pulled a wad of money from the front pocket of his tight jeans, gave her some bills, and she slipped back into the seat next to Merec.

She ducked her head and came up with the new pair of sunglasses on her face.

Merec chuckled. Jeremy's mouth twitched at the corner. They were wraparound glasses designed to shield the eye from all light, and they covered half her face.

When the cab pulled to a halt, a man wearing a uniform opened the door for her. She extended her hand to be helped out, and moving to one side, she waited for Merec to emerge. She kept her eyes closed behind her glasses to help her in her masquerade and reached elegantly, but sightlessly, for Merec's arm.

"Nice touch," he whispered to her. "No bags," Merec called to the doorman. As he led her away, he leaned over and said in her ear, "I want you to get yourself out of the lobby and up into the room as quickly as possible."

She nodded and let Merec guide her. "Steps,"

he said succinctly. Then, "Last one," and she was able to negotiate the distance to the check-in desk. She stumbled a few times, and at each occurrence her chin cranked one degree higher.

"May I help you, madame?" the clerk asked.

"We would like to book a suite," Merec interposed. "Adjoining rooms for myself, my wife, and our nephew."

"How long will you be staying?"

"A week," he said. "Possibly two if we decide to extend our visit."

"Name and address?"

"I am really so tired," Sarah broke in. "Darling, I'm sure you can take care of this." She patted Merec's arm, still threaded through her own. "I'd like the key, please. It has been a difficult trip."

The man behind the desk hesitated and said, "I'm not sure if the room is ready, and usually—"

"Give me the damn key before I faint," Sarah snapped.

The clerk handed Merec the key, and he gave it to Jeremy. "Take her upstairs," he said.

Jeremy took her other arm and guided her toward the elevators.

"Can I have your bags sent up for you?" the clerk called.

She stopped, turned. "Oh yes, please do. They're in Nashville or some ridiculous place." She groped for Jeremy's arm.

Merec said, "Airline screwup. I'm sure you know."

"Oh yes," the clerk agreed.

Merec leaned over the counter. "And could you, as a special service, remove the television from our room. Not our nephew's, just ours. It upsets her."

"Of course, sir."

"So helpful," Merec murmured and slid a folded twenty across the desk.

The clerk palmed it and smiled.

Merec slipped into their room a quarter of an hour later. Sarah was by the window. She was studying the horse-drawn carriages lined up along the north side of 59th Street. Jeremy sat in one of the bulky armchairs, his legs stretched out before him. His eyes were closed, and it looked as if he were napping, but Merec knew better.

With a sudden pang Merec felt the poignancy of it. They were both suspended, waiting for him. He had been leading people for a long time—senselessly violent, greedy, criminal types. These had been blunt, crude weapons, but under his direction they had been good enough to get the job done. But these two— thanks to them, when the time came for the next job—his own personal masterpiece—the whole world would be watching. About these two, he had no doubts. But for form's sake, he had to pretend that he did.

Sarah turned from the window. Jeremy opened one eye.

Merec closed the door behind him. "Did Jeremy tell you?" he asked.

"Tell me what?" She glanced quickly over at Jeremy in the chair.

"How marvelous you were. How many people can switch from hostage to fugitive in a moment *and* convince the Plaza staff that they're royalty while wearing—" he gestured at her rumpled clothes. "You were," he paused, "dangerously good."

She inadvertently took a step back, gathering the curtain close to one shoulder. "What do you mean?"

"What do I mean? Let me see, how can I say this?" He strolled into the room. "Okay, I'm going to tell you a story." He gestured for her to take a seat on the couch.

She seated herself but left her glasses on.

Merec clasped his hands behind his back and addressed his audience. "The story begins when a group of people decide—for whatever reason—to kill everyone in a rural nursing home. Their leader in depravity decides to play a game. It's called 'How Low Can Humanity Sink?' And things are going wonderfully. It's sinking satisfactorily, much according to calculation, until he gets to the last pair, when he receives a little surprise. He had witnessed other acts of sacrifice in his life, though not many. One hears of more than one actually sees. They are not so prevalent as the news would have us think.

"But back to my story. I must say, the irony of killing them both had its appeal, but the opportunity of a 'live one,' so to speak, was too much. So he decided to take her. To test her.

"He tried solitude. He tried beating. He tried torture. Nothing worked. But that's not all. More people are slaughtered around her. She is given the opportunity to leave. She decides to remain with her kidnappers and within an hour is calmly checking into the Plaza. She has everyone convinced she is blind and rich, and she makes it seem effortless. Questions pop up in the mind of her former captor, present colleague. Questions that had occurred to him before but return now more insistently."

"What questions?" Sarah asked.

"Questions like 'Where is the truth in this improbable situation?'"

"And?"

He gazed at her steadily. "A plant."

"A plant?" she repeated, confused.

"An agent. A spy, if you will."

There was a moment of stillness. Then Sarah began to shake. Her shoulders hunched up and foreword, her head bowed. The sound, at first low and intermittent, rose from a chuckle into peals of laughter. For at least half a minute she was unable to collect herself. Finally she took off her glasses and wiped her eyes, wet with tears. "Oh dear," she said. "I haven't laughed like that in years."

Merec wasn't smiling. He stood in the same spot, arms crossed, watching her with a slight frown. "I'm sure I'm not the only one to whom this has occurred. Jeremy?"

Jeremy shrugged, and that in itself was an admission.

"I'm sorry," she said, "but you must understand how ridiculous it sounded to me. I have been a housewife for thirty years. I spied on the dust and the dirty dishes and the laundry."

"Then how do you explain your . . . affinity for this lifestyle?"

Sarah slipped the glasses back on. "I can't."

"That's not very convincing," Merec remarked.

"The truth often isn't."

"Oh?"

"Well, how would I have known about the nursing home? And why wouldn't I have tried to save all those people?"

"Maybe you were a legitimate resident at the time."

She considered. "Why wouldn't I have turned you in when I had the chance?"

"You weren't absolutely sure of nabbing me, so you decided to stick with the case."

She threw up her hands. "I think you want to believe that I am some sort of female James Bond. Because then everything would fit nicely, wouldn't it? Then you wouldn't have to adjust your precious stereotypes one millimeter. A housewife could never possibly be courageous or adventurous, or want something more than the quiet life she's led—no, that stretches the limit of your narrow view of reality."

"Okay," he conceded. "Okay. Let's assume that you're telling the truth, and you've never been anything but a housewife. Why wouldn't you turn me in if you got the chance?"

"I didn't before."

He took off his jacket and pulled a pistol out of the waistband of his pants.

"You lied," she said, sounding surprised.

"About some things."

"You said earlier that you didn't have a gun. And that I could go if I wanted."

"I lied about those things, yes. But I didn't lie when I said I was tired of holding a hostage." He crossed the room and sat on the other end of the couch. "And I wasn't tired of you. I want to know," he leaned close, "why I should believe that you wouldn't turn me in if you got the chance? You would be a hero."

She locked her fingers together in her lap. "I'd be a hero, but for how long? A day? Two? What would they give me? A plaque? A check? A medal?"

He reached out and removed the thick plastic glasses, brushed away her hair so that he could see her eyes. "But what can we give you?"

She looked at him. "A job," she said.

Sacrifices
and Salons

Just before going to bed, Sarah sat at the dressing table running a brush through her hair. She had just taken a shower and dressed in the soft white bathrobe that she had discovered neatly folded on one of the shelves. Staring off into the air, she laid the brush down on the table and patiently worked through a knot with her fingers. Her mind turned over the events of the day. She felt like a sleepwalker who is awakened in the middle of their journey to find they have negotiated steps and doors and passageways, unconscious of the terrain.

She felt a light touch on her shoulder and looking up caught Merec's gaze in the mirror. He had come up behind her quiet as a cat. He lifted a damp section of hair from her shoulder and let it rest on his palm.

"Are you ready," he said, playing with the lock in his hand, "for the sacrifices that your new position will involve?"

"And they are?"

He grasped a piece of hair at the root, gently pulled it to its full length, then let it fall back to her shoulder. "Your hair."

Merec made the appointment for early Wednesday morning. Sarah slept deeply and woke with one arm stretched out across the expanse of the king-sized mattress. Trying not to wake Merec, she drew back her arm, rolled out of bed, and crossed the room to take a shower.

"You're going to turn into a prune," Merec called out. It was the third shower she had taken since they arrived.

"Too late," she said, and he chuckled.

When she emerged wearing the bathrobe, she looked with distaste at the sour-smelling clothes that lay in a heap on a chair. She sighed and bent to pick them up.

"You were able to pull it off yesterday, but today those clothes might be too much even for you." Merec laid a box on the end of the bed. "These should do for now. We'll get more later today."

She opened the box. It contained a pair of white gloves, a creamy silk shirt, fawn-colored trousers, stockings, and a bra and panties in soft pink. She blushed a matching color.

The salon was on the sixth floor of a building on the corner of Madison, not far from the hotel. Merec delivered her into Philip's hands.

Philip took off her hat, unpinned her hair, and raked his fingers through it. "Beautiful," he said. "Just a little trim, a little conditioner?"

Merec answered for her. "No. We want it cut short, something elegant, and dyed. What color would you say, Philip?"

"You are kidding, surely. This beautiful color dyed?"

"What color do you think?" Merec repeated.

"Well, most people going from white to color choose a light blond so as not to show the roots."

"Is that what you would suggest?"

Philip hesitated. "No. I think a strong color—dark brown, almost black. But there will be a problem with the roots, you know. Maybe I can give you a rinse that will help. But to keep it up you will have to come back often." He shook his finger at her, but of course she didn't see. Behind her glasses her eyes were closed, and she was enjoying the feeling of fingers in her hair.

"And yourself?" Philip asked Merec.

"Yes, I'd like a cut, and my friend too." He gestured toward the corner where Jeremy sat on one of the couches.

"Very good. Veronique, darling," Philip called out. "Veronique will take you to the dressing room, where you can change your blouse for one of the gowns. Let's get rid of these," and he reached for her glasses, but she stayed him hurriedly.

"Please, direct light is painful for me."

"Oh. We will work around it." He patted her on the shoulder. "Not to worry, my dear. I'm a professional."

When they returned to the hotel three hours later, Merec looked much the same. His hair was trimmed but remained on the long side. Jeremy rubbed his palm ruefully over his cropped head. His face seemed fuller, his features more visible, and he looked almost handsome. But Sarah's cut had taken years off. Even Philip had said at the end, "How old *are* you, darling?" before he remembered himself.

In the room, Sarah sat down at the dressing table and took off the hat. Then, more slowly, she removed the glasses and stared at herself in the mirror. She noted that the bruises had finally faded.

Merec moved up behind her. "What do you think?"

She looked at him in the mirror. "I've never had short hair. It feels strange."

"It makes you look quite young."

In the mirror she shifted her eyes from his face back to her own.

"I think it's time," Merec said, "that we know a little something more about you. Our application process is usually fairly rigorous."

"I can imagine."

"Possibly you can . . . but much of our decision is based upon what we find out about the applicant's past. From that we are able to tell what type of person they are and whether they'll suit."

"Are you really?" She seemed amused. "People aren't puzzles," she said. "The pieces never do quite fit together."

"You think you know more than I do about people?"

"No," she said. "I think I know less."

The Director's Screening

An envelope was delivered to the front desk at IBC's headquarters late Monday evening. It was sent up to the eighth floor on Tuesday morning, and the director's secretary brought it in on the top of a large pile.

"I didn't open any of your mail, as you said." She waited for a response. He grunted. "This one on top looks like another one of those amateur tapes." She placed the stack on the edge of his desk. "I wouldn't have bothered you with it, but you also said that you wanted all—"

"Thank you, June." He barely glanced up from the document he was scanning.

She left the room, closing his office door respectfully behind her. His eyes flicked up to make sure she had gone, and he grabbed the package. He slit one end carefully with his letter opener and eased out the cassette. There was no accompanying note.

Picking up the phone, he told June to get him the station manager on the phone, pronto. In less than a minute he was on the line, listening to the director's instructions.

"We need a private viewing room, and I want you and"—here the director named all the other key people in the studio—"to be there. And I want this to happen at nine-thirty."

"Nine-thirty," the manager agreed.

When the director descended to the viewing room fifteen minutes later, he found everyone settled in and waiting. Suddenly doubt leaked into his certainty. What if the tape wasn't what he thought? What if it *was* just another amateur reporter's tape?

He beckoned to his station manager. "Step outside with me."

The man paled but complied.

"I want to take a quick look at the beginning before we roll it," the director said. The station manager led him to a cramped editing room, flicked on some machines, and held out his hand for the tape. The director surrendered it and watched, concealing his anxiety beneath a frown.

There were a few seconds of static, which changed to black, and then Sarah Shepherd's face filled the screen. "Fine," he said. "That's fine. Rewind it and we'll join the others." He exited, leaving the station manager to follow with the tape.

The director took a seat at the back of the

room so that he could observe the reactions of his staff as he watched. They were all aware of his gaze on the backs of their heads, and they kept unnaturally still, waiting for the video to begin rolling. No one started or exclaimed when Sarah Shepherd's face appeared on the screen, but when the camera pulled back, they realized that they were watching new, unseen footage.

"Holy shit," someone whispered.

Someone else said, "Shhh," violently, and that was the last anyone spoke.

Filmed, cut, and edited, Sarah's performance was powerful. When Charlie hit her for the first time, she let out a soft grunt of surprise. Minutes later, the audience was chuckling at the sight of Sarah smoking her first cigarette.

The director realized that he had stopped observing his people and had transferred his full attention to the screen. That meant it was good, very good—he usually found it almost impossible to watch even a short clip.

On the screen, the camera position changed, and Sarah was staring straight into the lens, declining to ask anyone for money for her ransom. Then, back to a bird's-eye view, their eyes watered at Sarah's struggling attempts to walk. They gripped the arms of their chairs while she waited to be tortured. Someone gasped as the blood welled up around the first needle pressed beneath Sarah's thumbnail. They jumped and cringed at Lee's shattered screams when he felt the first bite of the steel under his own fingernail.

When the tape rolled to a close and the room flickered to black, no one moved to turn on the lights. With a grunt, the director himself rose and flipped the switch. He looked around smugly at the faces, dazed with emotion.

"We can't show that," someone said. "I've never seen anything more horrifying in my life."

"Or more glorious," another breathed.

The only woman in the room was quietly sobbing.

"Whether or not to air the tape is not under discussion," the director snapped.

"We'll certainly have to cut some of the—"

"We will leave it exactly as it is. I don't care if the FCC slaps us with a fine as big as the state of Alaska. It will not be cut. All I want to know is, can we get the exposure we need to air this tomorrow?"

"But we can't just air this and leave it at that. We have to *do* something," the woman cried out. The others looked away in embarrassment as she tried to catch their eyes. They were already shaking off their own response and turning to the mechanics of the business at hand.

"Ms. Fern is perfectly correct," the director announced. The others were startled. "And we

will do something. We here at IBC will personally spearhead the campaign to raise money to
ransom Sarah Shepherd." They were a quick
bunch. It took only an instant for the smiles to
appear. He could almost see the thoughts of free
promotion for the station, a huge boost in name
recognition, the priceless quality of goodwill,
and a reputation for responsible reporting.
Even Ms. Fern raised her glistening face and
looked thoughtful.

Headlines

It was late Tuesday evening when Tresler and Stanley checked into their hotel. They were both tired, and they rode the elevator up to their floor without speaking. Tresler fit his key into the lock and opened his door. He was about to disappear inside when Stanley stopped him with a "Hey."

Dutifully, Tresler turned around.

"What do we do now?" Stanley said, standing forlornly in the hallway.

"Sleep. You'll need it." Then he entered his room and shut the door.

Tresler and Stanley met early the next morning and headed out to get some breakfast. They

stopped briefly for Tresler to buy the newspaper
and then ducked into a nearby diner. They had
just settled down and ordered when Tresler
opened his paper.

"Stanley."

Stanley switched his focus from his coffee to
Tresler. Then he looked down at where Tresler's
finger stabbed the front page. He saw a large picture of Sarah Shepherd. Then he read the head-
line and felt a rush of excitement. "Well," he said,
"I guess I know what we'll be doing tonight at
eight o'clock."

"Ha," Tresler said, in agreement.

The news was splashed across every newspaper. IBC had constructed an elaborate last-
minute notification to hit the papers exactly
right, with just enough time before their dead-
line to get the story in the next day's edition.
The radio and TV newscasters had been easy;
IBC let them get the story from the papers.

The suddenness of the announcement was calculated to ensure that the authorities could do
nothing to stop the tape from airing. But it also
didn't give Merec much time. Soon after breakfast, he left Jeremy and Sarah and slipped outside. He walked ten blocks and made the call
from a pay phone on the corner opposite another
hotel.

Someone picked up and said, "Yes?"

"I understand that your father-in-law died recently in that nursing home incident," Merec began. "I wanted to give you my condolences. Such a tragic event."

The voice on the line said sharply, "Who is this? What do you want?"

"I have also heard that the death of your father-in-law means that the majority shareholder position in IBC passes to you." He clicked his tongue. "Such a responsibility."

There was a long pause. Finally the director said, "Merec?"

"So," Merec continued, "I never did get to ask you what you thought about the job you ordered. Didn't I say I would fix it so no one would suspect?"

"Yes. You certainly are thorough. There are not many who would kill an entire rest home full of old people to cover up one death. And that video . . . "

"Do I hear censure?"

"Oh no," the director said. "On the contrary. Brilliant work."

"Why thank you," Merec said modestly.

"I put some extra money in the account for the footage you kindly left behind. It was an entirely unexpected bonus. And I want to hire your cameraman away from you."

"But you couldn't supply him with the content that I do. Speaking of which, what are your plans

for this next installment? No more police inter-
views or hotlines, I hope." He said it in a friendly
tone, but it was an unmistakable warning.

"Oh no. We have other plans. We intend to do
some good works this evening," the director said.

"Do tell."

"We will start a ransom fund for Sarah
Shepherd's release."

"To be deposited into an offshore bank
account?"

"Of course," the director agreed. "The same
one?"

"No, a different account. It's much safer. But
you may have legal troubles with this ransom."

"That's what we have our lawyers for.
Tomorrow, after the broadcast, call this number,"
and the director read out the digits. "I'm sure you
realize the possibility that my phone will be
tapped, though this is not the number we will
give on the program for information about Sarah
Shepherd. You can give me the number of the
bank account tomorrow."

"Despite your lawyers, you take a risk in this,"
Merec observed.

The director's silence was an assent in itself.

"One more thing," Merec said.

"Yes?"

"I think that after tonight there will be many
praying for Sarah Shepherd. I was thinking of a
public vigil."

"Ahhh."

"This Sunday evening at St. Patrick's Cathedral. They can also take up a collection for the ransom there."

"I heard you were in New York." The director chuckled. "I see TV crews covering the event. Why didn't we think of this? You are a wealth of ideas."

"Do I have to tell you what will happen if you don't stick to our agreement?"

"Please, don't embarrass yourself. It is unnecessary. I will speak with you tomorrow." And the director hung up.

Merec held the phone away from his ear and looked at it. Then he smiled and hung it back on the hook. "I could almost like you, Mr. Director," he said. "Almost."

Planning Prayers, Drinking Whisky, and a Simple Black Dress

"**I've got something to do tonight,**" Merec said to Sarah that evening. "I hope I can trust you to stay here by yourself." He started toward the door.

"I'd like to watch it also," Sarah said.

"What?" Merec paused with his hand on the doorknob.

"I know there's something on the television tonight."

Merec shot a glance at Jeremy.

"Jeremy didn't tell me. I guessed. And as I said, I would like to watch it also."

"No."

"No?" She challenged him.

He shook his head.

"Why?"

He turned, leaning with his back against the

door. "This," he gestured to include the three of them, "what we have here, it is not a democracy. Do you understand?"

She stared at him, and her eyes narrowed.

"It works more like the army. To get through, you have to follow orders. Without question."

"I always thought I was particularly unsuited for the army."

"You make me tired, Sarah. Now Jeremy and I are both going into the next room. You will not go anywhere to watch the television, nor will you ask anyone anything about it, tonight or at any time in the future."

She regarded him, expressionless.

"Well?" he demanded.

"I didn't realize a response was required."

"I want your word."

She patted her pockets and came up with a pack of cigarettes. She extracted one but didn't light it. She twirled it between her fingers. "Is it the tape Jeremy made at Willowridge?"

Merec blinked once. "No."

"Because if it is—"

"I said," Merec cut her off, "no. I mean no. It is not the tape from Willowridge." He crossed his arms and waited.

Sarah crushed the cigarette in her hand. "Fine," she muttered between her teeth.

"Fine what?"

"I am not a child."

"Then stop acting like one, Sarah. Fine what?"

"I give my word."

"Thank you," he said. "Jeremy . . . ," and Jeremy walked past Sarah, his eyes averted, and slipped out of the room. Merec followed and shut the door softly behind him.

"Goddammit," Sarah muttered. She dropped the crumbled cigarette and went to take a shower. Stepping out of the tub, she wrapped a towel high around her chest and caught a ghostly glimpse of her face in the misty mirror. She moved closer and with a corner of the towel cleared a space. Even without the mist, the face in the mirror appeared almost youthful. It mesmerized her. Even as a young woman her hair had been ash blond, close enough to white to drain the vitality from her face. The transition from blond to white had not been dramatic. But now it was dark, and she felt, if not young, at least reckless. She stuck her tongue out at her reflection and went into the other room to dress.

But ten minutes later she had put on and discarded all the clothes Merec had bought for her—all beautifully tailored slacks and rich sweaters and shirts. She sat disconsolately at the edge of the bed in the bathrobe. Then she noticed the hotel directory on the bedside table. Pulling it toward her, she flipped through and tapped a page thoughtfully. She scooted over and picked up the phone.

"Hello? Is this the boutique? Yes, I was wondering if you had a black dress, size six. Nothing too revealing, but a little," she hesitated, "something sexy. You do? Could you have it brought up to room eight twenty-seven? Yes, I understand that's a slightly unusual request. No, I'm sure it will be fine. Thank you."

She answered the door to a haughty young woman with a swath of plastic over her arm. Sarah kept her eyes open long enough to see the woman's look of irritation change to understanding.

"Have you come from the boutique?" She pretended to adjust her gaze toward the woman's voice when she answered. "Wonderful. Thank you so much. Please come in," she said standing away from the door. "Maybe you could stay while I try it on and tell me how it looks."

"Of course." The woman stepped past her into the room, and Sarah shut the door behind her. She heard the rustle of plastic as the woman unwrapped the dress.

"Here you are."

Sarah held her hands out and felt the fabric on her palms.

"Do you need—" the woman began.

"Just show me where the zippers are."

The woman guided her hands on a short tour of the dress.

"Excuse me," Sarah said, and she headed for the bathroom. Once inside, she shucked the bathrobe and stepped into the dress. The material clung yet floated at the same time. She slipped the glasses on again, and now they didn't seem strange and out of place but mysterious, jarring, almost fashionable.

She emerged from the bathroom.

"It's perfect," the saleswoman breathed, truth leaking from her voice.

"Can I put this on my room tab?"

"Of course. Certainly."

Sarah found her purse and took out a bill, which she folded neatly and held out, saying, "Thank you so much for your help."

"My pleasure." The woman tucked the money away. "Have a good night, ma'am."

Sarah found her burgundy lipstick and her white gloves and slung her purse over her arm. She took the elevator down to the lobby and walked uncertainly out into the hall until she heard someone at her elbow.

"Can I be of assistance?"

She turned toward the voice. "Yes, could you show me to the bar?"

"Certainly."

She reached out for an arm and was conducted through the hall.

"Bar or table?"

"Bar, please," she said, and let herself be guided to a high stool.

"Thank you." She fumbled with her purse, but no one took the bill she proffered.

"He's gone," a voice said from behind the bar. "And you were about to give him a fifty."

She tucked the bill back in her purse.

"What can I get you?"

"Whiskey. And do you have cigarettes?"

"Yes. What kind of whiskey and what kind of cigarettes?"

"The best."

"That's often a matter of opinion."

"Then whatever you consider the best," she amended.

She heard the sound of a glass set on the counter before her, and the voice asked, "On the rocks?"

"Neat," she replied. "What am I getting?"

"You're not allowed to ask. Just drink."

She peeled the cellophane from the pack of cigarettes, and putting one to her lips, she sensed the tiny heat of the flame he offered. "Thank you."

She could hear him moving around behind the bar. She smoked her cigarette and located an ashtray with her fingertips. Thank goodness it was clean. "Quiet in here tonight," she said.

"Oh yeah. But I'm not surprised. I thought that everyone would be glued to the TV tonight. Why aren't you—" he stopped, then finished lamely, "listening?"

"To what?" she asked, wondering if those two words broke the promise she had made.

"To what? You've got to be kidding me. You

mean you didn't read the papers?" He realized what he had said and laughed, not at her but at himself. "I'm sorry. I mean, didn't you listen to the radio?"

"Not this morning," she said.

"It's another one about that woman, Sarah Shepherd. My roommate's taping it for me."

She nodded, afraid to pursue the subject any further. Instead she said, "Since we're the only ones here—at least I assume we're the only ones here—will you join me in a drink?"

"Thought you'd never ask."

She also offered one of her cigarettes, but he politely refused. "If you don't smoke, how do you know what the best is?" she asked.

"Do you always need personal experience to know?"

For over an hour, she sat with him at the bar. After their third whiskey, he leaned over the bar and took her gloved hand.

"Take off your glasses for me," he said.

"Why?"

"All evening you sat there all mysterious behind those amazing glasses. And I," he leaned even closer, and she felt the heat of his breath on her cheek, "want to see," she felt him grasp the glasses by the rims, "behind them." She didn't prevent him from pulling them gently off her face. But she did keep her eyes closed.

"Open your eyes," he said.

She shook her head.

"Please?"

"You can't see behind those. There's nothing to see."

He leaned forward so his lips were against her ear. "Has anyone told you that you are very beautiful?"

"Not recently," she said and was instantly submerged in remembrance. As from a dream she heard Jonathan's voice, through the hazy fog of sleep—"You are so beautiful."

"Are you okay?" The bartender grasped her wrists.

"Can I have my glasses back? It's the light. If I open my eyes even a little, it's very painful."

He fumbled with them and slipped them on her face, saying, "I'm so sorry. I didn't know."

"It's all right. Really."

She reached for her pack of cigarettes and took out another. He lit it for her.

"You have no idea what I look like?" he said abruptly.

"None," she replied truthfully, for she had not opened her eyes since entering the bar.

"Do you want to feel my face? I've seen on shows that's how blind people can get an idea of someone's features."

"That doesn't work for me. I've tried it, but in my mind people just come out looking like Picasso drawings. All eye sockets and noses and mouths in the wrong places."

"So you haven't always been blind—if you know what Picasso drawings are like."

"No. In fact it happened quite recently." She didn't offer any details, and to her relief, he didn't ask.

Instead he said, "What do you imagine I look like?"

"I hadn't even thought about it," she lied easily. She had in fact imagined him as incredibly handsome with dark hair, deep moody eyes, and chiseled features.

She heard him pour another drink.

"What is it like, losing your sight?" he asked, sliding the glass over to her.

She took a sip. "All you have is the sound you hear in your head, the touch you feel with your skin, and the smell that comes to your nose. And you realize how little you know, how little you have, outside yourself." That was what her blindness was like. But when she wanted the universe to take shape again, all she had to do was open her eyes.

"That's beautiful." She felt him lean in, and when he spoke next, his mouth was again close to her ear. He said, "My shift is over in about ten minutes."

She didn't reply.

"I would really like to take you out."

"Out where?"

"Anywhere. I could close my eyes, and we'd be blind together. Just us, just our voices and our hands." He had closed his eyes to whisper this into her ear and didn't see the man that approached the bar.

"Excuse me," Merec said. "Am I interrupting?"

The bartender straightened. "Not at all, sir. What can I get you?"

"My wife." Merec grasped Sarah hard above the elbow. "I've been worried, dear."

She could tell he was angry. Standing, she smiled at the bartender. "Could you put that on my tab? Room eight twenty-seven. I had a lovely evening." She put out her hand, palm down. The bartender took it and raised it to his lips.

Merec wheeled her smartly away. "What did you think you were doing?"

Sarah could feel the muscles tensed beneath the arm of his jacket. "I have no idea," she admitted.

They got into the elevator, and as the doors were closing, another man stepped in with them, so they were silent for their ride up to the room, silent on the walk down the corridor, silent when he opened the door. And when Merec finally spoke, it was not to her but to Jeremy.

At the opening of the door, Jeremy leaped up from a chair by the window.

"I found her," Merec said, and he sank back down.

"Jeremy," Sarah said, stepping forward and wrenching her arm from Merec's grasp. "What do you think of my dress? Merec hasn't said a word about it." She held out her arms and pirouetted.

"Where were you?" he asked, his voice rough.

Merec answered him before Sarah could speak. "I found her down in the bar picking up the bartender. God only knows what she was thinking. I mean she has two perfectly good fellows right here madly in love with her. What does she need with another? But he was terribly good-looking, and young, of course. He didn't stand a chance against our Sarah here. I saved him just as she was about to whisk him off."

Jeremy had dropped his hands from his eyes and was staring at her.

"What?" she said. "You don't believe him, do you? He's talking complete nonsense."

Jeremy lowered his gaze to inspect her dress. Suddenly self-conscious, she crossed her arms over her chest. When he said, "It's a nice dress," she blushed crimson. She started to say, "I didn't—" but Jeremy had already turned away and was listening to Merec. She scooped up her nightgown. All she wanted was to change and go to bed, but Merec intercepted her before she reached the bathroom.

"Didn't you hear me?" he said, barring her way.

"No, I wasn't listening," she snapped.

"Sarah," he said, grabbing her shoulder and shaking it lightly. "Don't worry about it, we'll make it okay."

"What are you talking about?" She tried to push him away. "I'm tired. I want to go to bed." He wouldn't budge. "Merec, get out of my way."

"Don't you understand? You can't go to sleep. Jeremy's going down to settle the bill. We're checking out."

"But I don't want to go."

"You should have thought about that before you dressed up in your slinky black number and went downstairs to charm the pants off Romeo."

"But I wore my glasses." Involuntarily she thought of how she had let him remove the glasses and take a good long look. "My hair," she said. "I'm sure he didn't recognize me."

"Not yet he didn't. But eventually he'll see what we watched tonight—maybe on a news program tomorrow or the next day, maybe on a rerun."

She didn't mention the fact that his roommate had taped it and that he might even watch it tonight.

"You were talking for a while. I could tell. And he'll go home tonight and dream of your voice . . . "

She thought of his words, ". . . just our voices and our hands."

". . . and then he'll hear that voice on the television. What are the chances he won't recognize it?"

Zero. She knew the chances were zero. "I just wanted to get out," she whispered. "I just wanted to sit down and talk to someone. I'm so tired of moving." She walked a few steps and sank into a chair.

"You want to get out? Then get out, but do it alone. You want to sit down and talk to someone? Talk to me. Talk to Jeremy. Tired of moving?" he crossed to where she was sitting and hauled her roughly up from the chair. "Too bad. Do you hear me, Sarah?" He shoved her back. "Now get some clothes and get changed. I'll pack."

Fifteen minutes later they were walking out of the hotel and sliding into another taxi. They all squeezed into the backseat, and Merec leaned forward. "To JFK, please. We're in a bit of a rush."

Sarah stared out the window at the lights of the city flashing by in a blur of red, yellow, and white. It was a city full of closed doors and drawn curtains. She thought that she must be the least of the secrets it held.

Half an hour later they pulled up to the international arrivals building at JFK. Merec produced a hat from his pocket and gave it to Sarah; it was a floppy black knit, and he reached over and pulled the brim low over her glasses. "Keep your head down," he whispered close into her ear.

Merec paid the driver, and Jeremy collected the bags. They all walked purposefully toward the entrance and passed through the automatic doors.

"Is he gone?" Merec asked. Jeremy nodded.

Before she knew what was happening, Merec had whipped off her sunglasses and deposited them in a nearby trashcan. On her other side Jeremy slipped a new pair into her hand. These were not sunglasses but eyeglasses with a very weak prescription, and when she put them on, everything jumped into sharper focus.

They passed the airline desk and headed for the escalator down to the baggage carousels. Halting before the line of hotel reservation desks, Jeremy gave her a woman's wallet.

"Take a look," Merec said. "Jeremy put it together for you."

She took the wallet, feeling the soft leather. She opened the snap and glanced down at a driver's license, bank card, credit cards, a phone card, even a library card, all in the name of Elizabeth Miller.

"That's you. You don't need a story, because you won't be talking."

"You did all this?"

Jeremy shrugged. "The license isn't very good. It won't stand up."

"But if you do your job right, it won't need to." Merec took her arm and moved her along. "Now go on and check into the Peninsula Hotel. Ask them to provide transportation." He gave her a little push between the shoulder blades.

She turned. "What about you?"

"We'll be checking into another hotel. This little trip to the airport might not put them off the scent. And now that they've got an idea of where we are and probably a pretty good description, any two men and one woman checking into a hotel in the next few days will be getting a knock on their door, I think. It's too risky. You're on your own, my dear. We'll come visit."

"What will I do?"

He shrugged. "Sightseeing?"

It was only later, much later, as she sat by the window in her new room watching the dawn lighten over the gray buildings that she remembered Merec's words: ". . . she has two perfectly good fellows right here madly in love with her. What does she need with another?" The words came back to her and echoed in her head. "Two perfectly good fellows right here madly in love with her."

She dragged her fingertips across her blouse,

feeling the smooth silk against the new skin. The skin was slowly toughening, but there was no sign of the nails growing back. At least not yet.

The
Sequel

When the video aired, Merec pulled a chair close to the television, and Jeremy sat on the floor, his back resting against the end of the bed. They watched all the news programs first, but it was mostly old information, and when it was time for the video, they switched to IBC and leaned forward.

There was a woman introducing it—soft-spoken, earnest, and very beautiful. She, Merec assumed, would pitch the ransom collection at the end of the program. Smart, he thought. Someone to catch both the men's and the women's attention. She spoke briefly and included a warning that the material was not suitable for young viewers or for the fainthearted.

"I'll bet that line keeps everyone glued to the

screen," Merec observed. "There's nothing like the promise of blood and gore to keep them interested."

They watched the familiar video, and as the final scene faded to black, Merec said, "Not a frame out of place. Right?"

Jeremy agreed.

"Right. Here we go."

The handsome woman appeared again on the screen. Her eyes were large and shining with unshed tears. She spoke about qualities. Jeremy groaned. "Didn't she watch? That wasn't about *qualities*."

Merec shushed him. He caught the words "give something back" and held up his forefinger to forestall any further comments from Jeremy.

"We here at IBC are committed to reclaiming one of America's latest, greatest heroes, and if it takes a ransom to do it, we say it's worth it. Since Sarah Shepherd was too proud to ask for herself, we ask for her. If she has in any way touched your heart, please contribute to our Lost Shepherd Fund."

"Very cute," Merec said.

"Let's show the power of the people. Just put one dollar in an envelope. Just one dollar and send it to," and here an address appeared and held steady at the bottom of the screen. "But whether or not you decide to contribute toward freeing this noble woman . . . "

Jeremy made gagging sounds.

". . . we ask that you pray for Sarah Shepherd. We urge you to organize services in your local place of worship. We will be conducting a simple service in New York City this Sunday evening at eight o'clock at Saint Patrick's Cathedral. All denominations are welcome." She managed a smile, but a sorrowful one, and they switched to a picture of Sarah over which they rolled the credits. At the end they showed the address once more. It hovered on a black screen for at least ten seconds before switching to a commercial.

"So what do you think?" Merec pressed the mute button on the remote and hauled his chair around to face Jeremy.

Jeremy rubbed his eyes. "Effective. No telling how much they'll collect."

Merec waved that away impatiently. "I don't mean that. What do you think about the service? Will they come?"

"Was that you?" Jeremy asked, staring up at Merec.

"Will they come?" Merec asked urgently.

"I'd say so."

"Then we have a lot of work to do."

Tresler and Stanley watched the broadcast in their own separate rooms. Tresler settled down in his armchair with a drink and a notebook. He began clinically enough, marking things down and taking small sips of his drink, but halfway through he stopped writing, and his drink was left untouched on the table. He remained motionless, staring into space, long after the program had ended, until a knock broke his reverie.

Tresler rose and went to open the door, leaving the chain attached. Stanley stood in the hallway.

"Wasn't that magnificent?" Stanley said.

"Let me open this up." Closing the door, he unlatched the chain and reopened it to let Stanley through.

Stanley strode in, his enthusiasm undiminished. "Wasn't she fantastic?" he said, slapping Tresler on the shoulder as he walked by. He collapsed in one of the armchairs. "Wasn't she . . ." He gestured with his arms in search of another suitable word. "What did you think, Tresler? What would you say?" Stanley looked up expectantly.

Tresler frowned and cleared his throat. "I say that it's best not to let emotions cloud your analysis."

"God, man, using your mind doesn't stop you from having a heart."

Tresler gave Stanley an appraising glance. "It might. Remember, it's the perpetrator you need to focus on."

"Is that all you think about?"

Tresler stared at him levelly. "Yes," he lied. "Now, let's get down to business. I thought this tape cleared up quite a few messy details."

"Like what?" Stanley said, interested despite himself.

"For one, we found out exactly how the suspects were informed of CIA involvement. We were able to see just how big a blunder Martins' group made by contacting that man Lee. The chances of success with that particular specimen as a recruit were low, even if they acted quickly, which of course we know they did not. Incompetence all around. Except from one quarter." Tresler paused and seemed to be waiting for a response.

"Us?" Stanley said.

The corners of Tresler's mouth twitched. "Merec," he corrected. "He didn't need to hear more than that one phrase recorded by the hidden camera. We knew from the first that we were dealing with a professional, but even professionals can get sloppy on their own turf where they feel safe. I think this proves that we are dealing with a criminal of the highest quality. Agreed?"

"A hidden camera," Stanley breathed. He had not caught the detail while watching, so absorbed had he been in the drama.

Tresler continued, "So we have established that Merec is a true professional. So why this abduction? Why these tapes, when they can give us more clues?"

"Didn't you listen? It's a ransom deal. He kidnapped the woman for the money."

"It doesn't fit," Tresler said. "Too elaborate a job for such a simple objective. An amateur might think up this scheme, but a professional would know how slight was the chance of success. No, if it were just for the money he would have gone for something simpler: kidnapping the CEO of a huge company or the daughter of a wealthy family."

"Okay, so?"

"So if ransom wasn't the objective, then what was?"

"I don't know. Do you?"

"Yes, I think I have a pretty good idea. But to make sure, I'm going to need to take a trip back to DC first thing tomorrow. And I need to take another look at the case file."

But it turned out that there was something else Tresler had to do before his trip to DC. The phone rang about two o'clock in the morning. It was Helen from the hotline with a call from a bartender at the Plaza Hotel.

Beauty
Tips

When Tresler arrived at the Plaza, it was almost three o'clock, and the traffic had thinned. As he got out of the cab and climbed the steps of the hotel, he noticed that the doorman on duty was leaning against the wall and the man's eyes were closed. He seemed to be dozing on his feet.

When Tresler spoke, the doorman started up. "Sorry, sir," he said and opened the door.

"Thanks, I don't want to go in just yet. I wanted to speak to you about some guests of the hotel that checked out about five hours ago." He flipped open his notebook.

"Oh, yeah, Karp on the front desk told me you were coming over. What do you want to know?"

"Do you know the group I am referring to?"

"Yeah, older guy with a blind woman and another, younger guy."

"*Blind* woman?" Tresler said.

"Yeah."

"Do you remember anything else about their appearance?"

"The older guy had gray hair. Couldn't see much of the woman with those glasses and the big hat she was wearing."

"Anything else?"

The man thought for a moment. "They didn't have many bags. Oh, and the lady, she was wearing gloves. But that's about it."

"Ah," Tresler said. "Did you overhear where the cab was going?"

The doorman looked skyward as though searching for help. "The airport," he finally pronounced.

"The airport?" Tresler said. "Are you sure you're not mistaken?"

"You asked me and I told you," the man said, screwing up his mouth.

"Yes, you did. Which airport?"

"Not sure about that one."

"Thank you for your help. An officer will be by to take your statement," Tresler said. "The airport," he repeated under his breath as he walked away. Though skeptical, Tresler sent men to the three area airports. Then he sat down to wait for the bartender.

It wasn't long before Peter hustled into the

bar where Tresler was tucked away at a corner table, sipping coffee. Peter spotted him and strode over. "Are you the investigator on the Sarah Shepherd case?" he demanded.

Tresler set his coffee cup carefully in the saucer. "I am."

"I know her," Peter announced. "I was with her most of the evening."

"So it seems. Please, have a seat."

Peter slid into the chair across from Tresler.

"I probably don't need to tell you that I had no idea who she was at the time," he said. "At that point I'd only seen the first video, and that only once. But I'll tell you something." He looked Tresler straight in the eye as though offering a challenge. "I'd know her again. I wouldn't even need to see her. One word, even if she spoke just one word, I'd know the voice." He smiled ruefully. "I'd know it in a second."

"What exactly did you talk about?"

"I did most of the talking," Peter admitted.

"Do you remember anything she said?"

He paused over that. "We drank a lot," he admitted, "so it's not all clear in my mind, you know. But I remember what she said it felt like being blind. Isn't that funny?"

Tresler asked him why it was funny.

"Well, because she isn't blind. Oh, and I remember one other thing. I remember her answer when I asked her what she imagined I looked like. She said she hadn't even thought about it. You see, I've always dreamed about just being ordinary. I never wanted to be ugly, just ordinary. But when she said she hadn't even thought about what I looked like, all of a sudden I wanted for her to know. I wanted her to treat me like I was something special. I thought maybe if she could feel my features . . . but she didn't even want to try."

"Maybe it was because she already knew what you looked like."

But Peter shook his head stubbornly. "People respond to me in a certain way. Most times positive, sometimes negative, but never just neutral. Think about it. You're trying to make everyone believe you're blind. What's the best, the easiest, most surefire way to do it? She kept her eyes closed behind her glasses. I would have known if she had opened them. And I think she knew that I would know—if you know what I mean. This is a little confusing."

Tresler reassured him. "I'm following you so far."

"You are? Great." He seemed truly relieved. "Okay, where was I?"

"You had asked her to feel your features."

"Right. It all comes back to this beauty thing. Everyone talks about how beautiful she is. Most of the time they don't even say 'for her age.' But I figured this out—that's because it isn't really about what she looks like at all. You see, it isn't just her face. It isn't even mostly her face. I can't explain it. You know that word *charisma*? I never really knew what that meant until I met Sarah. A word doesn't describe it, though."

He hesitated, then burst out with a torrent of words. "Do you believe that I met her?" As if afraid of Tresler's answer, he barreled on. "My roommate laughed at me. He said I was drinking too much. I am drinking too much, but I didn't make this up?" He made it a question.

"No," Tresler said. "You most assuredly didn't make this up."

"Thanks." He started to say more but needed to clear his throat first. "Was there anything else you wanted to ask me?"

"Yes. She was alone with you, by your account, for more than an hour. Can you tell me why she didn't admit to you who she was and ask for help?"

Peter was silent.

"Do you think," Tresler prodded, "that she might have been cooperating with her captor?"

"I've thought about that," Peter admitted. "And I can't answer for sure except to tell you that the woman I met was capable of anything."

A Life Built
for One

Sarah spent the night in a chair by the window watching the cars on Fifth Avenue. The headlights were blinding white; the taillights glowed a cherry red. If she looked left, they were bearing down upon her. If she looked right, all the cars were rushing away. She amused herself by picking a particular car—as far up the street as she could see—and following it with her eyes until it passed out of sight. The second when it flashed by below her window was so quick that she could miss it if she blinked.

Only when the sun rose did she lie down on the bed—on top of the covers. Not bothering to draw the curtains, she merely closed her eyes against the sunlight and wondered if she had the strength to make the journey back. She knew she could never return to the kind of life she had led with Jonathan. The life they had built together had been a life built for two. It was either too large or too small for just one person on her own.

Eventually she drifted off, and when she woke the room was dim and gray in the late afternoon light. She reached for the phone and called the desk to see if she had any messages.

"No messages, Ms. Miller."

"Thank you," she said and laid the phone in its cradle.

She emerged from the shower as the city was reclaimed by the long shadows thrown by the buildings. She toweled her hair dry while looking at the blank television screen. She had promised—no newspapers, no TV, no radio, but she itched to switch on the set and watch the evening news. Drawing a finger across the screen, she saw that it came away gray with dust. She rubbed it away on her towel and sighed. Among the clothes in the suitcase, she found a pair of jeans and a T-shirt. She put on her glasses and combed her fingers through her hair. Glancing in the mirror over the bureau, she didn't even recognize the woman staring back at her. Good, she thought. Good.

Silent
Trees

Tresler boarded a flight to Washington late the next morning, and within hours he was back at IBC headquarters. While waiting to speak to the director, he wandered around the hallway studying the pictures on the walls. In the back corner there was a formal photograph of the board of directors with the names listed on a small plaque beneath. Tresler idly scanned the names, and one in particular caught his eye. He returned to his chair and retrieved the file from his briefcase. Leafing through the material, he found what he was looking for—the list of the occupants of Willowridge Rest Home. Pursing his lips in a silent whistle, he picked up his cellular phone to make a call. Just as he disconnected, the receptionist called to him that the director was ready.

When Tresler entered his office, Director

Morgan motioned him to a chair but didn't rise.

"It's good of you to make time for me," Tresler said.

The director tapped one thick finger on the desk in front of him. He watched Tresler, and the sunlight caught the rims of his glasses. "How can I help you this time?" the director asked, with a slight emphasis on the words *this time*.

"I'll keep it brief. I just wanted to talk to you a little more about your Sarah Shepherd series."

"Surely the phone would have been sufficient for that. There was no need for you to come down from New York."

Tresler silently noted that the director had known his location. "I needed to return for other reasons," Tresler lied. "I thought I might just as well stop by."

The director's eyes narrowed a fraction, then he shrugged. "Ask away."

"About Sarah Shepherd. Having watched the videos, what do you think of her?"

"Wonderful woman. An icon." But the director's response sounded scripted. "And I'm proud that we here at IBC have been able to bring Sarah Shepherd to the people of this country. The public hungers for heroism, and we, here at IBC, have provided it."

"Didn't Sarah Shepherd do that?" Tresler suggested.

The director smiled at his simplicity. "Without us, no one would ever have known her name, heard or cared about her existence," he explained, as though to a child. "We were not responsible for her actions, but for her fame—I think we can claim a small share in that."

"But what has her fame to do with heroism?"

"If a tree falls in a forest . . ." He let the phrase trail off.

The discussion seemed to amuse the director, and Tresler took advantage of this. "All the millions of people in the world that never become famous," he said, "what about them?"

The director propped his elbow on the desk and tilted it slowly until it rested flat. "They are falling soundlessly."

Tresler raised his eyebrows in mild dissent.

"Why are you here asking me about Sarah Shepherd instead of Mary Higgins from Bottomswallow, North Dakota? You are here about Sarah Shepherd because of us. Because we put a microphone to her tree, so to speak." He leaned back in his chair, pleased with his argument.

"And the ransom and the vigil at Saint Patrick's Cathedral? A bigger microphone?"

"Exactly."

"Whose idea was that?"

There was the slightest of hesitations before the director admitted, "My own."

"Ah." Tresler paused. "What do you think about the person who made the tapes?"

There was a glint in the director's eye as he said, "That is a truly remarkable man."

Tresler waited for him to explain.

"He is one of those extraordinary people who does not need our services. He provides his own microphone; he makes sure he is heard."

"Do you think that's why he does what he does?" Tresler asked.

"What other reason could he have?"

"And his cameraman?"

"He could make us millions if he was on our staff."

"Anything else?"

The director heard the irony in his voice. "Millions are not to be taken lightly," he chided. "Those tapes are genius. Do you know how much money those tapes made me?"

"Is that how you measure genius?"

"No, certainly not. Genius doesn't pay. And neither, usually, does heroism. Now, if you don't mind, I've got some things I have to attend to."

Tresler rose. "Thank you for your time."

The director nodded before going back to his work.

Tresler paused in the doorway. "Oh," he said, "there is one more thing. I wanted to offer my sympathy on your father-in-law's death. You hadn't mentioned that you had a personal share in this tragedy."

The director looked up, startled, but Tresler was already gone.

Sightseeing

Her first day on her own, Sarah had spent sleeping. But the morning of her second day she went to the top of the Empire State Building, rode the ferry to the Statue of Liberty, and had lunch at a restaurant in Rockefeller Center. By one-thirty she had exhausted her patience with sightseeing.

Returning to the hotel, she asked eagerly at the front desk for her messages. The clerk said, "Sorry, Ms. Miller. No messages."

She tried to rest in her hotel room, but by three she was back out on the street. She put on her hat with the huge, floppy brim and wandered with her head down. She studied the black marks of gum on the sidewalk and the ankles of the people who passed her. She never knew that ankles could be so distinctive. When she got tired, she retreated into a nearby public library, pulled a book from the shelf, and sat at one of the crowded tables. She was surrounded by old men and women, also flipping through books.

The library, with its creaking chairs and aimless people, reminded her of Willowridge. A wave of nostalgia swept over her, and she wanted nothing more than to sit again with those old women on the lawn overlooking the hills. She realized that she still thought of them there under the birches, even though she had seen them sprawled on the floor of the cafeteria. She summoned up a picture in her mind to make it real. But she found it hard to concentrate—all she could think was "Why doesn't he call?"

Merec and Jeremy had rented a room in a hotel very near Sarah's—and just blocks from Saint Patrick's. They slept only briefly the first night and were up and out of the hotel early. First they collected all the newspapers and scanned every page, cutting out all the articles on the videotape. The clips resulted in a nice little pile, and they all mentioned the cathedral service scheduled for Sunday evening.

Then Merec made a list of all the things they needed to accomplish. "I want everything done by Friday evening," he said.

Jeremy studied the list. "It'll be tight."

"We will split the tasks. I will accompany you this morning in purchasing the supplies we need."

"And after that we'll check on Sarah?"

Merec stiffened. "Since when have you been asking questions?"

Jeremy shot him a quick look. "Sorry."

During the rest of the morning Merec often found his mind wandering. Where was she now? he wondered. Had she gone to the police? Or had she simply gone to the airport and caught a flight? And the most prevailing, the most recurring question—was she thinking of him?

Rose's Wish

During her two days on her own, Sarah did only one foolish thing. She blamed it on those wooden library chairs, whose creaking reminded her of Willowridge. Sarah called Rose.

She used a pay phone in the lobby of a restaurant. It was pure luck that she remembered one of Rose's acid comments about an unmarried daughter less than an hour away from Willowridge. That meant the same area code, the same name. She got the number from information, dialed, and asked for Rose.

"Is this another reporter?" the voice on the other end of the line asked sharply.

"No, it's an old friend."

"Your name?" The voice was still suspicious.

"Sarah."

There was a pause. "Just a minute."

"Yesss?" The voice that spoke sounded creaky, unused, and very faint. It sounded nothing like the snappy, acerbic Rose.

"Rose?" she said.

"Who is this?"

"It's Sarah," she whispered.

"Hello? Is anyone there?" The voice was almost fearful now. She must not have caught Sarah's words.

"It's Sarah," she said louder.

"What? Who?"

"Sarah," she shouted, disregarding safety.

"Sarah?"

"Sarah Shepherd."

There was silence.

"Did you hear me, Rose?"

"It's you," was all Rose said. There was another silence.

"Do you remember me?"

"Don't need to shout in my ear, girl," Rose grumbled, with evidence of her old irritability. It relieved Sarah so much that she wanted to burst out in nervous laughter, but she bit her bottom lip and waited for Rose to continue—to thank her. Instead Rose said, "So . . . what do you want?"

"Want?" Sarah echoed. "I . . . I just wanted to find out how you were."

"Well, I'm alive thanks to you." Rose didn't sound grateful.

"Is that so awful?" Sarah shot back.

"Yes, as a matter of fact, it is."

Sarah held the phone tightly to her ear.

"Did you ever for one second think what it would be like for me afterward? All my friends—everyone I cared about—they're all gone. So who exactly did you do it for, Sarah? Did you do it for me? Or did you do it for you?"

"I'm sorry," Sarah whispered. "You're right. You're absolutely right."

"I'm tired of being right. I'm just plain tired. But you wouldn't let me rest."

"Is there anything . . . ?"

"Too late for that," Rose said. "The only thing I want you can't give me."

"What is it?" Sarah asked.

"I wanted to die with fireworks."

"Good," Merec said to Jeremy, surveying the equipment they had arranged on the bed-spread. "That's everything. Now I want you to assemble it this evening. You understand how it should be done?"

Jeremy nodded.

"I'm going out for a while."

"Where are you going?"

"I," Merec said smiling, "am going to pray."

• • •

It was evening when Merec entered the cathedral. He looked around appreciatively. Outside, the cars rushed down Fifth Avenue and the sidewalks were thronged with people. But once inside the cathedral, there was a sudden calm, a hushed quality to the air. Hundreds of candles flickered, casting strange shadows against the immense stone walls.

Merec walked a way down the center aisle and slid into one of the wooden pews. Bending his head forward as though in prayer, he felt underneath the bench with his fingers. Karl had told him to look for small lumps the approximate size and shape of hardened gum, each about a meter apart. He was puzzled to find several right at the edge and clustered together. Bending even farther, he looked underneath and saw that he had been feeling actual pieces of gum and not Karl's clever fakes. He slid down a few feet, and there it was. Merec had to feel carefully to detect the wire that ran through it to the next little piece of gum-shaped substance a few feet down.

Smiling, he leaned back in the pew. Now, as soon as Jeremy finished his task, they would be ready.

When Merec returned to the hotel room a few hours later, he found that Jeremy had indeed finished the work assigned to him. It was laid out neatly on the bed—but Jeremy was nowhere to be found.

Weekend
Plans

When Sarah returned to her hotel room Friday evening, she found Jeremy lying on the bed, his eyes closed. She shut the door as noiselessly as she could and tiptoed across the room to the chair. Pulling it around so it faced the bed, she sat and watched him—his chest rising and falling in the deep, slow rhythm of sleep. About half an hour later he shifted onto his side, tucking one hand underneath the pillow, and slept on.

He might have slept all night, but the phone rang. Jeremy bolted upright and looked around wildly, but in an instant he had taken in Sarah sitting in the chair and the phone on the bedside table. He collapsed back onto the pillows. "You'd better get it," he said, his voice hoarse from sleep.

She caught the phone before the fourth ring.

"Hello?"

"Sarah."

It was Merec.

"Hello," she said again, she hoped calmly.

"Is Jeremy with you?"

"No 'How are you, Sarah?' No 'How have you been?' Don't you want to hear about the sights?"

He let out an explosive breath. "What the hell have you two been doing this entire time?"

"He fell asleep," she said.

The silence that followed was sharp.

"I mean, when I came into the room, I found him asleep on the bed. He just woke up now as the phone rang," she explained.

"Didn't wake up when you came in?"

"No. He didn't. Now, I don't know as you're the one who should be asking all the questions. Where the hell have you been for two days?"

"I am the only one entitled to ask questions, Sarah."

"I'm getting pretty tired of that business."

"Sarah." She could almost see him shaking his head. "Put Jeremy on."

She wanted to say, "No, not yet." But she held out the receiver. "He wants to talk to you."

Jeremy took the phone. His face was stern, but Sarah couldn't tell if it was from indifference or fear.

"Yes," Jeremy said, then "No," then "Yes" again. Try as she might, she couldn't hear Merec's words, just the rising and falling of his voice. Finally Jeremy handed the phone back to Sarah.

She brought it cautiously to her ear. "Yes?"

"We got off to the wrong start before. How are you?"

"All right."

"How was the sightseeing?" he asked.

"Dull."

"You can use your credit card, you know. Have you been shopping?"

"Do you think that would be more interesting?" She didn't even try to keep the sarcasm from her voice. "Have you used *your* credit card?"

"No. I've been shopping with cash," Merec admitted.

"Did you get anything good?"

"Oh yes. And I got something special for you. Thought you might want to practice with it a little."

She remembered the feel of a pistol in her hand, remembered the man's nose exploding in front of her. "Practice like back at the cabin?"

"No, not like that. That's not practice. I will come get you tomorrow." The phone at the other end clicked, and the dial tone hummed in her ear. She frowned, chewing her bottom lip. A movement in the corner of her eye made her start. She had forgotten about Jeremy sitting patiently at the end of the bed.

"You forgot about me?"

She shook her head. "No, Jeremy." What else could she say?

"What if," he stopped in mid-sentence, stood, and moved over to stand in front of her. He cupped her elbows, and a shiver went through her. She had forgotten the lightness of his touch, like a bird's wing cupping her skin.

"What if?" she prompted. But there must have been something in her voice, a hint of impatience, for he stepped back.

"What is it?" She took a step closer, and he backed away. "Jeremy—"

"I've got to go," he said, heading toward the door.

"Wait," her voice commanded. "You've forgotten something. What did you come for, Jeremy?"

He spoke without turning. "I haven't forgotten anything."

"Well?" She couldn't help but be exasperated.

She could see the curve of his cheek, the tip of his nose, the corner of his mouth quirked in what could have been a smile, or possibly the grimace that comes before tears. "I came to see you, Sarah. I just came to see you."

"You've seen me."

"Yes," he said, giving her the back of his head again. "I've seen you."

"And?"

"And . . . and now I'm leaving."

He had his hand on the knob of the door when she asked, "Merec didn't ask you to give me a message?"

He pivoted. His face was dead white. "I came because I wanted to. I came because Merec couldn't stop me." He spoke slowly, his voice sounding thick, as though he couldn't get enough saliva into his mouth.

"I figured he sent a message . . ." Her voice faltered at the blaze in his eyes.

"You be careful, Sarah Shepherd," he said. "Merec is . . . he isn't like other men."

She rolled her eyes.

"Don't do that. Don't make fun of it. I mean it. His brain doesn't work like other people's."

"He's smarter," Sarah jumped in.

Jeremy shook his head wearily.

"I thought you cared for Merec. I thought you admired him."

"That's not the point."

"Of course it is. It's the whole point."

Jeremy's voice was so low she could barely make out the words. "You don't know him," he said.

"What are you trying to tell me, Jeremy? What haven't I seen him do? What exactly am I supposed to be careful of?"

He appeared not to hear her. "Merec wasn't going to come see you tonight. He wasn't going to call. I don't think he was planning on seeing you tomorrow either."

Sarah crossed her arms. "Is that supposed to hurt my feelings?"

Again it was as if he hadn't heard. In a rush he said, "Leave tonight, Sarah. Check out of the hotel. Make sure you're not here when he comes."

"And where am I supposed to go?"

"Go to the police." At her expression Jeremy said quickly, "Or just go to another hotel. Be anywhere but here tomorrow."

"If you're trying to tell me that he doesn't care about me, that's not why—"

"No," he cut her off. "No. I spent a long time thinking about why he sent you off on your own like this. I know he said it would be too risky for the three of us to check in. But think about it. I could have checked in separately, and it would have been just you two—just a married couple. How many married couples do you think check into hotels in Manhattan? Or we could all have checked in separately but at the same hotel. He could have kept an eye on you. He should have kept an eye on you. What could be more risky than sending you off on your own? It's been two days since we spoke to you. I've been with him this whole time, and we didn't even call to see that you had arrived. Does that seem strange to you?"

She shrugged. "I thought he was trying to get rid of me."

"He has a different way of doing that, Sarah."

Jeremy's voice was harsh. "You saw that your-self."

"So why?" she challenged him.

"Why? I don't even know if he has admitted it to himself. But I think he's hoping that you will leave. He's praying that you'll be gone because . . . he doesn't want to have to kill you. And that is exactly what he is planning to do this weekend."

She didn't know what to say. She wanted to protest, but what Jeremy had said felt right.

"So?" he said.

"So?" she echoed.

"Will you go?"

"I can't."

He turned and left the room without another word, closing the door quietly behind him.

Tresler's
Audience

After his interview with the director, Tresler went straight back to the airport and caught a late shuttle to New York. He spent his time in transit trying to reach someone connected with Saint Patrick's Cathedral, but the only place he was able to contact at such short notice was the deacon's office.

Tresler returned to the hotel after Stanley had gone to sleep and was up and gone before Stanley awoke. He walked over to the cathedral and waited outside by reception while the deacon finished his previous appointment. It wasn't long before a young man and woman emerged. The deacon walked them to the door and shook both their hands before they left. "Good luck to both of you," he said, smiling genially. "You're going to do just fine."

When the door had shut behind the couple, the deacon turned to greet Tresler. "Sorry for the delay. They're getting married in the cathedral next week." He headed back toward the small office. "Is here all right for us to talk? I'm fitting you in between appointments, and I have another couple in about ten minutes."

"That's fine," Tresler said, following him into the room.

"So, Mr. Tresler, what can I do for you?"

"I work with the FBI and I'm following the Sarah Shepherd case."

"Oh, so you're here about the service."

"Exactly."

"Did you want to discuss the arrangements? A request for a special speaker?"

"Not quite," he said, and started to explain.

When Tresler began speaking, the deacon was sitting back in his chair with his hands clasped quietly in his lap and a pleasant smile on his face. But as he listened his brow furrowed. Then he sat up and began to fidget. Finally he interrupted.

"Sir, maybe I should explain. I work with weddings and christenings. This is not something I can handle. I imagine you would have to see the cardinal's office about this."

"The only problem is getting through to someone in the cardinal's office."

"Ah. Yes." The deacon sat, twisting his fingers in his lap. "All right. Wait here." He stood and hurried out of the room. When he returned almost ten minutes later, he didn't sit down again but remained by the door. "The cardinal's secretary will see you this afternoon at one," he said. "And now, if you'll excuse me, I'm late for my next appointment."

"Thank you." Tresler stood and started out of the room. But as he passed the deacon, he felt a hand on his arm.

"I wish you the best of luck. But I am praying for you to be wrong about this."

"So am I," Tresler said.

At one-fifteen, Tresler finished his speech to the cardinal's secretary.

The man leaned forward and said, "Excuse me, may I see your credentials again?"

Tresler took out his wallet and flipped it open to show his identification. The secretary received it and glanced down. Then he flipped past the driver's license and credit cards. He closed the wallet, and instead of handing it back, he placed it on the edge of his desk. Tresler picked it up and tucked it away in his pocket.

"I was hoping that this was a prank. I am assuming it is not."

"No."

"So," he said, tapping his fingers together, "tell

me if this is correct. You want me to close down
the cathedral and force a last-minute change in
location. Or alternately, you want the cathedral to
be closed for a thorough inspection by your people. And in addition, on the day of the service
you want to set up a metal detector in the front
entrance and search people as they enter, as well
as positioning a police team inside."

"Yes."

"And you have absolutely no concrete proof
of your suspicions?"

"We know that the perpetrator is in New
York—"

"*Was* in New York," the secretary corrected.
"You know that he *was* in New York."

"—and I think it is obvious that this special
service would be a target."

"Obvious to whom, Agent Tresler? Obvious
to you maybe. But it's not obvious to me."

"The cardinal might see it differently," Tresler
suggested.

"The cardinal?" The secretary's face flushed.
"Do you seriously expect me to bother the cardinal with this ridiculous request? The very
idea is ludicrous."

Tresler didn't respond.

"There will be no change of venue," the secretary continued. "If I find your men attempting an inspection of the cathedral, I will have
them escorted out. There will not, I repeat, *not*
be a search of our parishioners at the entrance,

and though your men are welcome to attend the service, they are not permitted to bring their weapons. Have I made myself clear?"

"Perfectly," Tresler sighed.

Tresler returned to his hotel room and collapsed into a chair. He knew he had only a short time to rest before he needed to begin what few preparations were left to him. The moment he closed his eyes, the phone rang. He picked it up.

"Tresler, where the hell have you been? I've been calling your room every hour since last night."

"Hello, Stanley."

"Hold on and I'll be right over." The phone clicked, and before Tresler had even managed to get up from his chair, Stanley was knocking on his door.

Tresler tiredly recounted his activities over the last two days. Stanley paced the room restlessly while listening and occasionally uttered an exclamation under his breath. When Tresler had finished, Stanley came and perched on the chair next to him.

"Listen, Tresler. You know I respect your work, but on this one I think I have to weigh in with the others. I mean, I know this guy is crazy, but we're talking about Saint Patrick's Cathedral. And really, what do you think he could do?"

Tresler rubbed his eyes. "I don't know,

Stanley," he said. "What went on around here?"

"Oh, I just followed up on some more Sarah Shepherd sightings. None of them panned out. We've been checking hotel registrations, but no one has two men and a woman checking in at that time of night. We're in the midst of reviewing passenger rosters for last-minute bookings on all the flights out of the three airports late that evening. But that will take a while. I hate to say it, but it's looking more and more like they skipped out of the city."

"They didn't," Tresler said.

"All right. That's your opinion. What are you planning to do?"

"I can still get some men in the cathedral tomorrow to take a look around. And I'll station a full team at strategic points outside the cathedral starting tonight. Beyond that . . ." He shrugged.

Double
Action

Sarah woke Saturday morning with a strange feeling of constriction in her chest, as though she couldn't pull enough air into her lungs. This is ridiculous, she thought. She showered quickly, called for room service, and found that she could not bring herself to sit down at the table by the window and chew. She paced the room, smoking one cigarette after another until she had almost emptied her pack, and tried to figure out why she was so excitable this morning. Was it Merec or the thought of what he was bringing her?

A light tap at the door froze her steps. She went to open it, and Merec sauntered in. The sight of him after four days was a revelation. In her mind he had grown in stature. His actions had, in her memory, invested him with a dark solemnity. But the second he stepped over the threshold with his offhand jauntiness and his aggressive mockery, he clicked back into place. And she thought, Oh yes, I had forgotten.

He placed a warm, dry European kiss on each cheek and moved past her into the room. She shut the door and leaned against it.

"Hello, my dear." Merec set down a bag and sat in the chair.

"Hello."

There was a small silence but not an awkward one.

"I see you haven't eaten." He glanced at the practically untouched platter of eggs and toast, now cold and congealed.

"No," she said.

"Not good," he chided. "You need to keep up your strength. But perhaps you need to work up an appetite."

"That might be it," she agreed, her breath coming short again.

"Would you like to see it?"

She took an involuntary step forward. "Yes."

He pushed the bag toward her with his foot. She approached and knelt, carefully pulling back the zipper. She peered in, then retrieved the revolver, gripping it firmly by the handle. Extending it to arm's length before her, she tilted her head to one side and examined it.

"It's beautiful," she said.

"It's a Smith and Wesson Chief's Special, 'airweight' model. That's why it's so light. Double action with a two-inch barrel."

She turned it over in her hands.

"Would you like to try it out?"

Her eyes were very bright as she nodded.

When they returned to Sarah's hotel room in the early evening, her arms were weak from the unaccustomed strain of holding them straight and steady before her. She had not shown any unusual talent but a concentration and focus that suggested the birth of a passion. Also, her head was light and fanciful from the wine they had drunk during a leisurely lunch that stretched into the early evening. A band had struck up at the restaurant, and they danced a slow, graceful foxtrot. Merec held her close enough that she could feel his handgun, a standard, practical Beretta in a shoulder holster, pressing against her ribcage.

He had done most of the talking, beginning with a short discourse on weaponry and gradually segueing into stories of his former jobs. She listened, elbows on the table, chin cupped between her hands. It was only when the dinner crowd started to filter in that they made their way out to the street. They meandered toward the hotel, and Merec accompanied Sarah to her room. She sat down in the chair, and Merec went over to the bed and picked up the phone.

"Do you want something to drink?"

She shrugged.

He set down the phone. "Tell me what you want, Sarah."

She gripped her pocketbook tighter and felt the shape of the pistol through the leather. "Don't you know?" she said.

The Sabbath

Sunday dawned with a fast, whistling wind that blew empty paper cups in arcing paths through the streets. The sky lightened slowly, the sun masked by low gray clouds.

Merec was awake well before dawn. He propped himself up on his elbow and watched Sarah. She stirred and opened her eyes to Merec's gaze. She smiled sleepily.

He stared back. His eyes, usually an icy blue, were now a soft gray. They matched the sky outside.

"Well?" she said to break the silence.

He hesitated. "Sarah . . ." Her eyes narrowed. "Last night . . . I mean, this isn't . . ." It required a significant effort on his part not to look away.

"All right," she drawled. "I'll try to remember that." He wished suddenly and fervently that he had not spoken at all. Reaching out, he traced a finger along her cheek. She permitted it for a second, then drew away.

He curled his fingers into a loose fist, then slid out of the bed and began putting on his clothes.

"Are you in some sort of hurry?" she said.

"As a matter of fact, I am. Today is a big day for us."

"Oh? What are we doing today?"

Now he smiled—a young, boyish grin of pure anticipation. "We're going to church."

The weather remained fitful, restless, with gusts that sometimes scattered sprinkles of raindrops. Jeremy had joined Merec and Sarah in the hotel room.

Sarah sat on the bed, her legs stretched out and crossed at the ankles. "Shouldn't we be hurrying?" she asked. "Most church services start about now."

"We're attending an evening service."

She frowned. "I didn't know they held evening services."

"This is a special one," Merec admitted. "Let me tell you about it."

"Please do." She spoke with a businesslike detachment.

Merec lied calmly. He said that they would be attending a memorial service for loved ones lost to random violence and that she would be mentioned in a prayer. "I thought you might like to make a public appearance," Merec continued. "And Jeremy's brought something very special for you to wear. Jeremy."

Jeremy hefted the big canvas bag onto the bed. What he extracted looked like something she'd seen in the movies. There was no mistaking what it was.

"How do you like it?" Merec asked. "It's the latest rage."

The garment Jeremy held up for Sarah's inspection was vestlike in shape, but it was the accessories that were the main feature. It was covered, trimmed, lined, crammed—with explosives.

"Are you sure it's my size?" she said.

Merec threw his head back and laughed—a little too heartily? Jeremy smiled, and to Sarah's eyes, he looked pained.

She examined it more closely. "Is it enough to blow up a whole church?"

"No, not nearly enough. You'd need a hundred times that amount. But this isn't for real. It's just to keep everyone in line."

"You mean it's not real explosives?"

"No." He pursed his lips. "The explosives are real enough. But in themselves they're harmless. Show her, Jeremy."

Jeremy tossed the vest toward Sarah but to the left of the bed. She couldn't help flinching as it hit the ground with a resounding thud.

"It is somewhat heavy, as you can tell, but as I said, harmless without the detonator."

"And who has the detonator?"

"I do," Merec said.

Did he speak a little too quickly? she wondered.

He fished something out of his pocket. "It doesn't work. We made sure of that."

"May I see?" From the corner of her eye, she saw Jeremy flash a quick glance at Merec, but Merec tossed it to her. It looked like a small black rectangular box. "Where's the switch?"

"You don't want to be able to thumb it by accident." He perched on the bed beside her. "You see, you have to open this catch." He took it from her, and it seemed to her as though he made sure their fingers didn't touch. "Flip this part back, and voilà." He uncovered a little red button. He snapped it closed.

She said, "I'd like to try." She fumbled with it but had it open a second later and placed her finger over the button. The curve of her thumb fit perfectly into the depression.

"So nothing will happen if I press this?"

Did they both turn to stone? Or was it her imagination?

"Nothing," Merec said.

She pressed. Nothing happened. They both seemed to breathe again.

Merec reached out and plucked it from her

hand. "Sorry, but we old timers get a little nervous around these things. We've seen too many work all too well."

She nodded, but she knew that there were many ways to deceive. However, she had already made her choice. There were whole days when she could have walked out, checked into another hotel, picked up the phone and dialed the police. She had made the decision, and she had no regrets.

"Of course the vest is not completely safe," Merec was saying. "It is never perfectly safe to walk around with ten pounds of explosives. For example, I would strongly advise you to avoid bullets."

"Who would be shooting at me?"

"Jeremy spent the night around the cathedral keeping watch. Maybe he could answer your question. Jeremy, how many agents does the FBI have stationed there?"

Jeremy held up five fingers. "But all outside the cathedral."

"You'll want to be aware of them, and we'll show you their location on the plans, but I don't see that they'll present a danger to you. Everyone will think that you're still our hostage. They don't know—" His voice dropped meaningfully. "They don't know that you're willing . . . and very able."

Sarah felt her face flame with heat.

"Not much for sweet nothings, Sarah?" he said lightly.

"Especially not in front of other people," she snapped.

"Who, Jeremy?" He feigned surprise. "Don't worry about Jeremy. He's a good loser."

"That's ridiculous," she said.

"You see, Jeremy. You never did have a chance." Merec brightened dangerously. "Do you want to hear a story, Sarah? I think we have time for a quick show-and-tell."

Both Jeremy and Sarah looked away from Merec, away from each other.

"I think I have told you something of the procedure of entering into this close-knit family. No? Well, part of the application process bears a resemblance to the game we played at the rest home. However, this game is a little more proactive than the one you witnessed. There isn't anyone to do the dirty work for you. It's two people, standing toe to toe, just waiting for the word to fire on each other.

"Now, there are some applicants I want to succeed, and some I don't. So I make sure that some have a full chamber, and some do not. In reality, the contest is no contest at all. Half are, what do you say, cannon fodder? But the applicants don't know it is rigged. They believe that both guns are loaded and they are facing death. A test like this is necessary. You don't want to take someone on a job and have them ruin the operation because you unexpectedly find that they don't have the nerve. It's happened to some of my colleagues more often than you would imagine.

"But in all the years that I have used this little scenario to test my applicants, not one has opened the gun to check the number of bullets. They were so trusting, these men and women. They didn't stop to think that if it was to be a true test—a real-life test—then it had to be unfair. When in life have you ever gone into something without the deck stacked either for or against you? It never happens.

"Well, Jeremy didn't think to check on the bullets either, but he did something else that no one had done before. He stacked the deck for himself. Usually I count to three, and they shoot. Jeremy, he shot on one. And he happened to hold the gun with the bullet, so it was very effective. It was cowardly, dishonorable, and very effective. He was my star pupil."

"Touching," Sarah said.

"Oh, but just wait. It is. That was not the part of the story that I wanted to tell. That was only the warm-up. Afterward we require the successful applicants to dispose of their victims, and after Jeremy's performance I was interested in what he would do. So I put my best shadow on him. Jeremy was ingenious. I won't go into the gruesome details of how he hid the body, but let's just say it was well done; it wouldn't have been discovered for weeks.

"We expect him to return for the rendezvous.

Right? Wrong. He makes an anonymous phone
call to the police, and they retrieve the body.
Jeremy barely stirs from his motel room for two
days. On the third day a story appears in the
local paper, and he takes off. He rents a car and
drives across three states, finally stopping in a
little town called Barton. According to my
source, he bought a bottle of Evian and a package of Fig Newtons and entered a Protestant
church. We believe he remained in the broom
closet there for thirty-four hours, until 10:00 A.M.
on Friday morning, when a minister stepped up
to the podium and said a service for Walter
Mitchell Storms. There were only three people
at the service: Jeremy, the minister, and an old
woman in an orange plaid skirt, rain boots, and
a pink wool sweater. The one thing the shadow
was not able to tell me was whether Jeremy
cried."

Merec finished the story. Jeremy's expression
was exactly the same as it always was—
guarded, immobile, aloof. But deep in his eyes
Sarah thought she saw a flicker.

"Well?" Merec asked.

But Sarah directed her question at Jeremy.
"Do you think that attending the funeral of the
man you killed makes you moral?"

"No. But it makes me human. He doesn't
qualify." Jeremy spoke about Merec as if he
weren't in the room.

"Isn't it funny that I mock you for having a

conscience, and you ... you ... what would be the word you would use?" said Merec.

"Pity." Jeremy enunciated clearly.

"My dear boy," Merec said, clapping him on the shoulder heartily. "After all this time I would have expected you to know me better. Pride is not something about which I am vulnerable. All right. Where was I? Oh yes, I mock you for having a conscience, and you *pity* me for having none. Am I correct?"

"I would challenge the word *conscience*. I would use the word *heart* instead," Jeremy said, moving out from under Merec's hand.

"If only that were true. If only both were true, I would be much happier. Simply because I am seemingly without morals does not make me less of a man." His voice roughened here. "No indeed."

"What is it they say?" Jeremy backed away. "We are doomed to disagree?"

"And we got on so delightfully before. What is it about a woman that destroys all peace between men?"

Sarah interrupted. "Shouldn't we be making plans?"

"Right as usual, my dear. All right, enough fun. Let's get to work."

Putting on Your Sunday Best

On Sunday evening, Tresler dressed slowly. Over his T-shirt he pulled on a bulletproof vest. Then he buttoned up a dark blue shirt and slipped into his shoulder holster. He had cleaned his pistol that afternoon, and now he carefully reloaded and made sure he had backup ammunition. Slipping into his jacket, he went to knock on Stanley's door.

"It's open," Stanley called from inside.

Tresler found him in front of the mirror knotting his tie. "Almost ready," Stanley said.

Tresler looked around the room and saw Stanley's bulletproof vest lying on the bed and his pistol in the holster slung over the arm of a chair.

Stanley picked up his jacket. "All set," he said, heading toward the door.

Tresler didn't move. "What about your gear?"

"I'm not wearing that into a cathedral."

"But we're not going into the cathedral. We'll be monitoring the event from an office in the building across the street."

"Well, actually, I've decided to attend the service," Stanley admitted.

"To *attend* the service?"

"Yes. That's what I was thinking."

"But didn't you hear what I said?"

"I heard, and I disagree. This is a service for an amazing woman, and I want to pay my respects."

Tresler rolled his eyes to the ceiling as if for help. "All right. I obviously can't stop you, but at least take your gun."

"Not in a cathedral. I'm telling you, nothing's going to happen. Come on, let's go." He led the way out, and Tresler had no choice but to follow.

Sunday Sermon

It was the time when day blends seamlessly into night, when the air seems crisper, the lines of buildings and trees seem clearer, and sound carries farther, echoing a little before dying away.

At the doors of the cathedral the light was as bright as day, the wattage supplied not by the sun but by the television camera crew. The wide lenses recorded the hundreds that shuffled through the doors to sit and pray for a woman they had never known.

The cameras were, of course, from IBC. They had arrived hours before to occupy this prime space. And as the people filed by, interviewers coaxed certain individuals to answer a question for the camera: "Why are you here tonight?"

Some of the responses:

"They said on the news there that she don't

got nobody else. No husband, no children, no family. So I think, Who will pray for her? Then I think maybe the whole world's gonna be her family."

"This is not even my religion. I have never set foot in a Christian place of worship. But my daughter was killed in a terrorist bombing in Israel. I came here so that I may . . . to support others who . . ." Tears choked off the sentence.

"I've just been diagnosed with prostate cancer. It was that night the first video aired. And when I saw it, and the next one, I knew that was how I wanted to go. I came to pray for Sarah Shepherd's courage."

Merec had been in place even longer than the television cameras. Dressed in a cassock, he had used the key supplied by Karl and climbed the stairs to the organist's balcony. Then, concealing himself behind thick drapes, he had adjusted the curtain so that he could see down into the cathedral. The view was enough to satisfy him that when the bullets came, it would seem to the people in the pews as though they were raining down from God.

Jeremy had been one of the first in the crowd to go through the enormous doors, but he had slid

into a pew toward the back. His video camera
was loaded with a fresh tape, a charged battery,
and he had an extra of each in the deep pockets
of his windbreaker.

The last of the people drifted through the doors
and took their seats. The cathedral was cav-
ernous, and though the crowd was quite large,
it was dwarfed by the space within.

From his hiding place, Merec gazed down at
the narrow bands of heads, ranged neatly along
the benches like ducks in a shooting gallery. All
those people had left their air-conditioned
homes, had gotten baby-sitters for the children,
had paid money for cabs or waited choking
with the heat in the airless subway stations.
Right now there were so many other things they
could be doing—watching the Sunday evening
movie on television, reading a book in bed, taking a cool shower, sipping a chilled glass of
white wine, spending time with their spouses,
their children, their friends.

Merec had always known in a vague sort of
way that there was something good in every
person. But until now he had managed for the
most part to avoid it. On the rare occasion when
someone had done something decent, something human, it had been such a tiny spark in
the vast sea that it had seemed irrelevant, an

aberration. But now he was confronted by all these people who were in this small but somehow profound sense good. Had Fritz been right? Did he really possess a genius for bringing out the worst side in people?

Was this really the time to begin to doubt?

Merec glimpsed the organist entering the balcony and ducked back behind the curtain.

A chord resounded through the cathedral, and the voices died away. Another chord, then a ripple of notes that blossomed into a song.

Some closed their eyes to listen, but Stanley tried to locate the source of the sound. He spotted the huge pipes of the organ in the dim light over the door. Then he settled back in the pew.

As the final notes were struck, pulsed, and faded, Merec slipped out from his hiding place, pistol in hand, silencer in place. In three swift steps he was behind the organist. He raised the pistol to the nape of the man's neck and pulled the trigger, catching the body so it wouldn't land on the keys. The only noise was a soft coughing sound and the light patter of drops.

Below, the cathedral benches creaked as people shifted in their seats, waiting for the service to begin. When the priest spoke, the words were familiar. He recited the prayer that even those without faith recognize. He spoke into the microphone in a soft, reverential voice that carried as though whispered into each ear:

The Lord is my Shepherd; I shall not want.
He maketh me to lie down in green pastures: He
*   leadeth me beside the still waters.*
He restoreth my soul . . .

Many joined him in reciting the words to the familiar psalm. When they had finished and the priest spoke again, his solitary voice echoed through the space.

"Thank you for joining me in the opening prayer this evening. Though we say it so often, and the words are so familiar, sometimes it takes a situation like this to remind us what they mean." He paused, sweeping the crowd again with his gaze. But he didn't look up to the shadowy balcony where Merec was swiftly assembling the long-range rifle.

"They mean that tonight we are here not only to pray for that brave, noble woman, Sarah Shepherd. We are also here to pray for the misguided people who are holding her. Jesus said, in his Sermon on the Mount:

You have heard that it was said, You shall love your
neighbor and hate your enemy.
But I say to you, Love your enemies, bless those
who curse you, do good to those who hate you, and

pray for those who spitefully use you and persecute you—

Merec balanced the rifle on the wooden rail.

"Think on these words," the priest said. "It is so easy to pray for Sarah Shepherd. She is good. She suffers. But she is not alone. She has found the way of the Lord, and He walks every step with her. Consider how much harder it is to pray for those men who have lost the way of the Lord. And consider also how much more they need our prayers tonight."

Merec's hand had dropped from the trigger. It was the last thing he had expected to hear.

He shook his head as though to clear it and fitted his eye back to the sights.

"This," the priest said, spreading his palms to heaven, "this is the way to rescue not just one deserving sheep but also the undeserving. We will welcome them back into the fold as the prodigal son was welcomed."

The priest smiled, and his throat blossomed red, a flower of blood spilling out onto the pages of the book in front of him. He was still smiling as he fell.

People gasped as the priest collapsed, but with no audible shot, they weren't certain what had happened. A figure in a raincoat and scarf climbed over the low barrier, mounted the steps, and went to stand beside the body of the priest.

Sarah looked down at the figure at her feet. Then she removed her scarf and let the raincoat drop from her shoulders so that all could see the vest she wore—with the ten pounds of explosives strapped firmly across her chest.

Before the priest's body even hit the floor, Stanley was on his feet, searching the crowd, sweeping the room for the gunman, and reaching for his weapon. His hand closed on empty air.

A ripple shook the audience like wind through a forest, and he heard her name whispered, "Sarah, Sarah Shepherd." He shifted his focus, and there she was. Her hair was short and dark, but there was no doubt. She stood over the body of the priest, and for one awful moment Stanley thought that Sarah had been the shooter. But then she slipped out of the raincoat, and he got a glimpse of what was underneath. Stanley was probably the only one in the cathedral who was reassured by what he saw.

• • •

Tresler had one eye on the television, but most of his attention was focused on the report of one of his operatives through the headset. Apparently someone in a raincoat and scarf had just slipped through the side door near the transept.

On the television Tresler saw the priest fall, but the cameraman who was filming hadn't tightened the focus, and the body was an indistinguishable heap. Approaching the set, Tresler squatted to bring it to eye level and stared hard at the body. Beneath it he was almost sure he could see a dark liquid seeping out, spreading in a slow amoeba shape. Then Sarah Shepherd climbed into the frame.

"Get some backup," Tresler barked through the headset before ripping it off. He didn't bother with the elevator. He took the stairs by twos and sprinted out of the building.

At that second a police car screeched around the corner and drew to a halt behind him.

"Damn," Tresler muttered. He had hoped for at least a few moments of quiet to study the scene. But with the arrival of the police, a crowd would gather. He pivoted and hurried over to the patrol car.

IBC's on-site reporter and the extra camera had left after the initial filming outside the cathedral. They were planning on wrapping up the footage with the anchors in the studio. There was only one camera left to cover the event and a single cameraman. The rest of the crew was out in the van.

In his initial shock, the cameraman had frozen on a single long-focus shot of the podium. And when Sarah stepped onto the stage, he had poked his head around the camera as though he didn't trust what he saw through the lens. But he did have an earpiece through which the studio could direct his shots, and they recovered a little faster than he did. He was prodded into action by shrill screams.

"Get the shot. Warren? Warren! Get the fucking shot!"

Then Warren realized what he had. He had been a teenager during Vietnam, and he had been turned down half a dozen times for work in the Gulf War, in Bosnia, in Africa. Now his dream was coming true right in front of him. The very thing a cameraman lives for. A live feed on a disaster.

The director watched alone in his office. He had tuned into the program at the start and watched as a background to other tasks. But he had been drawn in by the priest's sermon. The director had been raised a Catholic, though he had forsaken his religion long ago in place of more tangible rewards and hadn't been to church for decades. The familiar quotations, the unexpected focus on the kidnappers rather than the victim, pulled his attention from the stack of papers on his desk. He was watching when the shot tore the priest's throat.

The director cried out. It was little more than a grunt, but from a man who was known for his rigid self-control, it was significant. Immediately afterward, he glanced at the door of the office. It was closed. His eyes darted back to the screen.

There was Sarah Shepherd standing next to the body of the priest. She slipped off the raincoat, and the director's eyes narrowed with pleasure. He could see that his friend had set up quite a show.

Sarah looked out at the hundreds of eyes staring up at her. The blood on the floor had surrounded her shoes and was dripping down the marble steps. She would never be able to escape from this. They would just follow her footsteps, marked with blood.

Dignity, she thought, dignity. She extended one hand to the edge of the podium to steady herself, and when she spoke, her voice was miraculously clear. "Please stay in your seats. You will be safe if you remain where you are."

Those who had risen to get a better look at what had happened immediately sank down, hunching their shoulders, ducking their heads, trying to reduce their size in their new capacity as targets.

She continued, maintaining a calm, steady tone. "My name is Sarah Shepherd." She paused. "I don't know if all of you know my story. Two weeks ago I was living at the Willowridge Rest Home, down in Virginia. I thought that was where I would live out the rest of my life. At the time I didn't much care. My husband had died shortly before that, and I had nothing else, no one else. But you don't want to hear about that." She shook her head.

"I'm sorry, I'm not used to speaking before large crowds. I stayed four months at Willowridge. In my time there, we only had a handful of visitors. Most of the patients had passed into senility, so their relatives didn't bother coming by much. And anybody else, well, they wouldn't have been there if they had anyone who cared enough."

She focused on a woman's face in the front row. How did Sarah expect these people to understand? She hurried on, unaware that they, and almost everyone in the country, knew the details. "Then we had some very unusual visitors. As far as I know, they killed all the residents as well as all the staff on duty except for myself and one other woman. They left her, and took me, and I have been a hostage since." She stopped to take a deep breath and shifted her feet. They slid in the puddle of blood. The sound of a siren reached her faintly through the thick stone walls.

"Don't move," Sarah commanded. Her voice softened. "Please, don't move. I have been told that there's another man stationed outside with a clear shot at anyone who reaches the door."

Sarah heard a gentle sobbing from the mass of people before her. She smelled the fear. Or maybe it was the scent of the blood washing like a river around her feet.

Merec listened to Sarah with satisfaction. His prediction had, thankfully, been correct, and he did not have to pick off anyone in a run for the door. In his experience, the initial uncontrolled panic usually resulted in a deer-in-the-headlights freeze. By now Sarah's words would have registered, and they would stay put. They would sit and listen until she got to the lines that had been scripted for her.

Stanley craned his neck, desperately trying to locate the gunman. If he could locate him, he

could figure out how to approach him. It was
risky but within the realm of possibility. If he
couldn't locate the gunman, he would only be
able to save himself and—to his credit—he had
not even a thought of that.

But only one half of Stanley's mind was cal-
culating his position, his options, his strategy.
The other half was enthralled by Sarah's voice.
It was clearer, crisper, and paradoxically softer
than it had been on the tapes. It mesmerized
him. She seemed to speak not to his ears but to
his heart.

No one noticed Jeremy with his tiny handheld
camera. He filmed everything without distrac-
tion.

Tresler prowled through the maze of police cars
parked haphazardly across Fifth Avenue. He
organized a team for crowd control. He moni-
tored his operatives for anyone exiting the
building, and most importantly, he made sure
that every officer knew that they had a hostage
situation on their hands and heroes wouldn't be
appreciated. With these things completed, he
made his way over to the television van and
fought his way through the crowd to crouch in

front of the screen and watch the drama unfold within.

"I was told," Sarah said hesitantly, "that you all came here, at least in part, to pray for me?"

"Yes," a few hesitant voices floated up to her, thin with fear.

"Thank you." She cleared her throat. "I have a message from the man who organized this—" she was about to say "party" and realized how horribly inappropriate it was. She stumbled and said instead "—this spectacle. I can't describe him. I have never met anyone like him. As some people play with cards, he plays with lives. And he has burdened me with a message to all of you."

Sarah gripped the podium tighter. She found she did not like this part of the assignment. Merec had been able to deliver his demands with a mocking, sardonic twist that spun the words into whim, into fate.

She spoke slowly, seriously. "He says that he will release everyone here unharmed if ... if someone is willing to sacrifice their life. All that person must do is get up and walk out the doors of the cathedral. He promises that it will be quick."

The crowd was silent. Even the sobbing had stopped.

Then someone called out, "Will it save you?" But the voice was hard, not hopeful.

Sarah shook her head. "I don't believe I'm part of the bargain." She knew immediately that she had made a misstep. Someone snatched up her ill-chosen word.

"Bargain?" a middle-aged man said. "Bargain!" And the voice rose in a crescendo. "You call that a bargain?"

"It's not my decision," she tried to say, but her words were lost in the cry that had been taken up by the people before her. One man, with white hair and a bushy mustache, rose from the pew with his fist in the air.

A gunshot cracked. The old man collapsed onto the bench, unhurt. Everyone cringed. Merec had taken off the silencer and fired the pistol into the air.

It took a full minute before people began to raise their heads again. They were met with the sight of Sarah standing straight and stern.

"Who will go?" she said.

The night before, in bed with Sarah, Merec had dreamed. He dreamed that every single person stood after Sarah's words and that they all walked out of the cathedral together.

But now he waited. He stared at the crowd, and no one moved.

• • •

Sarah looked out over the heads. The seconds stretched taut, a tightrope of time.

Stanley twisted in his pew, searching the nooks and crannies for a glint of metal.

Merec pulled a small plastic box from his pocket. He traced a finger along its edge, opened it to expose the bright red button inside, then balanced it on the balcony. Reaching deep into his bag, he pulled out another identical box and laid it beside the first. Opening it he exposed a blue button. Finally he retrieved a third. Its button was white.

He picked up the first and casually pressed the red button. Nothing happened, for this was Sarah's decoy. He tucked it away. His hand was hovering over the blue button when his eyes registered movement below.

At first only a few people around Stanley noticed when he stood. He was seated toward the back, just a few rows in front of Jeremy. But soon the news rippled through the crowd and heads turned.

Sarah's eye was drawn to the movement, and she saw the man standing at the back of the church. She hailed him. "What is your name?" she said.

He gripped the bench before him. "Stanley Wall."

"Stanley Wall," she repeated and nodded at him.

He assumed that was his sign and reluctantly let go of the pew in front of him, wanting something more from her. The only problem was that he didn't know what. If he had been closer and had been able to see her more clearly, he might have been content with her shining eyes.

He sidled past the knees of the people next to him and walked down the wide marble aisle to the doors. His own movements seemed slow and dreamlike. He pushed open the huge door and stepped across the threshold, his eyes dazzled by the flashing strobe lights from the clusters of police cars and the spotlights of the TV crews.

Automatically he raised a hand to shield his face. He stood a moment in front of the door, then advanced a few steps to stand in the middle of the marble platform. He spread his arms, half invitation, half question.

The television camera had found and focused on Stanley by the time he reached the aisle. In the cramped van outside the cathedral, Tresler groaned. "What are you thinking?"

Merec had Stanley's head in his sights a second after he stood. He followed him with the barrel of the rifle as Stanley made his way out to the aisle and moved toward the doors. But then, as he got a direct view of his face, Merec recognized him from the introduction to the first video. And as Stanley walked forward, Merec let him pass underneath the balcony and out of his range of vision.

Laying the rifle on the floor, Merec retrieved the two detonators and flipped one open. Now. He had to do it now. Ducking behind the solid wood of the balcony, he closed his eyes and murmured, "Good-bye, Sarah," and pressed the blue button.

The stone walls boomed back the sound.

Merec fit his finger over the white button and thought of Jeremy, who knew nothing about this second detonator or the small gum-shaped pieces of plastique that Karl had attached beneath the benches. Then he pressed.

IBC's cameraman was still focused on the closed door, following Stanley's exit, when Merec pressed the first button. People all across the country, leaning forward on their couches and their recliners, heard only the echoing boom and then the screams. When the camera swung around, they got a blurred impression of white faces. The camera completed its pan and rested on the front of the church. The podium had been knocked over by the blast, and the intricate wooden chair that had stood a few feet behind now lay in fragments. And, of course, Sarah was gone.

A moment later there was another explosion, and people watching across the country were confronted with a snowy screen.

The roar of the first blast was faint, muffled by the stone walls of St. Patrick's.

Stanley heard the sound of the screams inside and started back toward the door. But a second deafening explosion made him leap back just as he was reaching for the handle, ears ringing.

Hesitantly, he reached for the door again. As he pulled it open smoke curled out in lazy, twisting ribbons, and there was a sharp, acrid smell that Stanley tasted in the back of his throat. The screams had stopped; from the interior of the cathedral there was nothing but silence.

Hints and Hymnals

Tresler sprinted out of the crowd around the television van and was close on Stanley's heels when he stepped across the threshold. Inside, the cathedral was smoky and dark—the explosion had blown out the hundreds of candles that had flickered around the walls. They blinked against the sting of the fumes, but they were still able to see that where there had once been row upon row of pews, now there was a thick carpet of splintered wood and broken bodies.

Police officers crowded into the cathedral behind Tresler and Stanley. They were talking as they entered, but once they saw the scene in front of them they fell silent.

Tresler turned to the person standing nearest him. "Get some help in here," he said.

The young man looked once more at the

destruction inside, his eyes wide. Then he nodded and fled.

"Everyone else fan out and try to locate anybody who might still be alive," Tresler directed
the small crowd.

"I can't imagine anyone's alive in that," someone whispered.

"Check anyway."

Tresler propped open the doors so the smoke
could clear and started down one of the side
aisles.

As he picked his way through the debris, he
scanned the sections to the right and left, searching for movement. A quarter of the way up, he
thought he heard something like a feeble cough.
He squinted through the smoke. Nothing. He
was about to move on when he spotted a weak
disturbance beneath a plank of wood. "Is there a
paramedic in here yet?" There was. "Someone's
alive over here," he said. He waited until the man
reached him and pointed out the spot. Then he
continued toward the front of the cathedral.

Climbing over the low barrier, he reached the
priest and bent over the body. The exit wound
was dead center in the back of the neck, so the
shot could not have come from the side of the
church. And it was too accurate for someone to
have fired from the crowd without something
to steady the rifle—even if they could have
done it unobserved. Tresler looked toward the
back of the church, and his eyes were drawn to

the long, shadowy balcony that housed the enormous pipes of the organ. He looked back down at the priest and up again. Then he yelled for Stanley.

They found the staircase leading to the balcony and crept up, Tresler first, with his weapon drawn, and Stanley just a step behind. They burst in on the quiet body of the organist slumped sideways on his bench. It took only a glance to see that Merec had come and gone.

Tresler lowered his weapon and crossed to the railing. "Perfect view," he muttered. "Dammit."

"Look at this," Stanley called.

Tresler turned around. Stanley was standing over the organist, but he wasn't looking at the man. He was staring at something beside the body, partially hidden by the folds of his robe. Tresler joined him and twitched the cloth away to uncover the little pile made by the rifle, pistol, and detonators that Merec had left behind. They gazed at the deadly little heap.

"This might yield something," Stanley said. "A fingerprint at the very least."

"Maybe." Tresler was skeptical.

"Well, we can at least try. I'm going downstairs to get some men up here to work on this."

Stanley disappeared down the stairs, leaving Tresler standing by the organ. His eyes wandered over the body and up to the blood, still slick and wet, that had splashed on the instrument. Idly he started to read the hymn open on the reading stand. He stopped reading halfway through, and a slight crease deepened between his brows. Leaning closer to the book, he studied the page, then looked at the stand it was propped on. The stand was covered with blood, but the open page was absolutely clean.

At that moment Stanley returned with two officers in tow. He was explaining to the men the things he wanted dusted for prints and saying he wanted the whole place scoured for any stray hairs or fibers when Tresler broke in.

"What hymn did the organist play at the start of the service?" he asked.

Stanley looked at him like he was crazy. "What?"

Tresler repeated his question.

"I don't remember," Stanley said.

"Did it go like this?" and, reading from the music, he hummed a few bars.

Stanley sighed. "Sing that again," he directed, and Tresler obliged.

"No, I don't think it was that."

"What about this?" and from memory, he hummed different notes.

"Yes, that was the one."

Tresler bent over the hymnbook propped on the stand and began reading the words aloud:

Lord, I care not for riches, Neither silver nor gold;
I would make sure of heaven, I would enter the fold.
In the book of Thy kingdom, With its pages so fair,

Tell me, Jesus, my Saviour, Is my name written there?
Is my name written there, On the page white and fair?
In the book of Thy kingdom, Is my name written there?

Lord, my sins they are many, Like the sands of the sea,
But Thy blood, O my Saviour, Is sufficient for me;
For Thy promise is written, In bright letters that glow,
"Tho' your sins be as scarlet, I will make them like snow."
Is my name written there, On the page white and fair?
In the book of Thy kingdom, Is my name written there?

When he had finished, Tresler waited expectantly.

"So?" Stanley demanded.

"Merec left that book behind."

Stanley was beside him in a moment. "How do you know?" he demanded.

"First of all, it wasn't the hymn that was played at the beginning of the service. Secondly, look at the bloodstains."

"There aren't any," Stanley said.

"Exactly."

It took a minute to penetrate. "Holy shit," Stanley whispered, leaning closer and reading over the lines again. "What does it mean?"

"I have no idea," Tresler admitted.

"Well, shit, Tresler. What good does it do us then? You know what I think? I think you're right, and he did leave it behind. But he just did it to drive us crazy. It doesn't actually mean anything."

Stanley returned to the other officers, but Tresler remained bent over the book, repeating the words to himself under his breath. He got stuck on the chorus and whispered, "Is my name written there, On the page white and fair? / In the book of Thy kingdom, Is my name written there?" He paused, then repeated, "Is my name written there?" He straightened, and his eyes glittered. Bounding to the balcony, he leaned out, searching the floor below.

"Watch out, Tresler, you don't want to ruin evidence," Stanley cautioned him.

Tresler paid no attention and leaned out even farther. Suddenly he gave a cry. "There it is." In a flash he had turned and was headed toward the stairs.

"What? There what is?" Stanley called after him. When he got no response, he looked at the two men dusting for prints and to the stairway where Tresler had disappeared. It took only a second of indecision, and Stanley was running down after him. He spotted Tresler kneeling beside a wooden pedestal that had been knocked over. But as he approached, he saw it wasn't actually the pedestal that Tresler was inspecting but a large book that lay just at the end of it.

"What's going on?" Stanley demanded.

"It's intact. The column must have protected it from the blast."

"Protected what?"

"The book of Thy kingdom."

"What are you talking about?" Stanley crouched down next to Tresler to get a better look. "Tresler, this is just the visitors' book."

"I know."

"So what do you want with the visitors' book? I doubt that Merec bothered."

Tresler didn't answer but continued flipping through the pages.

"Tresler, I don't think our man would have signed in."

"No? Do you remember when he called the radio station? At the end of our conversation, Merec said, 'When the time comes, I'll make sure you can find me.'"

"So?"

Tresler recited from memory. "Is my name written there, On the page white and fair? / In the book of Thy kingdom, *Is my name written there*?" Tresler waited patiently for the realization to hit.

"Oh," Stanley said in sudden understanding. "Oh." He sat back on his heels while Tresler continued studying the entries.

"It's not here," Tresler muttered. "Where is it?"

"You know, I signed in at the other one," Stanley said.

"What?" Tresler looked up sharply.

"At the other visitors' book. Just over there behind the other pillar." He jerked his head in that direction.

Crossing the floor, they had to stop to let a

stretcher pass. Then they both crouched over the other book while the bloody cleanup continued around them. Tresler pored over it, flipping back through the pages until he laid a finger beside an entry. "There," he said.

Stanley read the name. "Solomon Greer . . . You think that's him?"

"I know," Tresler corrected. "When we spoke on the phone, he told me I had the wisdom of Solomon."

Stanley followed the entry across and read out loud, "Hilton Hotel, room four thirty-five . . . You may have something here, Tresler." Stanley stood up. "So, what are we waiting for?"

A New American Hero

Half an hour later, Stanley and Tresler entered the Hilton Hotel with a few hastily gathered men as backup. Checking at the front desk, they found that room 435 was indeed occupied by a Solomon Greer. Commandeering the extra key, they rode up to the fourth floor, crept down the hall, and paused before the door. The team positioned themselves in a ring with their weapons drawn, and Tresler stepped forward to knock. There was no answer. He knocked again, louder. Still nothing. Tresler motioned to the men ranged behind, and unlocking the door, he pushed it open. As it swung inward, he glimpsed what appeared to be an empty room. He entered cautiously, weapon drawn. The other men slipped in behind him and, at Tresler's direction, scattered to check the bathroom, the closet, beneath the bed.

"He's not here," Stanley said. "Son of a bitch." He turned and kicked over a chair. "Goddamn it, Tresler, he's not here."

Tresler walked in a slow circle around the room and halted by the desk in the corner. With thumb and forefinger, he picked up a sheet of notepaper.

"What's that?" In two strides Stanley reached Tresler and plucked it gingerly from his fingers. He read aloud.

Dear Agent Tresler,

Didn't want to leave without giving you a bit of advice. "A good man can be stupid and still be good. But a bad man must have brains—absolutely."

As I've said before, you're in the wrong profession. It's been fun.

Merec

Stanley dropped the note back on the desk, disgusted. "So much for this lead."

"I'll call in forensics," Tresler said. He took out his phone and placed the call. Stanley dropped into an armchair. Tipping his head back, he closed his eyes. When Tresler got off the phone, Stanley was fast asleep and snoring. Tresler woke him with a light touch on his shoulder.

"I can wrap this up here. Why don't you go back to the hotel and get some sleep?"

Stanley looked up, about to say no, but he hesitated, then agreed. "Yeah, I guess I will. But you have to promise me, if you find anything you'll call."

Tresler nodded.

Heaving himself out of his chair with an effort, Stanley started toward the door. Just before leaving he stopped and turned around. "How much chance do you think we have of getting him now?"

Tresler shrugged.

"Really," Stanley pressed.

"Not much," Tresler admitted. "He'll probably be out of the country within a few days."

"That's what I thought." Stanley sighed and left the room.

When he arrived back at his hotel, Stanley found the avenue outside lined with media trucks. He was spotted through the glass even before he entered the lobby. Inside there was a scramble for equipment, and reporters came at a run with their cameramen and lighting people lumbering after. As soon as he pushed through the revolving door, they pressed around him calling out questions and waving their microphones.

"I can't hear a single one of you," he said. When they calmed down, he continued, "I'd be happy to answer any questions you have. But I have one for you first." Now they waited respectfully for him to speak. "Are you all really here for me?"

Everyone in the group surrounding him laughed. "Detective Wall, don't you know? Everyone's calling you the latest American hero."

"The whole country saw what you did," a woman in a turquoise suit threw in. "Now they're replaying your clip about every ten seconds."

It seemed as if the explosion had happened years ago and not just hours. "Oh," he said.

Everyone laughed again, holding out their microphones eagerly, and Stanley realized that they were recording.

"How does it feel to be a hero?" the turquoise suit asked.

"But I didn't save anyone," Stanley protested. Only myself, he thought.

"You were willing to sacrifice your life for strangers. What made you do it?" another reporter called out. They waited for his answer, the microphones swaying gently like heavy flowers in a wind.

"I'm a policeman. That's my job."

Then the questions started in earnest.

"You work down in the Washington area. Is it true that you were up here in New York pursuing the Sarah Shepherd case?"

"That's correct."

"Did you foresee something like this happening at the service? Is that why you attended?"

He was disgusted. "I should hope that I would have been a little more prepared if that were the case. I attended the service because . . . "

"Yes?" a reporter prompted him.

He tried to say it in as few words as possible. But his voice still broke. He said, "I went for Sarah."

That clip was played almost as often as his heroic walk through the cathedral doors.

Leftovers

It was only a short ride out of the city to where Merec had arranged to meet Karl. After getting off the bus, he stopped at a nearby liquor store and bought a bottle of expensive scotch. From there it was only a five-minute walk to the motel.

Entering the parking lot, he was rewarded by the sight of the familiar car parked outside one of the rooms. He knocked, and Karl opened the door, standing back to let him in. Merec entered and took the scotch out of the paper bag.

"Any glasses in here?"

Karl disappeared into the bathroom and returned with two. He set them down on a table, and Merec poured liberally. Handing one to Karl, he said, "I imagine you saw the news."

Karl accepted the drink and nodded.

Merec raised his glass. "Exceptional work."

Karl didn't respond to the toast. "What about the bonus?"

"Imminently forthcoming," Merec promised, keeping his glass in the air.

Karl raised his drink, and they both downed the contents in one swallow. Pouring another, Merec suggested, "Why don't you turn on the television, and we'll watch the latest."

Obligingly, Karl set his glass down and crossed the room to switch on the TV. "This okay?" he asked.

"Perfect," Merec replied.

They settled down in chairs on either side of the small table, watching the news and sipping their drinks. Fifteen minutes later, Karl's glass fell on the carpet with a dull thud. Merec glanced over. Karl's head was tilted at an uncomfortable angle, and his eyes had rolled back so that only a crescent of the irises still showed beneath his lids.

Merec stretched and rose. He felt for a pulse at Karl's neck, and having satisfied himself, he bent and picked the glass off the floor. Extracting a pair of gloves from his pocket, he pulled them on and proceeded to wipe the glass of all fingerprints. He pressed Karl's fingers around it again and returned it to the floor where it had dropped. He repeated the procedure with the bottle of scotch and the small glass vial that had contained the poison. He searched through Karl's belongings for anything that might connect him to

Merec or the cathedral. Finding nothing, Merec washed his own glass, returned it to the bathroom counter, and exited into the parking lot.

There was another hotel just a short walk down the street, and he took a room for the night. The first thing he did was call and book a plane ticket for the next afternoon. Then he took a long shower, shut off the lights, and lay down on the bed. He dropped off almost immediately, but it was not a peaceful, easy sleep.

The next morning, Merec bought several newspapers and found a café. He settled down at a table, ordered a light breakfast, and checked the papers. The story was on the front page above the fold in every one. Taking a sip of his coffee, he started to read. He scanned the account of events with satisfaction until he reached a sentence that stopped him dead. He opened the next paper, looking to verify the information. It was there also. Karl's wiring had not been flawless; there had been survivors among those sitting at the back of the cathedral. Neither article listed the names, but they did solicit information on one young man who seemed to have lost his memory as a result of the blast.

Merec sighed, closed the paper, and signaled for the waitress. It was a long shot, but nevertheless the possibility existed that the young man was Jeremy. It was not in Merec's nature to leave a job unfinished, and it seemed his work was not over quite yet.

Something Missing

Tresler remained in room 435 until the forensics team had finished their work. He wanted to be on site in case anything of relevance turned up. They were able to lift a few sets of fingerprints, and they retrieved a couple of hairs from the bathtub drain, but that was it. The head of the team promised that they would start the prints running on the computer tonight, but there was no telling when—or if—a match would come. Tresler nodded, thanked them, and went back to his own hotel room to catch a couple of hours' sleep.

He was up at seven the next morning, and stopping only to grab a cup of coffee and the paper, he headed back to the cathedral. As soon as the bodies were cleared, the salvage team had taken over. Tresler sought out the leader of the team and listened to his report. They had discovered that small amounts of plastique had been affixed to the underside of the pews, which meant that the target had never been the building itself—just the people in it. Consequently they were having trouble with identification, and much of it would have to wait until they got everything back to the lab.

Tresler asked if there was anything he could do to help.

The man shook his head.

"Okay, I'll get out of your way. Are you done with the balcony?"

The man said they were.

"If you need anything, I'll be up there." Climbing the stairs, Tresler was drawn over to the railing and stood gazing out over the cathedral's length. He remained there until the warmth faded from his coffee cup.

Several hours later, the head of the salvage team climbed the steps to the balcony. He found Tresler sitting on the edge of the organist's bench, staring out into space.

"Agent Tresler?"

"Yes?" Tresler said, focusing on the man standing in front of him.

"I'd like you to come down and take a look at something."

Tresler rose and followed him down the stairs and to the altar at the front of the church.

"Look here," the man pointed out. "The pattern of the debris from the explosion doesn't add up. Sarah was standing about here, correct?" He moved to the right of the podium, which was now lying on the floor. "But look at the way this podium fell. It should have been blown away from me. Instead, it's fallen toward me. And look at the pattern of the splinters. See, the explosion must have originated around here." He moved back and to the left of the podium.

Tresler watched this with growing interest but said only, "She could have moved just before the explosion went off. The camera was focused on Stanley."

"True," he nodded, "she could have. If not for one other little problem . . . we can't seem to locate any remains."

Tresler blinked.

"Sarah Shepherd is still alive," the man said. "Maybe injured, but definitely alive."

Complications

Of the people who had survived the blast, all lost at least one limb, and several suffered brain damage. But one young man was undoubtedly the worst. He had lost both arms and one leg, he was horribly burned across three-quarters of his body, and he seemed to be suffering from amnesia. It must have been the shock, his doctors concluded, because other than that his mind was unmercifully clear.

Merec entered the hospital through the main entrance. The woman at the front desk didn't even look up. "Do you know your room number?" she asked.

"Intensive care."

"Third floor, turn right. Take a pass."

He took a pink slip of paper from the top of a pile and continued down the hall to the elevators.

On the ride up, he fingered the thimble-sized syringe in his pocket.

Exiting the elevator, Merec turned right, pushed through swinging double doors, and found himself in the intensive care unit. There was a nurses' station in the center, surrounded by glass-walled rooms. The air seemed hushed, broken only by the low murmur of a voice and a quiet mechanical hum.

Merec walked up to the first room and looked through the window at the patient within. He could barely see the body through all the wires and tubes, but one hand lay outside the covers; it was small with pink polish on the nails. It was definitely not Jeremy's.

"Excuse me," a voice asked. "Who is it you've come to see?"

He turned to face a tiny nurse standing with her fists on her hips.

Merec opened his mouth to speak, but he didn't get a chance.

"I knew it. I've told you people that we do not allow reporters in here."

"I'm not a reporter. I read about the survivors in the paper."

"And?" she said, still aggressive, but her hands fell from her hips.

"And I think I might know the man who has amnesia."

"Oh." She still wasn't completely convinced. "Who is he?"

"I believe it's a coworker of mine. He doesn't have any family that I know of, so I thought I would come . . ." Merec let the sentence trail off.

"Describe him," she commanded.

"Black hair, brown eyes, and a mole here," he pointed to his left jaw.

The tiny nurse softened and laid a hand on his arm. "I'm sorry to have been so rude. If you'll come over to the nurses' station and give us some information . . ."

"I would like to see him first, if you don't mind."

"Of course," the nurse apologized. "He's pretty groggy from the drugs, but he's a tough one. He's down this way at the end of the hall."

She led the way and stopped in front of a room. "He's in here," she said gesturing.

Merec looked in through the glass and saw that he had misjudged in thinking he could identify Jeremy through his hands. He had none. The hospital gown's short sleeves fell like shoulder ruffles over empty sockets. There was also a suspicious lack of bulk under the covers where his legs should have been, and his eyes were swathed in bandages. Merec studied his handiwork. "No arms, one leg?" he inquired, his voice expressionless.

"I'm sorry, I thought you knew. But of course you wouldn't. They didn't say in the paper, did they?"

"No, they didn't."

Her mouth formed a silent "Oh." Then she said, "Well, I'll leave you . . ." She turned and bustled away.

Merec pushed open the door, crossed the room, and stopped beside the bed. He looked down into Jeremy's bandaged face.

The mouth moved, and Jeremy's voice, hoarse but still recognizable, said, "Who's there?"

"Hello, Jeremy."

There was a pause. Then Jeremy said, "Hello, Merec."

"So, didn't you think I'd come for you?"

"Yes. I knew you would—sooner or later."

"Then why didn't you tell them who you were?" Merec asked. "They would have given you protection."

Jeremy coughed hollowly. When he caught his breath, he said, "It's a little more complicated than that."

"No, Jeremy, you're wrong. It's very, very simple." Merec glanced up at the nurses' station. No one was watching. Leaning over, he inserted the syringe into the vein in Jeremy's neck and dropped it back in his pocket.

Jeremy's breath came out in a soft hiss as he felt the needle.

"That wasn't complicated now, was it?" He waited for a response. When he received none, he said, "I must admit, I'm disappointed in you, Jeremy. Somehow I expected more."

Jeremy smiled. "There is more."

"Oh really? Well, you'd better make it quick. You don't have very long."

"That's all right. This won't take very long. Remember the preparations for the service?"

"Yes," Merec said, glancing at his watch.

"Well, I rigged the detonator to a small explosive that I hid beneath the chair at the altar instead of to the vest."

Merec's whole body stilled. "What?" His voice was calm and very cold.

"Merec," Jeremy whispered, "Sarah is alive."

Merec remained motionless for some seconds before ducking his head in a strange, vulnerable gesture. "Well." He cleared his throat and looked down at Jeremy. Something made him frown. "Jeremy?" he said. There was no answer.

Undercover Cover-up

When **Tresler** entered the intensive care
ward, there seemed to be an emergency
under way. Nurses were running in every direction, and there were a number of people clustered around one doorway, accompanied by the
loud babble of voices. He stood for a minute
watching the spectacle, and when no one
seemed to notice his presence, he began inspecting the occupants of the rooms through the
glass. He had checked three before a tiny nurse
hurried by, spotted him, and stopped abruptly.

"I must insist that you leave at once. This
ward has just been closed to visitors."

"But—"

She cut him off, saying, "Absolutely no
exceptions."

He reached into his jacket for his identification. "I'm with the Federal Bureau of Investigation." He held out his wallet.

She reached out and took it, inspecting it suspiciously. "I can't tell if this is real or not," she said, handing it back to him.

"It's real," he assured her.

The nurse looked into his face, and she must have decided to trust him because she said next, "I think we've just had a murder."

Tresler's lips tightened. "One of the survivors of the explosion last night?"

"That's right."

"An older woman?" he asked quickly.

"No, a young man."

"A young man?" Tresler repeated, frowning.

"Yes, and I'm almost certain I spoke with the person who did it. It was an older gentleman, with long silver hair and an accent."

Now she had Tresler's full attention. "When did he leave?" he asked urgently.

"Only ten minutes ago."

Tresler relaxed slightly. There was no pursuing him now. "Go on," he encouraged.

"Well, he told me that he wanted to see the young man who was injured in the bombing and had lost his memory. It was in the papers," she explained. "And he described him perfectly. He claimed to have worked with the patient."

"Ahh," Tresler said.

"So he went in to see him, and the next thing I knew the young man's vital signs started to slip. I didn't even think about his visitor until after—when we lost the patient. Then I started putting things together. We called the police, but they haven't arrived yet."

Tresler took it all in, nodding. "Did the man visit any of the other survivors of the bombing?"

The nurse was startled. "Oh God, I don't think so."

"We had better check on them."

She agreed, looking frightened. They made the rounds of all the other survivors of the blast. The nurse checked to make sure they were all holding steady—they were. Tresler checked to see if any were Sarah Shepherd—they weren't.

"All right," he said, sighing. "Let's go see the victim."

She led him to Jeremy's room. Most of the crowd had broken up, but she still had to shoo people out of the way to pass through the door. By this time the nurse had regained most of her composure. She spoke above the murmuring voices, "Okay, people, back to work. We have other patients that need us more than this one now."

They filed out, and Tresler was able to cross to the side of the bed. He looked down at the young man.

"Who is he?" the nurse asked.

Tresler shook his head. "I have no idea. You had no luck in finding out?"

"We didn't have much to go on," she protested. "No fingerprints. No identification. He couldn't even tell us his name."

Or wouldn't, Tresler thought to himself.

"No one came forward to claim him. I mean, no one but that man."

It fit, Tresler thought. If this young man had been working with Merec, then no one else would have known he was there in the cathedral. And he obviously hadn't been meant to survive the bombing.

Tresler's cell phone rang. "Excuse me," he said to the nurse and stepped away into a corner of the room. "Yes?"

"Is this Agent Tresler?"

"Yes."

"This is Agent Patinsky. I said I would get back to you on the results of those prints."

It took Tresler a moment to remember that he was referring to the two sets of prints lifted from Merec's hotel room.

"And?"

"Well, nada on the first one. Probably just a random guest from a previous stay. But you won't believe what we turned up on the second set. It can't be a coincidence."

"What can't be a coincidence?" Tresler asked.

"The second set of prints came up as belonging to a CIA agent by the name of Alan Porter."

"CIA . . ." Tresler pivoted and looked at the young man in the bed. "Did that name come with a picture?"

"No picture. But we do have a general description—this is classified, of course."

"Of course," Tresler agreed.

"Six feet even, medium build, black hair, brown eyes, distinguishing marks include a mole on the left cheek. It's not much to go on."

"Oh no, it's plenty. Thank you."

"Pleasure. Do you want me to hold on to these hair samples?"

"Oh yes, I think those might come in handy," Tresler said. He hung up, checked his notebook, and dialed.

Zackman answered the phone.

"Agent Tresler here," he announced.

"Oh." Zackman sounded surprised, but he recovered quickly. "What can I do for you, Tresler?"

"Just a quick question. I need to know the name of the agent you sent into deep cover with Merec's organization."

There was a short pause, then Zackman said, "I don't suppose it can hurt him much now. His real name was Alan Porter. His code name was Jeremy."

Tresler remained at the hospital, ostensibly to oversee the police investigation, but really he was simply waiting for Zackman.

Zackman arrived less than two hours later with his own team of men. He bypassed the police detective in charge and instead sought out

Tresler. Drawing him into an empty room, Zackman asked, "Do the police know anything?"

"They suspect that the deceased was involved with the bombing. But that's all."

He nodded. "Well, that makes things easier. I'd like to talk to you a bit more. Can you wait?"

In less than twenty minutes, Zackman had dismantled the police investigation—though not without some bitterness from the men on the force—appropriated their files, and set his own men to work. Afterward he found Tresler and said, "My men have got everything under control here. What say we go get a cup of coffee?"

They went to the hospital cafeteria, and over cups of watery black coffee, Tresler briefed Zackman on what had happened since he had tracked Merec to New York.

Zackman listened to the whole story in silence, then asked a few precise questions. He seemed satisfied by Tresler's answers. "Well, I don't foresee any problems with this. It will be in the papers, of course, but they don't have the information to put it all together. It seems that the situation is well contained, thanks to you."

Tresler accepted the compliment with a nod. "May I ask *you* some questions now?"

"Go ahead. I'll answer you if I can."

"When I told you about Alan—"

"Let's call him Jeremy," Zackman said.

"Sorry. When I told you about Jeremy, you didn't seem to be very surprised."

It wasn't exactly a question, but Zackman knew what Tresler was asking. "No," he admitted. "I wasn't surprised, exactly. I had a funny feeling after that fire—you know, they never did conclusively identify a lot of those bodies. And," he took a sip of his coffee, "Jeremy was a bit of a wild card. We got him as a recruit out of the army. He was very good at taking orders. It seems that he wasn't as discriminating as he should have been about who he took them from."

"This man Merec," Tresler said mildly, "he seems to exert a powerful influence over anyone with whom he comes in contact."

Zackman gave him an appraising glance. "Oh, I'm not judging Jeremy. These situations are far too common for that."

"Oh really?"

"Well, we don't tend to advertise them. But it happens quite often when agents are asked to go undercover for months at a time. Their life depends on their becoming their role. And sometimes they do it too well."

"It's as simple as that?"

"Of course not. It just happens to be the excuse we use. You know the truth as well as I do, I imagine."

"No," Tresler said. "What's the truth?"

Zackman shrugged. "Exactly my point."

Fact
Checking

Tresler didn't return to his hotel room
until the early hours of the morning. He
had gotten less than five hours of sleep out of
the last forty-eight and had just undressed to
his undershirt and shorts when the phone rang.
Sitting on the edge of the bed, he rubbed his
eyes and picked up the receiver. "Hello?" His
voice was hoarse from lack of sleep.

"Late night?" the voice on the other end of
the line inquired.

Tresler's hand froze over his eyes, then
dropped to his lap. "Merec," he said.

"Still sharp as a tack."

"How did you get this number?"

"I've got the luck of the devil, you know."
Merec chuckled. "I only had to call twelve
hotels before I found one that had a guest regis-

tered under your name. Let me give you some advice. When I don't want to be bothered, I usually use a pseudonym."

"Yes," Tresler said dryly.

"Works like a charm, doesn't it?"

Tresler noticed that Merec didn't seem quite himself—his usual tone of smooth mockery seemed forced. "Are you all right?" Tresler asked.

"What? Of course I am."

There was a long pause.

"So," Merec said.

Tresler waited.

"I wanted to do a bit of fact checking."

"Fact checking?" Tresler repeated. He didn't know what he had been expecting, but it hadn't been this.

"Yes."

"You mean," Tresler said slowly, "that you want to ask me a question."

"Essentially, yes."

"Oh." He fell silent, thinking furiously. "Sure," he agreed.

"Well, how do I know that you'll answer me once I ask you?"

Tresler smiled. "You don't."

"Will you give me your word?"

He snorted.

"All right then, a trade," Merec suggested.

"That sounds a bit more like it."

"An answer for an answer."

"Two for one. And you answer both of mine first. Otherwise no deal."

Merec sighed. "You drive a hard bargain, my friend. But I accept. Ask away."

Tresler took a deep breath. "How did you turn him?"

"Turn who?"

"Alan Porter."

"*Who?*" Merec repeated.

"I thought you were going to answer my questions."

"I'm trying to. I will if you'll tell me what you're talking about."

"Alan Porter, the second undercover CIA agent." There was no response from Merec. "You knew him by his code name—Jeremy."

There was a dead silence on the other end of the line.

"You didn't know," Tresler said suddenly. "You didn't know, did you?"

Merec laughed, but it sounded pained. "No. I didn't know." He cleared his throat. "Next question."

"But—"

"Next question." Merec's voice was harsh.

"All right. What did you do with Sarah Shepherd?"

Again there was not a sound from Merec.

"Well?" Tresler prodded.

"I killed her," Merec said softly.

"No."

"Yes, I blew her up into little pieces."

"You can't lie about this one. There weren't any little pieces to find."

Merec felt as if the breath exploded from his lungs, but Tresler on the other end of the line heard only a soft sigh.

"Tell me the truth now. What did you do with her?"

"I was so certain that he was bluffing," Merec mused, almost to himself.

"Who was bluffing?"

"Jeremy," Merec explained. "Jeremy told me that she was alive."

"That was your question, wasn't it? And you have no idea where she is, do you?"

"No," Merec admitted. "But I can promise you one thing."

"What's that?"

"I will find her."

There was a click, and Tresler was left with a dial tone.

The Search
for Sarah

"**You had two questions** that he had to answer, and that's what you asked him!" Stanley said.

Tresler and Stanley were sitting together at a diner near the hotel the morning after Merec's phone call.

"What would you have asked him?" Tresler challenged.

"I don't know, but certainly not that."

"You wouldn't want to know where Sarah Shepherd is?"

"But that was *his* question," Stanley protested.

"There was no way for me to have known that," Tresler snapped.

Stanley was taken aback. He hadn't ever seen Tresler lose his unflappable calm. "Okay.

There's no point in talking about what we can't change."

"Exactly."

They sat a moment without speaking.

"So—" Stanley began.

"Don't," Tresler warned, "ask me what we're going to do now."

Stanley subsided, and they sat again in silence.

After a few minutes Stanley said reasonably, "Well, we've got to do something."

"What would *you* suggest?"

"I say this thing isn't over yet. I say we find him."

"And tell me, how are we going to do that, Stanley?"

"You're the one who knows how he thinks," Stanley pointed out.

Tresler sighed. "All right. Yes, there is a way to track him. It's very simple. He said he was going to find Sarah Shepherd. We don't have to find him. All we have to do is find her."

"And you think that's going to be simple?"

"Don't you?"

"No. I mean, not necessarily."

Tresler's eyebrows rose. "Why not?"

Stanley's brow wrinkled, and he chewed on his thumbnail. "Well, this is how I see it. Merec hasn't got her. And Jeremy's out of the picture." He paused for confirmation.

"That's right," Tresler agreed.

"So she's alone. And if she's alone, why hasn't she turned up?"

"I don't know. You tell me."

"It's obvious. Because she doesn't want to be found."

Tresler waited. "So?"

"So . . . it just might not be so easy."

Tresler looked up at the ceiling for a brief moment, then down at his hands. "Don't worry, I'll find her."

"You know, you're starting to sound like Merec."

Tresler's eyes darted up to meet Stanley's gaze.

"Sorry."

Tresler shook his head.

"Okay, any ideas on where to begin?"

"One or two," Tresler admitted.

"Well." Stanley stood and clapped him on the shoulder. "Let's get started."

Comfort or Curse

Years later, Tresler received a letter with a foreign stamp buried among the junk mail. He opened it with curiosity, and he caught his breath as he read the short note. The next day he booked a flight, and the day after, he arrived in a small town near a famous sanitarium. He checked into a hotel, dropped off his bags, and asked for directions. He found the long graveled drive leading to the institution without much difficulty and parked in the shade under a stately row of trees.

Walking up the path, Tresler wondered what name to request. He asked for Merec. That was enough.

Tresler would have asked about Merec's visitors and his habits, but no one he encountered spoke enough English for a conversation. He followed the soft-shoed attendant down cool, dim corridors through the building and out into the garden beyond. The attendant motioned him down a flagstone path leading into a grove of trees. The air itself felt hushed.

Tresler found Merec in a wheelchair by a quiet pond, shaded and wept over by willows. Merec looked worn and frail, but his blue eyes were still sharp.

"So you came," he said.

Tresler spread his arms. "As summoned."

"I thought you might."

Tresler noted that Merec's once smooth tone had turned scratchy. It was the voice of an old man.

"Still catching criminals?" Merec asked.

"Still trying."

"That's good. A man needs a profession."

"Word was that you . . ." Tresler searched for a word, ". . . retired."

Merec nodded slowly. "Yes, that's right."

"May I ask why?"

"You can ask. Can't say that I can give you an answer. Well, no, that's not exactly true. Let's say that I just got tired and didn't see the point anymore."

Tresler leaned forward. "Was there ever a point?"

Merec chuckled. "There was, but it sounds foolish now. Then again, everything sounds foolish now."

Merec fell silent, and they sat for a long time, listening to the buzz of crickets.

Without taking his eyes from the placid water, Merec spoke. "Do you know where she is?" he asked in a low voice.

Tresler shook his head.

Merec turned toward him suddenly. "If you know you must tell me."

"I don't."

Merec sank back into his chair. "I've looked everywhere. It's all I did . . . until I came here. I followed rumors—a woman who went to hunt tigers in India, another who won over two million in a casino in Monte Carlo and then lost it all on one enormous wager."

"I heard that she gave it all away to charity."

Merec pounced. "So you looked too."

"Yes, I looked," Tresler admitted.

"And?"

"The same as you, I suspect."

Merec nodded. "How long?"

"They took me off the case after six months." He paused, and added, "But I looked a while longer on my own."

"So . . . you're still looking," Merec observed.

Tresler didn't deny it.

"You know, the reason I asked you here is that I had a dream that you had found her and that you two were together. Isn't that crazy?"

"What would you have done if you had found her?"

Merec smiled. "I started out thinking that I

would kill her. At least that was what I told myself. Now I just want to see her. Just to see her once more." His voice faded. Then, with something of his old élan, he shrugged it off. "But look, she has brought us together in the end."

"That's why I began searching for her in the first place," said Tresler. That, at least, had been his excuse.

"Well, let's make the best of it, shall we?"

"Yes," Tresler agreed.

He stayed until the day faded into dusk. Finally, when the first fireflies hovered over the garden, Tresler stood. "I should be going."

Merec nodded. Staring down into his lap, he said, "I am sorry to have brought you all this way for nothing."

"Not at all," Tresler protested.

Merec continued as if he hadn't heard. "But I thought that you might know something, and if you saw me here, like this . . ." He shrugged. "They say I am dying," and he looked up at Tresler with his old twisted, ironic smile. After a moment it trembled and broke. "She was so beautiful," he said in a husky voice, "heart-breakingly beautiful."

Tresler left him dying by the willows with Sarah Shepherd's face before him—a comfort or a curse, Tresler did not know.